BIG RED

BIG RED

• A NOVEL STARRING •

Rita Hayworth

and

Orson Welles

JEROME CHARYN

Liveright Publishing Corporation

A DIVISION OF W. W. NORTON & COMPANY

INDEPENDENT PUBLISHERS SINCE 1923

Frontispiece: Rita Hayworth and her "hubby," Orson Welles, at the Mocambo, November 11, 1945. Photo: Associated Press.

•

To Robert Warshow, In Memoriam

He had not been to so many places, but wherever he went, he always went to the movies.

—SHERRY ABEL

CONTENTS

· ONE ·

The Kid from Kalamazoo, 1943

1

I WAS AN ACTRESS who couldn't act, a dancer who couldn't dance, a singer who couldn't sing. So I went straight to Hollywood after my sophomore year at college in Kalamazoo. Still, I wasn't much of a maverick. I had grown up on a farm in southern Illinois. Both my parents couldn't read a word. I promised myself that I would become a reader, and I did become one, with a fierce regard for language. But language alone couldn't imprison me with its pleasures. I saw every film that reached our rural town. There were no picture palaces on the plains, but we did have fifty-seaters in every nearby hamlet. That's how I discovered the world, watching William Powell and Myrna Loy eat breakfast in their pajamas. . . .

I lived in a roomette at the Hollywood Hotel, right on the boulevard, near Musso's and the trolley car line, with the constant hiss of overhead wires, and despite the racket, I still felt like a grand duchess. I worked in the basement of the Writers' Building at Columbia, belonged to a shadow crew. We were attached to the Publicity Department, but we barely existed at all. I was paid seventy-five clams a week to dig up dirt on the directors and stars of every studio, including our own. I was hired as a common clerk until the studio realized I was the best damn digger on the lot.

Columbia had swallowed up all of Poverty Row on Gower Street by then. It occupied an entire avenue of barns, storage facilities, soundstages, and half-empty lots. Its Administrative Building was a converted stable. I'd never been invited to the commissary, not once. The head of our crew, a shifty character named Archibald, kept trying to get into my pants. "Rusty, you don't have much of a future here."

"I'll take my chances," I said.

I couldn't imagine *ever* returning to Kalamazoo. I was a fanatic about *Photoplay* and *Modern Screen*. All the dirt I collected was gold to a tomboy raised in movie houses. I knew where Gable and Lombard had their hideaway in a penthouse on Hollywood Boulevard before the King got rid of his first wife. I also knew about his dentures.

There was a deeper tale to tell. Carole and her mother had been killed in a plane crash while returning from a war bond rally in '42, and Clark was inconsolable. Louis B. Mayer had to put him on leave at MGM. I once saw Rhett Butler in rags, tottering along the trolley tracks, and I had to lure him into the Hollywood Hotel, with its long verandahs and steeples that looked like a witch's lair. The bellboys couldn't believe it. His speech was so garbled, even I couldn't understand a word. I fed him hot milk, and finally he sobered up. "Say," he said, "you're a swell kid." He left a twenty-dollar bill on the table and marched out of the Hollywood Hotel.

The King wasn't my only customer. I could point to the table at Musso's where Ty Power sat with one or two of the cowboy extras he'd picked up at Gower Gulch. I could talk about Tallulah Bankhead's conquests at the Troc, where she'd wrap a tablecloth around herself and her latest catch, a starlet from one of the minor lots. She lived at the Garden of Allah on Sunset, and it was said she loved to swim in the nude. . . .

I didn't get fired. Archibald, who had once been a sergeant inside some crackpot sheriff's office in Sonoma County, smirked at me. "The boss wants to see ya, chicken." Archibald's smirk spread across his face like a lantern on fire. "I'm talking about the big guy—Harry himself."

I was bewildered in that dank row of cubicles where we worked six days a week. What the hell would Harry Cohn want with me? But I never bothered to ask. I didn't have to go back out onto Gower. I took the underground passageway to Cohn's castle. He occupied an entire floor in the Administrative Building. He rebuilt his offices after visiting Mussolini in 1933. Cohn had even done a documentary on Il Duce, *Mussolini Speaks*, and the dictator had decided to decorate the president of Columbia Pictures in Rome. Harry never quite recovered from that trip. He kept an autographed picture of Mussolini on his mantel until the beginning of the war.

The walls of his entire suite were white-on-white, like Il Duce's. The outer office was as big as a baseball diamond. A receptionist sat at the far end behind a tiny desk. Hers was the only chair in the room. A bleached blonde in a tailored outfit and a teal necktie, she didn't bother to look up as I approached.

"Rusty Redburn to see Harry," I said.

"*Mr. Cohn*," she rasped, correcting me in a clipped British accent she must have picked up in an elocution class on Hollywood Boulevard. "Do you have an appointment, young lady?"

"I believe *your* boss is expecting me."

The receptionist ambled out of her seat and sashayed into an inner office with all the aplomb of a starlet on Poverty Row with stiletto heels. I waited at least fifteen minutes for her to come back. Then she squired me into an inner office with a bump of her derriere. This office had the same barren white-on-white walls. It was occupied by the boss's number-one secretary and her assistant, with deep suspicion in their hooded eyes. Both of them could have just stepped out of Max Factor's Hollywood salon, that's how artful their pancake had been put on.

Again, there were no other chairs in the room.

They murmured to one another as if I were a pimple that Max Factor could make disappear.

"Rusty Redburn, honest to God, I can't locate her file."

"Do you think she polishes saddles at the Columbia ranch?"

Then a buzzer sounded, and a curious door, without a door-knob or a keyhole, clicked open.

"Enter, please," the assistant said.

And I stepped into Harry Cohn's private office, which was twice as large as his secretary's, with a Steinway near the door. It had a semicircular desk at the far end, on a platform, and two chairs that were much lower than the desk and looked as if they belonged in a nursery. But Cohn wasn't sitting behind his desk. He stood near a picture window that opened onto Gower Street. It was his way, I had been told, to check when his employees arrived at his fief-dom. Cohn himself never appeared before noon. He often stayed until midnight, wandering across the studio to make sure that no one had left a light on. He liked to think of himself as Harry the First, or King Cohn, but the other studio heads called him the Jan-itor behind his back. I'd also been told how crass he was, but the Janitor didn't seem crude to me.

He was a handsome man in his fifties, with muscular shoulders, an assassin's clear blue eyes, and an angelic smile. He'd once been a streetcar conductor. He wore a houndstooth jacket from a haber-dasher in Beverly Hills, and a Sulka shirt open at the neck to reveal a hint of his hairy chest.

He dug into me with his blue eyes. "You're a dyke, ain't ya?"

"Suppose I am."

He laughed, and I could spot the amazing symmetry of his dental work. His teeth were whiter than white, like a mouth made of Chiclets.

"Sweetheart, what do you think of Orson Welles?"

I wasn't an idiot. Rita Hayworth, Cohn's prize property, had just moved in with Welles on Woodrow Wilson Drive, in the Hollywood Hills. I adored *Citizen Kane*. We Hollywoodians had our own second-run movie house, the Regina, right on the boulevard, wedged between Grauman's Chinese and Grauman's Egyptian. I wrote reviews for all the classics shown at our little box of a theater, plus tidbits about the stars, and signed my pieces Regina X. There had been nothing like *Kane*, before or since. It exploded onto the screen—and into my head—from its first shot. I couldn't catch my breath until after the final credits. But I didn't tell that to Harry. You had to lie and lie if you wanted to remain in Hollywood, even as a basement clerk in the Publicity Department who lived in a roomette.

"Welles is a has-been," I said. But I was puzzled. "Mr. Archibald couldn't have told you about me. He hates my guts."

"Who's this Archibald?" Cohn asked, with a sudden gruffness in his voice.

"My boss in the basement of the Writers' Building."

"I'm your boss," he insisted, and then licked his lips with his serpentine tongue. "It was Louella. She said you were reliable. I could trust you *not* to be a rat."

He meant Lolly Parsons, Hollywood's premier gossip columnist and bitchiest bitch, with her wattles, her notorious triple chin. She had her own booth at the Brown Derby on North Vine, where she could snub you or greet you according to her own whimsical delight. The chef had to prepare a special grapefruit pudding for Louella, who was finicky about her weight. She lost a little of her allure after she became Hearst's toad. Lolly had massacred

Welles' first film because she insisted that Charles Foster Kane was modeled after the Chief, as the newspaper tycoon was called, and that *Citizen Kane* was a parody of Hearst and his mistress, Marion Davies. But it was the Chief himself who had wrecked Marion's career, trying to turn a comedy star with a stutter into a cross-eyed tragedienne, who couldn't really play Elizabeth Barrett Browning *or* Marie Antoinette. And Lolly was too thick to understand that Kane's megalomania was more about Welles, the Boy Wonder, who had played the Shadow on the radio—Lamont Cranston, a vigilante with a deep-throated roar—than about William Randolph Hearst, a reclusive pasha with a girlish voice. Still, I moonlighted as one of Lolly's stringers. I fed her tidbits from time to time, and she would toss a crumpled ten-dollar bill into my lap while she sipped her vodka martini and spooned her grapefruit pudding.

"Shucks," I said, playing up to the Janitor, "has Lolly ruined my reputation?"

He ignored my remark. "Louella has assured me that you're reliable, and I have an assignment for you, Miss Rusty. I don't like the Boy Wonder and what he might do to Rita's career. So I recommended you to Rita. You see, my redhead needs a secretary."

"But why would Miss Hayworth ever want *me*?" I asked, growing more and more suspicious.

"Jesus," Harry Cohn said, "you can spell, can't ya?"

I stared right at the Janitor. "You don't really want a speller, sir. You want a spy."

He laughed again. "I can tell that we'll do wonders together. The job pays a hundred and fifty a week—more than some of my writers get."

"And all I have to do is become Miss Hayworth's gal Friday and report back to you about her and the Boy Wonder? I don't even have to think about it. I'll take the job!"

I didn't intend to spy on Rita or the Boy Wonder, but I was as grand a liar as anyone in Hollywood, and I had taught myself to be selective about details. Half-truths never hurt a soul.

"I'm delighted," he said, stifling a yawn with his fist. "Rita is expecting you."

Yet the manner of my compensation was full of mischief, to say the least. It seems that Rita and perhaps Orson would pay *part* of my salary, but the Boy Wonder was broke. And the lion's share would come from the Janitor himself. It was pretty obvious. I was working for him. That was Columbia Pictures in 1943.

Cohn put me right into his planner. I would report back to him every Wednesday afternoon at four—without fail—unless I was presented with other instructions. His blue eyes fluttered, and he looked a little insane. It wasn't hard for me to realize that he was in love with Rita, and he couldn't bear the idea that she was with Orson Welles.

"You won't fail me, will ya, kid?"

"Mr. Cohn, I *never* fail."

I heard an odd sound, like a cricket crying. His door opened, and I knew I was dismissed.

A resurrection had occurred during my time with Cohn. I had *risen*, the kid from Kalamazoo. Cohn's secretary and her assistant leapt up the moment I reappeared.

"We'll be in touch, Miss Redburn," his secretary said. "Welcome to the executive club. I'm Sally Fall, and my assistant is Josephine."

I didn't acknowledge their sudden interest. I walked away from those barren white walls and returned to the tunnels. I felt much cleaner among the cockroaches and the rats.

2

ORSON WAS EASY. Declared a genius by the time he was six, Welles seemed to live without a sense of boundaries. He stormed into the Gate Theatre in Dublin and became a star at sixteen. He returned to America, captured radio in 1936 with his booming voice, rode from studio to studio in a hired ambulance, frightened half the country with his *War of the Worlds* broadcast, and stripped theater down to its bare essentials and then rebuilt it with whatever baroque or barren world he wanted. The Boy Wonder appeared on the cover of *Time* at the age of twenty-three and was courted by Henry Luce himself. He went out to Hollywood a year later with his own company of players and worked on *Kane*, the first studio film that defied the studio system. Louis B. Mayer and the other Hollywood moguls believed in strict, linear narratives, and *Kane* was a sarabande of moments and set pieces—flashbacks within a flashback. I had no idea what was coming next. *Kane* invented a grammar and a syntax I had never seen before.

Yet Welles was irrevocably wounded in the process. He couldn't seem to understand that even a Boy Wonder had *some* limits. The

Japanese warlords had attacked Pearl Harbor, and Orson couldn't enlist on account of his flat feet. FDR was worried that the relentless propaganda of the Axis powers might sway Latin America to declare war on the Free World, and he wanted Orson to go to Brazil as a goodwill ambassador. Orson was in the midst of editing *The Magnificent Ambersons*, based on Booth Tarkington's saga about the fall of a wealthy family in the Midwest. But he abandoned everything to prepare a documentary about the carnival in Rio. He plunged into the carnival with an entire crew and spent a month filming in the *favelas* outside Rio.

Meanwhile, *Ambersons* was ripped apart and reshot without Welles. It sank into oblivion as the second feature—at the bottom of the bill—in random movie houses. It played at the Regina, and I went to see it, of course. The film wasn't completely ruined. *Ambersons* still had the Orson touch, but it didn't have Orson. He should have played Georgie Minafer, a spoiled brat, just like himself. What the film lacked was the Shadow's roaring radio voice. *Ambersons* was really a film about Orson's patrician childhood in Wisconsin, filled with nostalgia and loss. Eugene Morgan (Jo Cotton), an inventor, was modeled after Orson's own father, Richard Welles, also an inventor, who drank himself to death. Eugene was in love with Georgie's mom, Isabel (Dolores Costello), who was the replica of Orson's mother, Beatrice, a mysterious and magnetic lady of the arts who died young. Orson's tracks were all over the place. But *Ambersons'* homage to a lost time could never compete with the pyrotechnics of *Kane*. . . .

He filmed and filmed in Rio with his usual fury until he was fired by RKO for wasting so much footage on the *favelas*, and his ensemble, the Mercury Players, was thrown off the lot. He returned to Hollywood without a studio behind him. For a while I thought he would end up at the Hollywood Hotel, another misbegotten soul, like the silent film stars who couldn't make the transition to sound and waited in line to become an extra in some epic by DeMille. But Orson still had one resource—radio. And he could always broadcast from the CBS studios near Hollywood and Vine with his Mercury Players. They did *Treasure Island, Heart of Darkness*, and other classics—in miniature, of course. And the Boy Wonder, now twenty-eight, had a new passion. Before he left Rio he glanced at a photo of Rita Hayworth in *Life* magazine, kneeling on a bed in her negligée, and he fell in love with the sweep of her magnificent shoulders. *I'm going to marry that girl.* That's what Orson declared on the spot.

There was one little complication. Rita was in love with Vic Mature, or so the studio said. But Vic, who had appeared with Rita in *My Gal Sal*, joined the Coast Guard, and was now stationed in Boston. Both he and Orson were giants at six feet two and a half, but Vic was sleepy-eyed and sluggish, with a debonair attitude, and Orson was merciless in his pursuit of Rita, who wore the bracelet Vic had given her with a solid gold heart.

Orson secretly arranged to have Rita invited to a cocktail party at Jo Cotton's ranch house in the hills. Rita was shy and barely uttered a word. She wore a black dress that revealed her long neck and the incredible line of her shoulders. She walked with a dancer's gliding grace, as if a panther had come to the party out of the wild, a panther with a mane of red hair.

"I intend to marry you," Orson announced with a rogue's smile.

Rita fled. Relentless, he phoned her for a month. Her maid said that Miss Hayworth was indisposed. Finally she picked up the phone.

"What do you want?" she asked with a slight tremor in her voice. "And if you talk about marriage, I'll have Harry Cohn hire someone to run you out of Hollywood."

He laughed—at least that's how the legend goes. "You hate Harry."

"But he hates you as much as I hate him."

"Then let's conspire, shall we? And we can hate him together."

So off they went to Romanoff's. They sat at a secluded table, where Rita, in a red shawl, wouldn't be noticed, or pestered by the cocktail crowd. He never mentioned his films or hers. He talked about his childhood in Wisconsin and about his beautiful mother, Beatrice, who turned all yellow at forty-three.

Rita stifled a sob at her corner table. "You must have adored her."

"I did," Orson said in his deep, melancholic voice.

Their romance was very swift. She stopped wearing Vic's bracelet and moved into Orson's rickety ranch house on Woodrow Wilson Drive, though she still kept her apartment near Wilshire.

3

RITA WAS A less complicated creature than the Boy Wonder, but her own tale is sadder, and hard for me to tell. She was born Margarita Carmen Cansino, in Brooklyn. Her father, Eduardo, who was illiterate, came from an illustrious family of Sephardic Jews; the Cansinos were once counselors to the kings of Spain. They had to convert to Catholicism during the Inquisition, and practice their Judaism in secret, as Marranos, or so I discovered while researching Rita's roots for Harry Cohn and Columbia.

The Cansinos gave up all ties to their Sephardic past sometime in the seventeenth century and also lost their high station within the royal house. They turned into a tribe of flamenco dancers instead. And Eduardo arrived in America in 1913 with his sister as part of a team, the Dancing Cansinos. He fell in love with Volga Hayworth, a tall beauty from the Follies with the longest legs in Manhattan. He married her, and Rita *arrived* in 1918, less than a month before the Armistice.

The Cansinos prospered until Eduardo's sister returned to Spain with husband and child. Stuck without an income, Eduardo moved

the family to Los Angeles and opened a dance studio on Hollywood and Vine. There were problems. Volga was chronically alcoholic and had an uncontrollable rage that Rita would soon inherit.
Eduardo's studio disappeared during the Depression, and he was
forced to revive the Dancing Cansinos, but this time with Rita as
his new partner. She was a chubby twelve-year-old who spoke in
a whisper. But Eduardo had her dark brown hair dyed jet-black,
and arranged it in a bun at the back of her neck. Shy as she was, he
turned her into a tornado on stage. They danced at military hospi-
tals and floating casinos off the shores of San Diego. Eduardo had
her wear a provocative black dress or a suit with a wide-brimmed
hat. Men were immediately drawn to little Margarita. Eduardo
locked her in the dressing room after each performance, while he
pissed away most of their money at the gambling tables.

Eduardo's favorite haunt was the Foreign Club, a casino-café
in Tijuana, where Eduardo performed with Margarita, advertising
her as his wife, since the clientele would have been disturbed by
a father doing the flamenco with his twelve-year-old daughter.
The Foreign Club was as grand and luxurious as a hacienda, and
attracted Hollywood stars, producers, and gossip columnists. The
chubby child was gone once Margarita was out on the checkered
dance floor, and her body swayed in rhythm with Eduardo's. I
had heard many stories about the sensation that the Dancing Cansinos had caused at the Foreign Club, and something bothered
me, didn't feel right—father and daughter in what seemed to most
like a sizzling embrace. Archibald, my boss in the basement of the
Writers' Building, got wind of it, and he thought Harry might
notice him if he had some dirt on Rita. So he sent me down to
Tijuana in my Ford coupé that I had picked up for a song at a junk-
yard in San Pedro.

By that time, the Foreign Club had closed, and Tijuana had
lost most of its Anglo customers, at least the wealthy ones, while

the "hacienda" sat there like a ghost ship on dry land. I rummaged about on a street of dance halls and saloons near that dead casino and managed to find several folks who had once worked there—a hatcheck girl, a waitress, a master of ceremonies, a cook—and they all said there was something "unnatural" about Eduardo and his daughter. The hatcheck girl was more explicit.

"I didn't like the way he touched her. I caught them once in their dressing room. She was naked, and he was biting her neck."

My research ended right there. Eduardo had molested his own daughter, like a vampire who danced with silver teeth on the soles of his boots. As much as it pained me, I still left that out of my report to Archibald. I didn't want Rita blackmailed by the Publicity Department—or Harry Cohn. But I understood the toll it had taken on the Cansinos, and especially on the girl who had been her father's concubine. Volga must have turned to alcohol because she couldn't protect her only daughter. Margarita had become the Cansinos' meal ticket. She helped feed her two younger brothers. And she fed them well. The president of Fox Pictures had seen her dance at the Foreign Club and offered her a movie contract when she was fifteen. Margarita became Rita Cansino, a Spanish beauty with black hair, though she was half Irish on her mother's side. . . .

I happened to be at the Hollywood Canteen when I ran into Jane Withers. A teenager now, with a strong following, she had once been Shirley Temple's only rival as a child star. Jane, I soon discovered, had also been one of the chief motors of Rita's career. In 1935, while Jane was preparing for *Paddy O'Day*, in which she had the title role of an Irish immigrant girl, she wandered onto the set of a Charlie Chan film and saw a beautiful young dancer. This girl was "dynamite," Jane told me. There was a part in her own film for a young Russian dancer, and Jane used all her pull to get Rita the part. Jane had already become a dynamo at Fox by playing spoiled brats, and was allowed to have her own cameraman and other crew members follow her from film to film. Even Shirley Temple didn't have such power.

Shrewd as well as talented, Jane attended a Hollywood writers' conference when she was eight. Some of the writers objected to having her there, but Jane had more prestige at the studios than they did. "Honest injun," she told the Hollywood writers, "you don't know the first thing about writing dialogue for kids." But they taught her things about dialogue, too, and made her realize that the words she had to deliver were like lyrics that she could sing as she recited them. Jane, who was ten at the time of *Paddy O'Day*, noticed Rita's nervousness on the set before every take. Rita could dance like a dervish, but was morbidly shy as soon as she had to utter a line. So Jane taught her the art of "lyrics," how to find the rhythm for every sound. And the child star served as an acting coach to sixteen-year-old Rita. Jane, who was quite spiritual for a little girl, prayed a lot. She whispered to the Lord that Rita was frightened of dialogue, and asked Him to stick with the young dancer and teach her how to sing every sentence. It worked. Rita prevailed in *Paddy O'Day*.

But she didn't have Jane Withers on the set with her for every film. The studio dropped Rita after a while. Her hairline was too low. It made her look primitive, and managed to hide her stunning features. And then a strange man came into the picture—Eddie Judson, who was thirty-nine years old and wore expensive suits; tall, with a fine crop of hair and a salesman's smile, he promised to make a star out of Rita. No one knew what the source of his income was. He seemed to arrive without a discernible past, as so many in Tinseltown do. He must have heard about Rita from a friend of his at Fox and decided to "prey" on her in his own manner. He approached the family, said he would like to take Rita to the Trocadero, and show her off to the movie crowd. Rita was seventeen. She'd never been on a date before.

It was an odd courtship; he never once declared his love. Still, she eloped with Eddie the moment she turned eighteen. It was the only way Rita could unfasten Eduardo's grip on her.

Eddie was a wizard. Within four months she had a seven-year contract at Columbia. But starlets were little more than indentured servants whose contracts could be canceled at Cohn's mere whim. So Eddie bargained on her behalf. He went to Helen Hunt, Columbia's top hairstylist. He knew that Rita would never succeed with that low hairline of hers. Hunt suggested an electrolysis studio on Sunset. There, Rita had to endure a whole series of painful treatments, in which each follicle was removed with a charge of electricity, until the roots were destroyed, one by one—and it took two years. Hunt also changed the color of her hair from dark brown to a rich, vibrant red. Now Cohn began to notice her. He snarled at Rita, called her "Big Red," and insisted that he couldn't *sell* Rita Cansino. "It's too fuckin' foreign," he supposedly said, and the Publicity Department had Rita usurp her mother's maiden name. A new Columbia starlet was born, Rita Hayworth, with her signature shoulder-length red hair.

She now played Doña Sol, an aristocratic vamp, in *Blood and Sand*, seducing poor Ty Power with each sway of her hips. Her accent was ridiculous, but when she danced with Anthony Quinn, Ty's rival as a bullfighter, each movement was like a savage musical note. Rita was noticed. Rita was adored.

She danced with Fred Astaire in two lavish Columbia musicals, *You'll Never Get Rich* and *You Were Never Lovelier*, the first in '41 and the second in '42. Her dance steps made him look like a little boy stuck in a whirlwind—that whirlwind was Rita. But Fred was as nimble as she was. He did finally catch up with her, though he never danced with Rita again.

Alas, she still had the same rotten husband to deal with. Eddie played her up to the Hollywood press. He told her what to say at each interview. He groomed her, told her what to wear. I should have sensed her hysteria, the blank, terrified look in her eye when Eddie wasn't around. But I didn't know then about the incestuous life Eduardo had forced upon her. . . .

Eddie made it worse, much worse; he pushed her to sleep with other men to help her career. Orson would call him a pimp, and a pimp he was. Eddie arranged to have Rita spend a weekend with Cohn on Cohn's yacht. But Rita backed out at the last moment. Cohn never forgave her. Yet that's how her independence began. Eddie wouldn't give her a divorce. He threatened to disfigure her, throw lye in her face, if she dared leave him. He reportedly had a letter she had written to him that could damage her career. In the letter, which had become a kind of legend in our basement at the Writers' Building, Rita had listed the producers she had slept with on Eddie's orders, and why she didn't want to do it ever again. The thought of Rita's "purloined" letter enraged me. It stank of all the power male producers had over starlets in Hollywood.

Eddie demanded $30,000 for the work he had done in making Rita a star. It was pure ransom money, but Harry Cohn, one of the cheapest men alive, paid the thirty grand just to get rid of him, and Rita finally got her divorce in '42. It wasn't charity on Cohn's part. Rita was now the biggest star on Columbia's lot. And that's why I was brought in—to protect the Janitor's investment in Rita, and feed his own delight in having me spy on her.

4

I RODE MY FORD jalopy into the hills. Woodrow Wilson Drive might just as well have been Mount Parnassus. This was a gated wilderness and wonderland far removed from the flat surfaces of Hollywood Boulevard, with its plebeian sensibility and all the bits of slow, irrevocable decay—it was a rallying point for those on the way up or on the way down: unemployed scribblers, actors, directors, and neophytes who had landed some petty job on one of the major or minor lots. There were "vultures" of every sort, half-mad secretaries, clerks, and cowboy extras who lined up at the latest Hollywood premiere outside the Egyptian or Grauman's Chinese, or watched Ty Power and Loretta Young leave their handprints in Sid Grauman's cement, and then the whole crowd would vanish into a mousetrap like mine. We Hollywoodians had secondhand bookshops along the boulevard, as well as delicatessens, bars, lingerie shops, and drugstore counters with all the aroma of decay, and with the dust, the dirt, and the constant racket of the streetcar lines.

There were no streetcars on Woodrow Wilson Drive, just a single stagecoach from the depot near the Hollywood Hotel that allowed tourists to gawk at the castles, haciendas, and ranch houses of the stars tucked away in the hills. I knew the stage-coach driver, Byron Brown, an unemployed stuntman who had crippled his leg in a bad fall, working for Tom Mix, King of the Cowboys during the silent era. Byron was a familiar sight, with his company of tourists; that coach, borrowed from one of Columbia's back lots, could carry nine or ten adults and a couple of kids.

I was mystified when the coach stopped right in front of the gate at 7975, Orson's rented home. Orson wasn't much of a plan-etary figure and shouldn't have interested Byron and his stage-coach full of star worshippers. Both of Orson's films had been flops. I held back in my coupé, remained hidden; I didn't want the Boy Wonder to think that I had directed Byron to Woodrow Wilson Drive.

Of course, Byron wasn't concerned with Orson Welles. He climbed down off the seat of the coach in his cowboy boots and dragged himself in front of the gate, tugging on the tails of his bandanna. He'd had so many falls he could barely walk, but he was the best Hollywood guide in the business. Folks had to sign up weeks in advance for one of his tours. He'd once been the highest-paid stuntman in Hollywood, part of every Tom Mix deal. That cowboy in the tall hat wouldn't do a film without Byron Brown written into his contract.

And here he was gimping along that gate.

"Ladies and gents, this Art Deco chalet, constructed in 1937, with its oval-shaped pool, is where Hollywood's love goddess, Rita Hayworth, lives when she isn't working at Columbia. It's Rita's hideaway, not her official residence. She swims here and sunbathes in the buff, I'm told, on the porch at the back of the chalet, with deer from the forest nibbling on the lawn. I'd call it paradise, wouldn't you?"

"Will Rita wave to us, Byron, if you call her out?" asked one of the tourists in a gray mackinaw that matched the grayness of his skin.

"I couldn't do that, sir. It would be violating Rita's privacy. And no one would ever trust me again."

The man in the mackinaw wasn't getting his money's worth. He'd come to Hollywood in the middle of a war, from a narrowing universe of ration stamps, and wanted his moment of glory.

Byron spotted me in my coupé, and I couldn't avoid him now. I left the car at the side of the road.

"Hey, meet Rusty Redburn, a neighbor of mine. She works at Columbia," Byron said with his usual swagger. "Maybe Rusty can introduce us to Rita."

The tourists encircled me and pawed at my leather jacket like a pack of wild animals. I was angry at that bastard, and I'd always liked him.

"Miss Rusty, is Rita's hair as red as fire?" asked a woman who accompanied the man in the mackinaw. "That's what I was told."

I couldn't abandon Byron, a fellow habitué of Hollywood Boulevard. "Oh," I declared, "it's so red, sometimes they have to follow her around the set with a fire extinguisher."

"Gawd," the woman said. "I knew it."

I must have lightened Byron's load, since the tourists returned to the stagecoach.

"Byron, take this stop off your itinerary, or you might lose your stagecoach. Mr. Cohn wouldn't like you pestering his biggest star."

"Rusty," he said, with a startled look, "you wouldn't rat on me."

"But Rita might," I said. "There's only one tour guide in these hills with a stagecoach, Byron, and that's you."

He climbed back up onto his seat and had to serenade his team of pintos before the damn horses would move. The stagecoach rumbled deeper into the hills with its rusty springs and rickety doors and wheels.

I didn't move. I loitered for fifteen minutes, worried that Rita might think I had arrived with the star worshippers. Then I rang her intercom.

"Miss Hayworth," I said. "It's Rusty Redburn, from Ophelia."

Ophelia was the most celebrated employment agency and secretarial school in Hollywood. Located on North Vine, it supplied a host of stars at the major studios with a cavalcade of secretaries and assistants. The agency was very secretive about its list of clients. And Harry Cohn must have paid the owners quite a bundle to have them claim me as one of their hirelings. But that wasn't my affair. The Janitor and all the other studio chiefs did whatever they damn pleased. It was wartime, and the studios thrived—the movie palaces were packed with people.

Rita buzzed me through the gate.

I walked past the oval pool with its dark green glaze, as if it were covered with a ripple of glass, and rang the doorbell of Orson's "Art Deco chalet." Rita met me at the door in a rumpled white blouse and rolled-up blue jeans, without her socks. She wasn't wearing any Max Factor, like Cohn's assistants. And she was far more vibrant than she appeared onscreen—a sweet temptress, a softer Doña Sol from *Blood and Sand*. And she didn't have any toreadors like Ty Power or Tony Quinn to play with, just a counterfeit secretary from the Ophelia Agency.

There were tiles in the hallway, and the staircase had a mahogany rail. We went into the kitchen. She had a gliding step. Her shoulders swayed. Her red hair had its own natural cascade.

She poured me a cup of coffee, and we drank it together, out of the very same cup. She apologized. She had fired her maid.

"Angela was a busybody. She read all my mail."

"Well, Ophelia is a full-service agency," I bragged. "We can find you another girl."

Rita had an odd request—I felt as if she trusted me on the spot.

She confided that she hadn't hired me to help her write letters. She felt embarrassed, bewildered even, around Orson. "I had so little school, Miss Rusty, and Orson is such an intellectual. You've heard of him, I suppose."

I'd found my heavenly match. "Yes, Miss Hayworth. I'm a devoted fan."

Her eyes lit with flecks of enchantment. Then she pouted. "I'm Rita here in this house. Orson has given me *Hamlet* to read. And I can't make heads or tails. . . ."

"Well," I said, with a sip of coffee from the same cup, "where should we begin?"

Rita was quite serious. "Who is Hamlet and what does he want?"

I'd read my Shakespeare at Kalamazoo. And so we went into the guiles of Hamlet, while Rita was at the stove, cooking dinner for Orson Welles. She had a dimple of deep concentration as she added paprika to the spicy chicken dish she was preparing. I was suddenly the sous-chef. I helped her snap a pot of string beans and cut the eyes out of a pile of potatoes.

"What about that crazy girl Ophelia?" she asked. "Why does the prince let her drown?"

"That's the problem. He loves her and loves her not."

Rita laughed with a deep-throated innocence. "Hamlet is not that different from most men. They will chase a woman right up to the moment of capture and then pull back."

"Cowards," I said, "cowards all."

Suddenly she looked at the clock on the wall. And that sensuous face, with the big brown eyes, froze with fright.

"I didn't realize . . . he'll be home in half an hour."

She disappeared into her bedroom, and within a flash she returned wearing a lace-edged negligée—I recognized the label, Juel Park's, with its high-class lingerie shop on Wilshire, in Beverly Hills. It was where all the Hollywood divas went to buy their lace pants. Juel Park's was the premier house of seduction, pure and simple.

"Oh, Orson," she said with a wink, wrapping herself in a very sheer silk robe—from Juel Park's. "He likes me to *dress* for dinner."

"Shouldn't I leave, Miss Rita? I wouldn't want to intrude. . . ."

"Don't be silly. We still have lots to do. Besides, you haven't earned your salary yet."

There was a welter of sadness on her face that was hard to reconcile. All the intensity had gone out of her eyes.

"I'll never learn," she said. "I'm just not smart enough. I don't have the gift."

"What gift?" I asked like a dumbbell.

"The gift of words. Orson *sings* every sentence. I've tried. But I can't really do it."

"Nonsense. You sing with your shoulders, with every step," I said. "That's your gift."

Rita stared at me. "It's not the same thing," she said in a voice that was like a whisper.

"Miss Rita, I'll teach you whatever I can."

That orphaned look was gone. I cursed myself for coming here. I was sentenced to stare at her beauty.

"I'll memorize sentences—about *Hamlet*. And then there's *War and Peace*. It hurts my head just to count the pages. Natasha and Pierre . . . and Napoleon's army. And then there's *Pride and Prejudice*."

"We'll read them all," I said, "every word."

She didn't feel beautiful, not even in her Juel Park's. Perhaps that's why there was only one Rita Hayworth. She had very little vanity at her vanity table. Gentle as she was, she combed her hair like a half-wild animal. She was Big Red, as the Janitor called her, unlike any other creature on or off Cohn's lot.

And then, in the midst of our archiving what she should read and when, the Boy Wonder arrived. He was a giant with a tiny, turned-up nose and a clumsy gait. In fact, he had the biggest shoes I'd ever seen on a man. But he also had a calculated charm. He meant to win me over without a hint of who I was.

"Darling," he said in that wonderful basso of his, "you wear a nightgown in front of strangers. You'll give all my secrets away. Miss Whoever-You-Are, you might as well know that I buy Rita the flimsiest lingerie I can find at—"

"Juel Park's."

"Ah," he said, kissing my hand, "you are an aficionado of women's undergarments. Now, who are you, and what the devil are you doing here?"

Rita, the shy one, intervened in my behalf. "Orsie," she said, "meet Miss Redburn, my tutor and secretarial assistant. I just hired her. And you'd better be nice to her. She's one of your biggest fans."

I saw the same roguish smile of Charles Foster Kane that I'd met on the screen. "And what is your movie theater of choice in Hollywood, Miss Redburn?"

"The Regina," I said.

And he roared, as if I had revealed something beyond my own power to reveal. "You're my heart of hearts, you really are—the hidden queen of that movie house, Miss Regina X. Damn it, I read your reviews all the time. You're so much better than that shit Louella. But why were you so hard on *Ambersons*, darling? You know I didn't cut that film. It was stolen from me—and massacred—while I was in Rio."

"Mr. Welles, you could have reworked every scene and it wouldn't have mattered."

His pugnacious demeanor disappeared and Orson retreated a bit. "Explain yourself," he said, "or I'll have you shot."

And now I had that big baby. "What's missing is your voice, Mr. Welles."

"But I narrate the film," he said.

"Narration, sir, is not enough."

Rita suppressed a giggle with the cup of her hand. She was having the time of her life.

"It's a frightening yarn, Mr. Welles, the unraveling of a dynasty. But the rhythm is wrong. It needed you as Georgie Minafer."

The Boy Wonder wasn't disturbed at all. He was onstage in the Hollywood Hills, playing Orson Welles. "You know how to wound a man, Miss Redburn. I'm too old to *inhabit* little George."

"Oh," I said, "you would have inhabited him well enough, sir. If you could become Kane as an old, old man, you surely could have been young Minafer at twenty—and twenty-five—in one of your false noses. Then we would have had all the sympathy and the sadness that the part required."

"She's a witch," he said. "Rita, you've hired a witch. And I'm in love with her, madly in love—"

Rita was alarmed.

And now Orson soothed her. "But in the most fanciful way. Tell me what she has taught you."

Rita held her arms behind her back and signaled to me with her thumbs.

"Hamlet is a madman who chats with ghosts, a killer prince who wants to bring down the Danish monarchy."

"Yes," Orson said, "a lad who wants to tear things apart, a schoolboy with anarchy in his rapier."

Like Orson himself. Destruction hovered over all his projects. He was a dynamiter, not a Hollywood director.

"I'm starving," he said. "Let's eat."

They invited me to sit with them at the table. And that's when I felt Hamlet's rapier in my own belly, like a razor ripping into a bag of blood. I wanted to confess that the Janitor was paying me to spy on them. But I would have lost my place, my *nearness* to Rita and Orson. And I'd have become one more Hollywood drifter without a job. That's when I decided on my course of action. I would finesse Harry Cohn, feed him a few morsels, but nothing that would hurt Rita and Orson, or reveal my true identity. Ah, Lady Hamlet was at the table, the most universal of liars, bloody bag and all.

"Tell me," Orson asked, with morsels of chicken in his mouth, "since you're such a scholar, I want some hard facts. Where did you go to college?"

"Kalamazoo," I said. "But I could only afford the first two years."

"(I've Got a Gal in) Kalamazoo" was last year's number-one hit, performed by Glenn Miller and his band. And I was the victim here. I kept getting shoved right into the thick of that damn song.

"Rita," Orson roared, triumphant now, "look what you brought into the house—our own little gal from Kalamazoo. Rusty's a real pipperoo."

Orson was satisfied. He'd labeled me, and now he could finish his meal.

5

ORSON HAD A valet, Shorty Chivallo, a half-pint who lived in the guesthouse above the garage. But there was no need to feel sorry for Shorty. He was a regular troubadour with the ladies, always in the middle of a love affair—or two. He was quite agile, and had once been a cat burglar. He could crawl through any window or hole in the wall. Shorty was also a Shakespearean. He grew up on Manhattan's Lower East Side and spent six years in Sing Sing. That's how Shorty first discovered Shakespeare. He became a scholar in the prison library, teaching himself whatever had to be taught—with the fever of ritual and religion. He followed Orson out to California and showed up at Woodrow Wilson Drive before Rita had moved in. Shorty made an odd proposal.

He offered to become Orson's valet without the least mention of a salary.

"That's ridiculous," Orson said. "I can't allow you to work for free."

"No, maestro," Shorty said. "I'll pay you for that privilege."

Orson wailed at Shorty for his insolence, and finally they

settled on a solution. Orson would borrow money from his new valet from time to time; he was always desperate for cash. And Orson let him have the guesthouse. Shorty also drove Orson from place to place in his own prewar Cadillac, with wooden blocks on the pedals. Shorty couldn't have gotten behind the wheel without those wooden blocks. The two of them were always arguing and dreaming of projects.

Shorty had a child's perverse, mischievous face. That's why the Hollywood ladies loved him so much. But something else possessed him. He wanted to play the Fool in any future film or stage production of *King Lear* directed by Orson.

"But you're unschooled," Orson would moan. "The only training you've ever had is as a cat burglar. People will laugh at me, hiring my own valet to be Lear's Fool. It's the most compelling moment in all of literature. A king in his dotage, giving all his property and treasure away, and wandering here and there with his court jester and a handful of knights. The knights are nothing. Lear and the Fool are wild men, naked to the bone, and they speak the poetry of rage and absolute despair. We laugh, we cry. We don't know how to relate to the wonder of them."

"I'll quit if you won't have me," Shorty said. But he remained in the guesthouse, chauffeured Orson with the help of those wooden blocks, and attended to his wardrobe. It was an unfortunate period in Orson's life. While other directors worked, or went overseas, Orson was idle. He'd lost the fealty of RKO, and no other studio would hire him. He did act as Rochester—with a false nose—in *Jane Eyre*, but Selznick wouldn't let him sit in the director's chair. He was considered a wrecking machine, and perhaps he was. Louella alone hadn't ruined his career.

And so he reverted to a childhood enchantment. His father had introduced him to magic, and that's what possessed him now. It didn't surprise me at all. He'd directed *Kane* with all the art of a magician, and his hocus-pocus had troubled the studios. The moguls didn't want any narrative tricks on the screen. Yet wasn't Kane his own King Lear, left in a deserted palace, without a Fool to comfort and badger him?

Orson decided on a spectacle, the Mercury Wonder Show, to entertain servicemen who were waiting to be shipped out to the Pacific from San Pedro, with Rita as his star attraction and Shorty as his assistant. He found a small, abandoned theater in Hollywood where he could rehearse—it was on North Highland, near the Max Factor salon. Orson had all the seats ripped out, so that he could duplicate a carnival atmosphere. He'd gutted the entire house, turned it into a cavern—a dark, empty circus. The chandeliers were gone, and he brought in hurricane lamps to light his cavern, with shadows on the roughened walls.

He had Jo Cotton from the Mercury as his fellow performer. Orson used a little of his own money, and lot of Shorty's excess cash from his days as a cat burglar, to buy thirty-six thousand dollars' worth of equipment, including a calliope from a beached riverboat.

The Janitor knew about Rita's planned participation in Orson's spectacle. I told him so. Like other artful liars, I played on the truth as much as I could, without having Cohn grasp how fond I was of Rita and Orson. I did end up meeting with Cohn every Wednesday at four, as we had arranged, flying right past his little fleet of secretaries. The Janitor seemed to thrive on these encounters, as if I were revealing unholy secrets when I revealed nothing at all.

"She cooks for him in her underwear?"

"I never said that, Mr. Cohn. That's her way of dressing up."

"And they live with a shrimp?"

"Nothing of the kind," I said. "Shorty is his chauffeur and his valet. He has a room above the garage."

"*Shorty Chivallo*," Cohn pronounced with contempt. "An ex-con.

And a safecracker. The little bastard has slept with half the girls on my lot."

His venom was misplaced. Cohn didn't give a damn about Orson's valet. He wanted Rita. He still hadn't recovered from the fact that she wouldn't spend a weekend with him on his yacht. He must have relived that ill-fated weekend every day of his life.

"Big Red," he would mutter with a maddening glaze in his blue eyes. "Big Red." He planted microphones in her dressing room at Columbia, mocked her on the set—he was always in a rage about Rita—and his minions also mocked her. She was filming *Cover Girl* at the time. Since she was so distraught, Rita asked me not to watch her scenes. She had enough people gazing at her, she said. She preferred that I sit in her dressing room. It puzzled me that it was such a shoddy place. But that was Cohn's means of humiliating the star of his studio. Rita's mirror had a curious yellow tint. The paint on the walls had begun to chip. And she had a child's electric train set with half a mile of tracks winding across the floor. She'd had the same Lionel railroad when she was a little girl. It was the only toy Eduardo had ever given her. The sound of the whistling trains seemed to soothe her, and still did. And I had to dodge those whirling locomotives while I waited for Rita in her dressing room.

She was always frazzled after the first half a dozen takes. She would return to the dressing room with chalk-white lips and a blank stare on her face.

"I hate them all," she said. She'd cry in my arms, and slowly that alabaster look would disappear.

"Rusty," she'd whisper, "you're the only one I can trust."

"You're living with Orson," I had to remind her.

"Oh, Orsie's nice," she said. "But I could never trust him the way I trust you. He's a man, for God's sake. I have to perform for him, play the naughty girl every other night. . . ."

But she was always much less somber once we left Gower Street. Anything to do with Columbia rattled her. And she was superstitious, perhaps from the time she had danced with her father at casino after casino. She spat three times into her handkerchief and twisted about like a kite with red hair. "Good riddance to bad rubbish," she shouted, pretending to salute the Janitor's window.

Shorty would pick us up in his Cadillac and drive us to the theater across from Max Factor. We entered that cavern with its hurricane lamps. I had become Orson's booking agent for the Wonder Show. I had to hire clowns, acrobats, showgirls from MGM, barnyard animals from Columbia's ranch, a tiger, a lion, and a leopard from the Paramount lot. We were meant to rehearse for sixteen weeks. Orson had an entire circus and magic show in mind. But we didn't have enough available cash to hire the clowns and acrobats until the very last day of rehearsals. Orson raided Juel Park's as often as he could and wrapped Rita in the finest lingerie, yet he never even glanced at the bottom line of his bank account. He thrived on chaos, and he made his magic show more and more complex, as if chaos and randomness were built right into the fabric of his art.

Most important, Rita could breathe in this dusty cavern, away from Columbia and Harry Cohn. I'd helped sew her costumes— the Boy Wonder had choreographed six sequences, which meant six changes of costume, and I served as her dresser. That gliding step of hers had come back, and she danced across the cavern, among the hurricane lamps. She wasn't paid a cent, but she was happiest here. She was working with Orsie, and this fantastic carnival in the dark meant more to Rita than her career. She had never wanted to be an actress. And signing her autograph on glossy shots of herself in a lace gown to satisfy the insatiable hunger of her fans seemed almost like a death sentence to Rita, as if she were signing away the rights to her own flesh.

And it was curious. She had a carnality in front of the camera. Was it part of the same repertoire that Eduardo had taught her when she was twelve? Or was it another kind of brazenness? Margarita Carmen Cansino Hayworth—Big Red—declared her freedom by making love to a camera lens.

6

O RSON'S CARNIVAL WENT up in the heart of Hollywood,
on Cahuenga Boulevard, near the Hollywood Canteen,
where Rita had spent her nights preparing sandwiches, washing
dishes, and dancing with servicemen. Rita could relax there. She
didn't have to play Doña Sol—the temptress from *Blood and Sand*—
at the canteen. She could tell the servicemen about the electric
trains in her dressing room and not feel a bit embarrassed. But now
she had to rehearse for the magic show, rehearse well past midnight
when Orson was at his best. He'd always been a nighthawk. He
slept until noon unless he was on call for *Jane Eyre*, and even then
he was always late. . . .

The tent was on a lot that belonged to one of the majors; at least
that was what I had been told. It was a vast circus tent that looked
like a series of sewn-together sails assembled by circus men with
deep ripples in their backs; they used sledgehammers, stakes, and
piles of rope. At first the canvas lay on the ground across the lot;
and suddenly, with one terrific pull on the ropes by the circus men,
twenty strong, the tent billowed out with a perfect snap and rose

above the boulevard. And Orson had his Wonder Show with red circus wagons, sawdust, a midway, and with bleachers and camp chairs stacked in rows that reached to the roof—it could have been the roof of the world, that's how high the tent swayed on its central pole along Cahuenga Boulevard.

Orson thrived on illusion. That was his masterstroke, the secret to whatever he did. Soldiers and sailors entered for free, of course, and all the others paid as much as five dollars; even Louis B. Mayer of MGM had to show his hawkish face, as part of the moguls' patriotic duty. It was Shorty who collected the tickets, standing on a stool, Shorty who had to find strands of order in the Boy Wonder's extravagance. There was bedlam even before the show began. Barnyard animals, braying all the time, wandered about, accompanied by bare-chested acrobats in skin-tight pants and clowns in gaudy costumes, who lunged at people until Shorty led them away. He was the lone constable under the tent.

Orson climbed onto the stage wearing a fez and a long black-and-white robe, as Dr. Welles the Magnifico, ringmaster of the Mercury Wonder Show. He made no patriotic pleas to the servicemen. "We're here to entertain," he warbled into the microphone in a voice that resounded off the upper tier. "If there is confusion, or if I fail at a trick, please forgive us. Ambition is what drives me, the need to do more and more. That is my weakness—and my great gift."

A leopard passed in front of him on a silken leash held by a little girl in a nightgown. It could have been a mirage as the leopard and the little girl vanished into the wings.

While the crowd roared above and the acrobats performed cartwheels below, and wagon masters drove their wagons across the midway with reckless speed, and the clowns clung to the high wires, hurling their wigs at the audience, Welles the Magnifico put a rooster in a trance with a few whispers and a wave of his magic wand. The rooster stood on its perch, stiff as the dead. A sailor taunted it.

"Wake up, stupid!"

And Orson chided the sailor. "You really ought to be polite to Little Magnifico, or he could remain there forever."

Another sailor salaamed and said, "Wake up, little darling, please."

The audience cheered him on. Orson tapped the rooster's beak, and the bird ruffled its feathers, started to make an ungodly racket, flew off its perch, and fell onto the ground. The audience barely had time to clap, as a marksman arrived out of nowhere in a storm trooper's uniform, stood in the stands, among the soldiers, sailors, and civilians, aimed his rifle at Orson and fired. The report of that rifle reverberated through the corners of that canvas tent like the crack of doom. The soldiers and sailors were stunned. But I was privy to Orson's monkeyshines. The bullet was real enough, and the marksman even realer. He had aimed slightly off-target, and his bullet landed without the least ruffle in a mattress secreted away in the wings.

Orson had hid another bullet under his tongue while he was waking the rooster, and with a sudden snap of his head right after the rifle's report, he gave the illusion that he had caught the bullet in his mouth. He spat it into the sawdust. Otherwise the soldiers and sailors might have ripped off the rifleman's arms. Once they realized he was another illusionist, they let him run into the narrow tunnel under their seats.

While Orson swallowed fire and threaded needles with a flick of his tongue, clowns fell off their unicycles and were buried in sawdust, and servicemen stamped their feet as their frustration grew. They'd come to see the love goddess, not a fire-eater in a fez. "Where's Rita, where's Rita!" they chanted over and over again. "Rita, Rita, lovely Rita."

"Patience, my children," Orson muttered into the microphone, wrapping his robe around him like a bat's wings. "And now for the pièce de résistance, a trick that Houdini himself never quite mastered, the Death Defier, performed by Jo-Jo, Wizard of the West."

Jo Cotton arrived from the wings in top hat and tails, followed by Shorty and a pair of acrobats, who were dangling a large sack. Shorty tied Jo-Jo's hands as tight as he could, stuck a gag in his mouth, so he could barely breathe, then bundled him into the sack, while two other acrobats carried out a steamship trunk. With delicate maneuvering, Shorty and the acrobats locked Jo-Jo, gagged and bound, inside the trunk. And as an added measure, the acrobats wrapped the trunk in thick cords of seaman's rope and left the stage with a grandiose flourish of their arms, abandoning Orson and the steamship trunk.

Now we saw the mastery of his art. Orson never once looked at or mentioned the trunk. He danced with several chorines, plucked a goose out of his hat, while the audience could think of nothing but that lone trunk on the stage, with Jo Cotton's lungs about to burst for lack of air.

Finally Louis B. Mayer himself stood up. "We cannot bear it, Welles. You must do something. Mr. Cotton will choke to death."

"Nonsense," Orson said. "Jo-Jo is fine."

There were rumblings high above, among the soldiers and sailors; a woman fainted, and Shorty had to supply an oxygen mask. Orson was amused by the murderous look in the audience's eyes. He was a dynamiter, as I said, a provocateur. He'd been that way ever since he was a child. And a moment before the servicemen were about to rebel, rush to the stage, and cut the cords, Orson bowed, removed a jackknife from his pocket, ripped away at the ropes, smiled once, and uncovered the trunk.

Then Rita's head popped up with her magnificent red mane.

Her shoulders were bare in a sequin dress designed by Marshall Page, couturier to the stars.

Orson clutched Rita's hand, and she leapt genie-like out of the trunk in high heels.

With a single, sudden coup, the Mercury Wonder Show had become a success, as long as Rita was onstage. She danced with Orson and sang "Long Ago (and Far away)" in her own natural voice, which was soft but a little scratchy. Rita had been feuding with Harry Cohn at Columbia. The Janitor wouldn't allow her to have any voice lessons. It was Martha Mears who dubbed the same song in *Cover Girl*, stealing Rita's shadow, and the shadow of her voice. But she could still sing at the magic show with a bandstand behind her, and a full orchestra. The soldiers and sailors were intoxicated by this girl who'd climbed out of a steamship trunk when she shouldn't have been there at all. But I knew all the mechanics behind that trick. Jo-Jo's hands hadn't really been tied. He pulled on a string and wiggled his way out of the sack. And he escaped from a push-out panel in the rear of the trunk and crawled into the wings unnoticed, while Rita crawled through the same panel wearing a cape covered in sawdust. She removed the cape once inside and rose out of the trunk like an ebullient jack-in-the-box.

It didn't really matter now what Orson did. He was only the manager and chief magician of the Mercury Wonder Show. Rita was its soul. She was outside Orson's abracadabra. Clowns careened off their unicycles. Acrobats tumbled off the wires. Lions roamed without their trainers. A calliope arrived in a coach with horses covered in silver; its steam-pipe music had a deafening screech; but none of that noise could harm the presence of Rita onstage; it wasn't her beauty alone that thrilled the audience; it was the perfect glide of every step, the lyrical sweep of her broad shoulders, as she helped the maestro perform his tricks; handkerchiefs flew in every direction; a robin nestled in Rita's lovely hand.

Transfixed by Rita, caught in her spell, none of the servicemen wanted to leave that tent. They followed the lyrics of "Long Ago (and Far Away)," begging her to sing the song again. Suddenly all motion stopped. The clowns and acrobats stood in Rita's wake. The calliope went dead. The leopards and lions preened and licked themselves, while Rita sang in the softest voice.

After almost three hours the servicemen finally started to leave. A messenger from Rita's studio arrived with a sealed letter. "What the heck is this?" Rita asked, frightened by the formality, knowing the Janitor's tricks. She ripped open the envelope and dug out the letter.

"Orsie, what is this?"

"A cease-and-desist letter. You're Cohn's property, and if you continue to perform, he'll sue."

I could see the furrows gather around her eyes. "The hell with him. He can take his *Cover Girl* and shove it. He won't let me sing. I'm his puppet, Big Red." A fit was brewing; it was the first time I'd seen her temper flare. She didn't have the same glide. She moved with a whiplash. I might have tumbled had I gotten in her way.

"What's your opinion, Rusty? What do you think?"

I had to be cautious.

"Orson's right. Cohn could ruin your career with one stroke of his pen."

She sought comfort in my own unambiguous glance, while her spine quivered like a serpent under her skin. Shorty drove us back to Woodrow Wilson Drive, with his feet on those wooden blocks. Rita sat like a zombie, as if the blood had gone out of her. I was so damn ashamed. Cohn couldn't have crafted that letter without my reports. Rita, it seems, had been having too good a time at the tent show.

7

MARLENE DIETRICH HAD volunteered to serve in Rita's place at the Mercury Wonder Show. She, too, wore a sequin gown designed by Marshall Page. Furious, Rita fell into a jealous fit.

"You're fucking that Nazi. I can feel it in my bones."

"That's ridiculous," Orson said. "Marlene hates Hitler. She's been at more bond rallies than any other actress."

"You're fucking her."

Orson loved to be at the center of a storm. "You told me how much you liked her at the canteen, how you both washed dishes together, shared a cigarette."

"That's not the same thing," Rita said. "You're fucking her behind the curtain, every night."

Orson laughed his Shadow laugh, his earsplitting roar. "She's with that Frenchie, Jean Gabin. He watches every move I make. He could slit my throat. He's practically a gangster, Gabin is. Rusty, don't you agree?"

I idolized Gabin. He was my favorite actor in the world—the

French Gable, as critics called him, but Gable couldn't touch the sadness in Gabin's eyes, the deep pessimism of his portraits. Gabin dies in almost every flick. That was his signature, his charm on the screen. He came to America after the fall of France in June of 1940 and fell in love with Marlene. Hollywood didn't know what to do with Gabin. He wasn't suited to American success stories. So he acted in a film or two—both were flops—and escorted Marlene to the Hollywood Canteen and the Mercury Wonder Show.

Finally Rita's temper subsided. She accompanied us to Cahuenga Boulevard in Shorty's Cadillac and sat in the bleachers wearing a blue veil. The soldiers and sailors adored Marlene, but the excitement never built under the tent the way it had with Rita. And the show finished in less than an hour and a half.

But the Janitor had miscalculated. He'd created his own time bomb. His attempt to sabotage the Mercury Wonder Show and penalize Rita had only brought her closer to Orson Welles. They were married that September of '43, in the midst of *Cover Girl*; copying Welles, Rita arrived later and later at the studio, and there was little Harry Cohn and his production chiefs could do about it. They had to acquiesce to Rita—their Big Red—or hold up production indefinitely, and the Janitor couldn't afford to do that; he would have been lost in a maze of light bulbs.

It was like an elopement out of a fairy tale, as if Orson and his accomplice, Shorty, had rescued Rita from Harry Cohn. Shorty's Cadillac appeared on Gower Street minutes before Rita's lunch break. Rita wasn't wearing her *Cover Girl* costume. She left Gene Kelly flat on Stage Nine and walked out of the lot in a tan suit with padded shoulders and a floppy hat with a "bridal veil." Orson looked like a groom in chalk-striped trousers, a pink shirt, and the bow tie that he favored. They arrived at the municipal building in Santa Monica, where they were met by Jo Cotton, the groom's best man, and Dr. Maurice Bernstein, known as

"Dadda," Orson's former guardian and a mysterious figure out of his past.

Dadda was a Russian Jewish orthopedist from Chicago who got into a scrape with a fellow surgeon and had to move to Kenosha, where he befriended Orson's parents, Richard and Beatrice Welles, and soon became Beatrice's lover. He was a handsome devil, with dark hair and dark eyes, who made it a habit of seducing other men's wives, particularly if they had a musical bent, as Beatrice did. He discovered Orson at six months and put himself in charge. As his protégé grew, Dadda showered him with gifts—an actor's makeup kit that Orson still used, a violin, a painter's box that he always carried with him, a magician's kit, a puppet theater—and composed a nickname for him: *Pookles.* Dadda still called him that. There had been some conflict between them, as Orson told me in private. Dadda was very stingy in doling out the boy's inheritance, keeping a good portion for himself. Despite the conflict, "Pookles" never gave up his affection for Dadda. That was revealed in *Citizen Kane*, where the publisher's finance manager and most loyal friend is also named Bernstein. . . .

They all went before the superior court judge on the fourth floor of the municipal building, where Rita could barely whisper the ceremonial words, and Orson the Magnifico couldn't seem to get the wedding ring out of its box. The judge had to help him extract the ring. I wondered where Eduardo and Volga were, why Rita hadn't invited her own parents to the wedding. Big Red didn't want them there on what must have been the first truly happy day of her life.

She stared at the ring on her finger. "Rusty, make a wish."

I wavered.

"*Please,*" she said with tears in her eyes.

So I wished that Orson would be faithful to her until the last day of her life. But I'd researched the maestro too well. He'd discarded his first wife and seldom met with his daughter, Christopher Welles, who was five years old. And he'd tossed away sweethearts like twisted flowers. He was devoted to Rita now. That's what mattered.

Reporters were waiting for them outside the building.

"Miss Hayworth, where are you going on your honeymoon?"

"Mrs. Welles, you mean. . . . It was my lunch break. I have to report back to Harry Cohn."

Orson had become an outlaw, banned from the lot until Columbia declared him a bit of a genius once he was married to the studio's biggest star. Suddenly the wrecker could do no wrong. Harry Cohn invented tales about Orson directing a sequel to *Gone With the Wind*, with Rita as Scarlett O'Hara. Of course, he didn't have the rights to the book or any of its characters. But it was a "morsel," as Hollywood columnists liked to call it. And wartime audiences loved to imagine their favorite redhead returning to Tara without Vivien Leigh. Many of them didn't know what a director was or what he did. They imagined that an actress like Rita directed herself. So Orson Welles didn't exist in their minds except perhaps as the magician who was married to Rita. . . .

Red invited me to watch a rough cut of *Cover Girl* in the Janitor's private screening room. Harry wanted to show her off to the "Big Boys," the Manhattan bankers and brokers on Columbia's Board. They ogled Rita from their velvet cushions, hypnotized by her red hair. Harry didn't even bother to introduce me to these sultans in Arrow shirts and argyle socks. They all had hairy hands.

I hadn't been on the set of *Cover Girl*. But I had a premonition of what the film was all about—girls in skimpy attire parading in front of a panorama of male characters—bit players and stars—who ogled them with utter amusement and as much lust as could make it onto the screen in '43. That's what Rita had to contend with. No matter what part she was meant to deliver, she was still Salome with her seven veils. Producers, directors, cameramen, and fellow actors all "undressed" her as she danced.

Harry was selective in what he revealed about the film. He didn't feature Danny McGuire (Gene Kelly), whom he borrowed from MGM at a hefty fee to dance with Rita and woo her a little. Harry didn't feature him at all. He concentrated on Big Red as *Rusty* Parker—no relation to me, of course. The bastards at Columbia had swiped my name. But I didn't care. There was room for more than one Rusty in Hollywood.

We first see her as a chorine, half-naked, at Danny McGuire's nightclub in Brooklyn. All the chorines have one ambition—to become a cover girl for *Vanity* magazine's Golden Wedding Anniversary issue. One night *Vanity*'s publisher, John Coudair (Otto Kruger), arrives unannounced at Danny's club with Broadway impresario Noel Wheaton (Lee Bowman). Coudair hasn't been able to find the right cover girl for *Vanity*. He's interviewed hundreds of girls—thousands, perhaps. But he's instantly struck by Rusty Parker, his eyes glued to her with both lust and a terrible sense of loss. It seems that Rusty Parker reminds him of a showgirl he had met forty years ago, Maribelle Hicks, also played by Rita (in a flashback) with great aplomb. It's the most poignant part of the film. Coudair tried to woo Maribelle, but she marries her own accompanist, a piano player. As it turns out, Maribelle is Rusty Parker's grandmother, who had recently died. There's even a touch of incest in Coudair's attraction to Rusty Parker, but I'm not sure anyone else noticed it in that screening room, not even Rita herself.

Rusty Parker becomes Coudair's Cover Girl, of course. Danny McGuire is jealous, and accuses her of betraying his nightclub and all the chorines. Rusty is now dancing in one of Noel Wheaton's exclusive uptown theaters. She agrees to marry Wheaton, the debonair Broadway prince with his suave manner, who had made her a star and believes he has the right to possess her. But Rusty Parker rebels. She sneaks out of her own wedding to Wheaton as *Vanity's* Cover Girl and returns to Brooklyn and Danny McGuire.

The film enraged me, left me boiling mad. It was a venomous fairy tale. All the girls in the film were fleshpots—merchandise for the men.

"Beautiful," one of Columbia's sultans said, puffing on a Havana from Cohn's humidor. "Harry, I commend you. What gams Rita has."

"You can't miss," said the second. None of the sultans congratulated Rita. It was Harry's film, not hers.

The sultans were wrong. Rita was an enchantress, a girl with diamonds in her legs, as she moved with a furious glow that left every other dancer in her wake. Not even poor Gene Kelly could match the magnetic sweep of her "gams." Rusty Parker was all alone up on the screen on Harry's front wall.

I clapped at the end of the screening to satisfy the sultans in their in argyle socks. But I mourned Rita, despite the diamonds in her legs. Rusty Parker was *regulated* throughout, preyed on by Coudair and Noel Wheaton, perhaps even by Danny himself, as much as she loved him. No one seemed to care what Rusty Parker wanted. And Cohn wouldn't even allow her to ask that question.

She was *his* property, and Danny's, too, in the film. Still, I wore the satanic mask of a smile. I was damaging Red, not protecting her. I didn't want to get fired. Fact is, I was mortally afraid. Perhaps it was the aroma of the humidor, and the sultans' hairy hands, or the plushness of that screening room, but I abandoned Big Red to her own silence.

8

A DAY OR TWO after the screening, someone showed up at the gate on Woodrow Wilson Drive. Orson happened to be at home preparing a script for the radio when the buzzer sounded. "Lamont Cranston here," Orson said in the Shadow's somber voice. "Who is it?"

"Eddie Judson."

Rita was bewildered. Her arms flapped like the wings of a crazed bird. "Orsie, don't let him in—please."

"Darling," Orson said, calming down his wife, "he'll only come again. He wants something. Let's find out what it is."

"I know what he wants—my blood. Orsie, he'd drink it all if he could."

Orson laughed. "Well, let's meet the vampire face-to-face. We'll dig a pitchfork out of the shed and jab him in the heart— right, Shorty?"

"Yeah, boss," Shorty said. "A pitchfork can do wonders."

And so Shorty buzzed him in.

Eddie looked like a down-and-out salesman. He was wearing

a herringbone suit with a torn cuff, an unclean white shirt, and a canary-yellow tie, while he clutched a bouquet of exotic tulips in one of his manicured hands. That bouquet must have cost him a pretty penny, unless he had swiped it from a flower shop in the lobby of a high-class hotel. I could imagine that he hadn't prospered without Rita, his number-one "client." Slightly gray at the temples, he was beginning to grow bald; I suspect he used makeup to soften his grim pallor.

"For the new bride," he said, but Rita wouldn't accept his bouquet. She stood crumpled up in the corner.

"Darling," Orson said, "don't be rude. That's not like *my* Rita."

She came out of the corner to curtsy once and grab the flowers. I undid the wrapping paper and put the tulips in a vase. Eddie's flowers began to breathe like succulent creatures. I didn't like his smile. He was here to menace with his crooked mouth.

But he didn't have a menacing voice. He began to plead with the falsetto of a choirboy. "Mr. Welles, I made your wife into a star. I ought to have some compensation—a slice of the pie."

"You son of a bitch," Rita said. "Harry Cohn gave you thirty grand just to get the fuck out."

"Ah, darling," Orson said in an actor's modulated voice, "you mustn't be mean to poor Eddie. He brought you a bouquet. Thank him, dear."

I could feel Rita's fury the second I recalled how silent she had been all through their marriage, how Eddie Judson had bullied and abused her, sent her to sleep with other men. "I'll thank him," Rita said, as she turned to slap Eddie's face. The bastard never even flinched. She'd left him with two deep marks in the pancake he wore.

"Hey, I'm the innocent party," he said, patting his cheek with a clown's red handkerchief he pulled out of a hidden pocket.

"Innocent," Rita said, rage distorting her features. "You piece of shit, you pimped me out to your producer friends and half the gossip columnists in Hollywood who had a prick in their pants. You would have had me sleep with Harry Cohn, spend a weekend on his yacht."

Eddie tapped his forehead. "You slept with the others, so why not him? He would have made me a producer on the lot."

"Enough," Orson said. "Judson, we don't need to hear about your tactics with Harry Cohn. Now, what the hell do you want?"

"A little respect. Rita is *my* creation, not Columbia's, not Harry Cohn's. She would still be floating around in some string of 'B' pictures without me. The electrolysis was my idea. I paid for those treatments, follicle by follicle, out of my own fucking pocket. I calmed her before every audition. She would have been incoherent without me—incoherent, you hear? I want to become her manager again—at a thousand a month. Believe me, Mr. Welles, I have plenty of tales to tell about your . . . wife."

"So it's a bit of blackmail," Orson said, lunging at Eddie, but he wasn't much of a gladiator with his big flat feet. He was clumsy, as he had always been. Eddie shoved him aside with a sinister laugh. Shorty, however, had grown up under different circumstances on Manhattan's Lower East Side. He hunched his shoulders, and butted both of Eddie's kneecaps like a billy goat.

Eddie groaned and collapsed to the floor. "I'm crippled," he said, "crippled for life."

Orson and Shorty helped him to his feet.

"I still have my contacts," he said, hobbling about. "She's finished, I'm telling you."

"I sincerely doubt that," Orson said. "You're the one who's finished. Your little circus is over, Mr. Eddie Judson. Hollywood has slammed its door."

"But I have pictures," he blurted.

Orson rubbed his chin. I knew his tactics. He was stalling for time. Eddie had unnerved him.

"I hired a photographer when that slut was sleeping with other men."

Orson punched him and nearly cracked a knuckle. "You won't call my wife a slut—not in this house."

Eddie laughed. "Call her the Mother of God, what do I care? I have the pics."

He was bluffing, with a gob of blood in his mouth. We were as keen as cannibals in our basement cubicles. Louella and I would have known had any such pictures of Rita been for sale. There was an unbroken market for "nudies" of that nature. And I had heard of none.

"Throw him out," I said with all the swagger of a professional snoop.

"Don't come back," Orson said, and Eddie hobbled to the door.

There was an electric spark of silence in the living room, a moment beguiled by sharp static.

Then Shorty spoke. "Listen, boss, I don't trust the bastard. I can do the number on him, do it myself."

Orson glowered with his deep-set eyes that made him look like a Mongolian warlord. "What are you talking about?"

"The number," Shorty said. "Have him put in a pine box."

"We're not barbarians," Orson said.

"If you don't want me involved, don't worry. I can find other talent."

"And you want to play the Fool," Orson said. "You're a small-time hustler, just like Eddie Judson, when you say things like that. You have no dignity of character—none. I'll banish you to the guesthouse."

"Big talker," Shorty said. "But suppose he has the ammo? Then we're up the creek."

9

NONE OF THE "nudies" surfaced, or so it seemed. But the bastard began to give unflattering interviews about Rita to his network of gossip columnists. There was a sudden barrage of articles about Rita's electrolysis, images of her with a Neanderthal hairline, as if she'd been born in a cave. "There is no Rita Hayworth," Judson said to columnist Sidney Skolsky at his headquarters in Schwab's on Sunset, where all the unemployed writers met at the counter and feasted on their ice-cream sodas and tuna fish sandwiches for thirty-five cents. "She's a fabrication."

"I'll kill him," Rita said.

Shorty began to weave his angelic smile. "Exactly my sentiment."

"And where will that leave us?" Orson asked. "My wife with handcuffs to complement her wedding ring? No, thank you. We'll wait out his little brush fire."

Rita went to work; Orson continued with the Wonder Show. But then Lolly Parsons got into the fray with her usual poisonous drip in her syndicated column, Flickerings from Filmland.

*What's this that we have been hearing about our Cover Girl? Are
there lewd photographs of La Hayworth up for grabs? Will our boys at
battle in the Pacific have to reconsider their favorite pinup? I wonder.
Maybe you should, too.*

I was summoned to the Brown Derby on North Vine, where
Louella sat at the queen's private booth with her wattles and frazzled hair. North Vine wasn't like the original Derby on Wilshire in
the shape of a stupid hat. The Hollywood Derby was designed like
a Spanish mission, with chandeliers that shed the soft, shadowed
light of a church, and it was where all the moguls met to make their
deals because of its proximity to the studios. Wilshire was too far
away. No one, not even Louis B. Mayer, could enter the Hollywood Derby without kissing the queen's hand. But the queen had
a rival now. She had to share her grip on Hollywood with Hedda
Hopper, who was tall and blond and didn't look like a malevo-
lent toad. Hedda had been an actress, had appeared in more than
seventy-five films. Hedda had a silky voice and her own syndicated
column. She was on national radio, and had narrated no fewer than
six shorts on Hollywood for Paramount. She didn't have Hearst
behind her, like Louella, but "Willie," as his friends called him,
was now fading fast with his galaxy of newspapers. His mistress,
Marion Davies, had to bail him out of bankruptcy with a million
dollars of her own and all the jewels he had given her.

But Louella still had her booth, which commanded the entire
Derby. No one could get in without a nod from Louella, who
despised cutlery and loved to nibble with her fingers. I wasn't
allowed to sit until she looked me up and down with her mean
little eyes, set deep in her skull, like a luminous cavern. The first
thing I noticed was the tulips on the table, and I realized where
Eddie had gotten his flowers—from Gilles, the manager of the
Derby, at Louella's request. She was in cahoots with that swindler.

He was another one of her stringers—her informants, her rats—now that he had no income. And Gilles must have wrapped the flowers himself, assembled that bouquet with a willfulness all his own. He often plotted with Louella and planned the demise of this actor or director who had withheld whatever she desired and was on her unwanted list.

The toad stared at me with her deep-set eyes. "You've been working for Rita as her secretary, haven't you, my little pet?"

I stared right back. "I'm not your pet, Miss Parsons."

"And you're spying on Rita and that miserable Mr. Welles for Harry Cohn, aren't you?"

I realized I was on a precipice at Woodrow Wilson Drive. Louella could have informed on me at any moment, but she wouldn't. I was much more valuable to her hanging in midair. She was the real spy. She'd been ratting on Marion Davies—her very best friend—to Mr. Hearst for two decades now, had told him about Marion's fleeting romance with that Little Dictator, Charlie Chaplin, as well as all her other love affairs. And it was Marion who had introduced Louella to Hearst, who had convinced him to hire her as a columnist. But Louella was loyal to no one, and "Willie" didn't seem to mind the love affairs. He treated Marion as a naughty child.

"You will tell me *everything*," Louella insisted, "*everything*, you hear?"

I was still on that precipice. And I would fall, whatever I did.

"Rusty, dear, what does the Boy Wonder say about me? Now, no lies."

The thing about Louella was that she did have a sentimental streak. She came into prominence as movieland's gossipmonger during the silent era. And she had a soft heart for those Hollywood-ians who didn't survive the transition to sound. Many of these casualties ended up as pensioners without much of a pension at the

Hollywood Hotel. And on Friday nights Louella would appear in the lobby with a ten-dollar bill for every single one of these ghosts. She'd written about them in her columns, had talked about their stardom in some moribund DeMille epic.

But I still had to be careful with the toad, who clung to her booth in her silver fox coat and diamonds that reminded me of tattoos, as I talked about the Boy Wonder.

"You disabled him, Louella."

"Evidently not enough," she said. "He wooed and won the biggest star in Hollywood, stole her from a true patriot, Vic Mature, after that poor boy enlisted in the Coast Guard. I wrote to Welles' draft board, I had Louis B. Mayer complain, but it seems that the Boy Wonder has fallen arches. The goddamn Armed Forces won't take fellahs with flat feet."

I had to compete with her cunning. I'm sure the toad had read my reviews, published in the Regina's mimeographed broadsheet. I was now part-owner of that little firetrap on Hollywood Boulevard, ever since the Janitor, with Rita and Orson's help, had doubled my salary—I invested every spare penny I had in the Regina. It had become more of a home to me than my roomette at the Hollywood Hotel. I was Rita's confidential secretary *and* Regina X.

"Miss Louella, come on, you know that *Kane* is a good film."

She tapped the ashtray with her cigarette holder. "A great film, perhaps the greatest of all time."

"And still you destroyed it."

"I had to, child. He attacked the Chief and made fun of Marion—compared her to a silly opera singer. A wiser man would have chosen another subject. What does he say about me?"

I looked into those caverns, but couldn't see a glimpse of her dark eyes.

"He calls you an inexorable shit."

"*Inexorable?* No, I am not," she said. And that's when Eddie

Judson slid next to her in the booth. His outfit wasn't rumpled this afternoon. He was the same dapper guy I remembered, with a silk handkerchief and a starched collar.

"Hello, Rusty—hello, hello." His baritone had miraculously come back. All the thinness had gone out of his voice. He now had Louella Parsons as his protective codpiece.

"You haven't lost your handle," I said. "You're as much of a swindler as you've ever been. And clever as you are, you've attached yourself to Miss Louella at the Brown Derby."

The toad sat there with her burning eyes. "You ought to be nicer to Eddie. Your mistress's entire career is at stake. Not even La Hayworth could survive the publication of 'nudie' pics, popular as she may be. He's considering a 'nudie' calendar, and Columbia would drop her in a flash. But I've asked him to postpone the calendar, as a personal favor to me."

I didn't like this unholy alliance. She used her column for all kinds of vendettas—Louella always tried to even some score—and she was willing to break Rita just to get back at the Boy Wonder and his refusal to abandon *Citizen Kane*, a film she herself admitted was a masterpiece. She'd backed Orson at first, but he'd made a fool of her in front of Willie. So she had to demonize him.

And I had to fight back, demonize Eddie if I could.

"Miss Louella must have told you," I said. "I was paid to dig up dirt at Columbia. I dug as hard as I could, and all I could find was how you mistreated your wife. There was never a single mention of any pics."

Eddie guffawed in my face. Then he put on a pair of white gloves, pulling on every finger, as a surgeon might, testing the pliability of his fingers, and he removed a manila envelope the size of a postcard from his breast pocket. Inside the envelope were several photographs in plastic slips. He tossed one onto the table with his newfound assurance that the toad was on his side. He gave me a

jeweler's loupe to wear. I scrunched my eye and saw a woman sitting in a chair in her lacy underpants. There was nothing provocative about her pose, nothing meant to tease or seduce, but the
woman was definitely Rita before she'd had her scalp redone with
electrolysis, before she had become a redhead.

"That's the first," he said. "I have another dozen—for my calendar. And the poses get better and better. You wanna see her bush?"

"Watch your language, Mr. Judson," the toad said. But she was
much fouler than he was, particularly when she played craps in the
lobby of the Hollywood Hotel. She was the best craps shooter in
movieland, and she had a whole mantilla of curses whenever she
blew on a pair of dice.

The toad turned to me. "Child, talk to Rita. Tell her she's
licked. She'll have to hire Eddie at a thousand a month. That
includes my cut."

I left them there to gloat. And I walked back out into the sunlight. I listened to the electric buzz of the streetcar a few blocks
away. I couldn't save Rita from Eddie or the toad.

10

WHENEVER THE BLUES HIT, I ran to the Cat's Paw, a lesbian bar and lounge on the boulevard, right across the street from Musso's. There was the usual sign in the window.

OFF LIMITS

ALL MILITARY PERSONNEL

FORBIDDEN TO ENTER THESE PREMISES

The sign meant little or nothing at all. The bar was full of WACs dancing with WAVES. Still, I never once saw a military policeman intervene or raid the Cat's Paw. Management paid off the vice squads, both city and county, but the bar couldn't afford a first-rate swing band of its own, and it didn't want a bunch of amateurs, so Glenn Miller or Benny Goodman was piped in. And it was just my luck that Glenn Miller was serenading me with "(I've Got a Gal in) Kalamazoo."

I wasn't wearing my usual corduroys. I hadn't come to flirt. Just to lick my wounds. And then I saw her at the imitation zinc bar—

Sally Fall, the Janitor's posh private secretary, who had worked at the Bon Marché in Paris during her junior year abroad. Her mom was a film cutter at Columbia and her dad taught philosophy at UCLA, and Sally herself had studied for a semester at the Sorbonne. I had a feeling that Sally Fall was the culprit who had ratted on me to Louella. Who else could it have been? Only the Janitor and his private secretary knew about my relationship with Rita.

She was wearing a dress from Columbia's own collection, a discard from Adrian, Hollywood's top costume designer, with a velvet jacket and white gloves, all smug with the knowledge that she and Harry Cohn could ruin an actor's reputation at will with one phone call. She was sipping a sidecar and swaying to the sound of "Kalamazoo-zoo-zoo." She had several of her "sisters" with her, executive secretaries to one mogul or another. The Cat's Paw was perfectly safe. La Dietrich dropped in from time to time; so did Tallulah, and actors like Ronald Colman and Robert Donat and their wives often went slumming and sat for a while at the zinc bar. That's why there were never any arrests or raids. The studios' publicity teams were much too powerful. They could override any maverick police chief with a call to the mayor, or even the governor, Earl Warren.

But I didn't care about the logistics of the Cat's Paw. As I said, I hadn't come here to flirt. I watched Sally like an attack dog toying with its prey. She was all lovey-dovey with her girlfriends from the other studios. But she didn't leave with any of them. I waited until she went to the side door of the lounge, and I followed her into the alley.

She swiveled around on one hip and said, "Rusty Redburn, have you been following me?"

I grabbed the lapels of her Adrian jacket and shook her as hard as I could.

Both her arms flailed as I let her fall. She seemed lost in that alley, bewildered, half-wild. Then the wildness went out of her eyes.

"You're crazy. I'll tell Mr. Cohn. He'll have you fired."

She clambered to her feet and I shook her again.

"Yes, *chérie*, tell him how you sold me out to Louella, how you betrayed his trust."

"I did nothing of the kind," she said with a fake French accent she'd probably picked up at the Bon Marché.

"I was nice to Miss Parsons," she said, "that's all."

I abandoned Sally and returned to the Cat's Paw. And that's when I had my first real surprise of the day. Louella's one and only daughter, Harriet, an associate producer at RKO, was dancing with one of the service gals, a sergeant in the WACs. I'd never seen Harriet here before. She'd had a colossal wedding at Lolly's small estate in Beverly Hills. I'm told that David O. Selznick had to put off a screening of *Gone With the Wind* because it conflicted with Harriet's wedding and he didn't want to offend La Parsons. *Everyone* was there, under one of the makeshift tents—Gable, of course, and all the other stars of the major studios, plus entire cadres of publicity departments.

The marriage didn't hold, I guess. I'm not sure what the reason was, but Harriet's eyes were riveted on me, and I wasn't even a service gal. She wasn't as plump as Louella; she was a bit taller and had the same frazzled hair. I wasn't attracted to her in the least. But I hadn't lost my cunning at the Cat's Paw. I had to find a way to get back at Louella. So I watched Harriet dance with the service gals. Some of them had been drummed out of the military for being too brazen in their pursuit of a "butch" sergeant or nurse, and had been presented with a "blue ticket," which was sort of a dishonorable honorable discharge. They could still wear their uniforms and apply for any job they wanted. A blue ticket was the Army's diabolic method of making a gal invisible. But they were all visible enough at the Cat's Paw.

And then there was that other tale about the Supreme Allied Commander himself. When he was advised to get rid of certain damsels in a particular battalion, his own WAC sergeant said she would have to put herself at the top of that list, and that he would have to give the blue ticket to every file clerk and member of the motor pool. And so General Eisenhower, who was overseas, shook his head and left every damsel in place. That's how it was in the service and at the Cat's Paw.

Finally, Harriet found herself in my arms, dancing to "Moonlight Serenade." A deep shiver came up from her toes. She looked away and said, "Oh, you're beautiful, you are. Haven't we met?"

"Yes, Miss Harriet, we have. At the Vine Street Derby. I'm a stringer for your mom . . . and Rita Hayworth's private secretary."

She was still pulsating like a lizard. "But I would have remembered you. You're—"

"Rusty Redburn."

She still couldn't look into my eyes. I rubbed Harriet's shoulders a little. I'd swear she was about to swoon.

"My place?" she whispered in my ear.

Harriet was the most bewildering seductress I had ever met. Louella's limo—a deluxe lime-green Packard—was waiting outside with Louella's own liveried chauffeur. I didn't touch Harriet once as we sat on the upholstered cushions. The chauffeur only had to drive three blocks along the boulevard, and not a single streetcar to dodge at this hour. Harriet lived at the Garden Court.

It had once been the swankiest address in all of Hollywood, the former home of Lillian Gish, Gloria Swanson, Louis B. Mayer, Stan Laurel, and John Barrymore, with its lush gardens, its ballrooms, its Beaux Arts corbels and porticos. But the Garden Court had lost a lot of its glamour. The corbels were beginning to crumble. One of its ballrooms had closed. There'd been a rash of burglaries, and the stars had fled long before the war. It was no longer on the tourist route of the Hollywood stagecoach. But it was still swanky enough for an associate producer like Harriet.

She occupied an apartment on the second floor. The furniture was in the style of some famous French king, I suspect, on loan from Louella—with armoires and mirrors that reached to the ceiling.

"I've never done this before," she said. "I'm still legally married, you should know."

She stripped to her undies—they were nothing compared to Rita's lingerie, weren't silky to the touch, like Juel Park's. I could read the Bullocks Wilshire label on her skirt and blouse. Her thighs were quite thick. She should have played in the girls' softball league that we had at the studios.

She must have met her coworkers at Bullocks' Art Deco tea room several times a week. That damn department store looked like a miniature Empire State Building in the midst of Beverly Hills. I only went there for the "uniforms" I wore at work. Otherwise I went to the vintage shops on North Vine and the cowgirls' emporiums near the Farmers Market. I once saw Garbo there arguing with a merchant over the price of a peach. . . .

I was kind of miserable. I didn't know what to do with Louella's daughter, except to make her fall desperately in love with me. That was my mission. I sat with her on the sofa.

She was all starry-eyed. "God, Rusty, where'd you get those biceps?"

From playing softball, I should have said.

I had to work up the raw courage to kiss Harriet's neck. . . .

I spent the night with her at the Garden Court among all the fancy furniture. Harriet was already gone when I woke under her satin sheets. She left me a pot of coffee and a love note, accompanied with an envelope of cash. She couldn't have known that I worked for the Janitor. She probably thought I didn't have a penny in my pocket.

When can I see you again, dearest?
My hunger is without end.
Infinitely Yours, Harriet

I tore up the note and returned the cash in the same envelope, addressed to her at RKO. I wasn't out to blackmail Harriet or harm her, or perhaps that was the lie I told myself. But somehow, I had to hit Louella as hard as I could. And her daughter was the only weapon I had. So I saw her daughter again.

It was Harriet's idea to take me to the tea room at Bullocks. We had black tea and scones in that Art Deco masterpiece of a room with its pillars and fluted windows. The waitresses wore white smocks and had ribbons in their hair and the service pins of their sweethearts.

"Darling, we can't touch," Harriet said. "We can't neck. Mama's pals hang out here."

That's all it took—one scone.

I was summoned to the Hollywood Derby. There was devilment in Louella, a blind fury. I sat down at the far end of the booth. "I will crush you," she said with spittle on her tongue. Her spine was growing crooked, and she had a touch of kyphosis in her back that seemed to flare.

I couldn't have gotten very far if Hedda Hopper hadn't diminished Louella in the past two years. She looked like the maddened toad of North Vine.

"You will never go near my Harriet again. Is that understood?"

"Yes, ma'am," I said, sounding like a schoolmarm.

"Even if she comes to you and begs you on her knees, you are to shun her."

"Yes, ma'am."

"It's hard enough to find her another husband without you getting in the way. You are a menace, Rusty Redburn, and a slut at heart."

"Yes, ma'am."

She hadn't come to the Hollywood Derby for lunch, but for a vendetta. She was bedecked in white gloves and a blue veil. She flung Eddie Judson's manila envelope at me like a projectile. Louella meant to scratch, and she did. The sharp corner of the envelope cut my lip. I didn't howl with pain. I wouldn't give Louella that kind of satisfaction.

She lent me her handkerchief, monogrammed, of course, with perfume from Bullocks Wilshire's shelves. "Wipe your mouth, Rusty. Gilles can't abide blood. It scares his customers away."

I patted my lip with the handkerchief and returned it to Louella. Her face froze in disgust. She balled up the bloody handkerchief and tossed it into the waste bin that sat near her booth.

"Rusty, if you ever even wink at Harriet I'll have you run out of every studio in town."

"Yes, ma'am."

There was no point in dueling with her. I could tell how pale she was under that satin mask. She was losing her hegemony over Hollywood. Louis B. Mayer had become closer to Hedda than he was to her. She no longer had twenty-four-hour exclusives on every lot. She was out-scooped half the time. She had to rely on tipsters like me.

"Eddie Judson won't bother Rita anymore. I've *invited* him to keep out of her red hair. You can have all the pics." She clapped her hands. The gloves made a dull thud in the cloister-like silence surrounding her booth. "Bravo. You're a worthy opponent, Rusty. But don't you *dare* follow Harriet around."

"Miss Louella, I didn't find Harriet—Harriet found *me*."

"That's a shabby excuse," Lolly said. "She's a defenseless girl—now go! I'm getting tired of you."

And so I slid out from the edge of the booth. Diners at other tables stared at me. Not everyone had the privilege of sitting with the queen, even if that queen was turning brittle and had a tarnished look.

I didn't bother glancing at the "nudies," as long as Eddie didn't have them.

I wasn't a sentimental gal. I'd shot craps with Louella in my own fashion, and I won the entire pot. Harriet didn't deserve to be swindled by a desperado like me. She was a gentle creature, silly and naïve. She was better off being with a man, who would make love to her in the old missionary way, and give her an orgasm, once a month. But he wouldn't wander over half her body. I'd given Harriet an anatomy lesson. She wouldn't get that from a man.

Why did I feel so soiled? I'd gone to war with Louella, and took advantage of the only vulnerable thing she had—frail Harriet, who'd fallen for me and lacked her mother's instinct to kill; she would remain a minor figure at RKO until Louella's power waned enough so that they could fire Harriet and suffer no consequences. I didn't need any tarot cards to tell me that. Her future would whiplash right into her face.

11

THE MERCURY WONDER SHOW went deep into October, and soon the Christmas season of '43 was upon us. Medallions of Santa were hung from the crisscrossing wires of the streetcar lines right after Thanksgiving, and Christmas trees appeared all along the boulevard. I missed the Tanakas and their grocery at the corner of Wilcox. It was all boarded up, a wonderland of manicured debris. The Tanakas had been gone for almost two years. Julie Tanaka and her father had both "adopted" me, a rustic from Illinois. The loss I felt was like a punch in the heart that never healed. Julie had been one of my best friends. She studied chemistry at UCLA, graduated summa cum laude, and was elected to Phi Beta Kappa, but she couldn't even get a job as a lab technician on account of her Japanese heritage, so she worked in her papa's store. Papa Tanaka, or the "Baron," as we often called him, was the kindest man I'd ever met in movieland. I was starving when I first arrived, and the Baron fed me for a month. He wouldn't accept a dime.

"But I have to repay you, Mr. Tanaka. I'm working now."

"Not an issue," he said. "You spend time with us, Miss Rusty. . . . You laugh. That is my reward."

I wanted to hide them in my tiny roomette when the military cops and the FBI stomped through the grocery store, but I couldn't have saved Julie and the Baron, not at a hotel where clerks and patrons called the Nisei "Nips" and "yellow rats." I tried to get through to the War Department and failed, so I asked a leftie lawyer at Columbia to call, and he found out that the Tanakas had been sent to Manzanar. It was near an abandoned Shoshone reservation in Inyo County, at the foot of the Sierra Nevada, in northeastern California. The county leased Manzanar and its six hundred acres to the War Department—soon it was a barracks town with tons of barbed wire and tin shacks.

I wrote to Julie in care of the relocation camp, told her that I'd like to visit; the postcard I got in return was all bent and had ink-blots, and most of it had been blacked out. It read like a modernist poem that featured the words "this" and "that."

I sent her packages, yet every single one was returned. I called the main office at Manzanar, but no one seemed able to find Julie and accompany her to the phone. So I had to survive with the knowledge that she was less than two hundred and fifty miles away and I couldn't get near her.

Half the stalls at the Farmers Market were now empty, and Orson and Big Red had lost their Japanese gardener, their Japanese cook, and their Japanese maid. Rita cursed Mayor Bowron and Governor Warren; those two pols had rejoiced over Roosevelt's Executive Order 9066, signed in February of '42. It allowed the President's commanders on the West Coast to designate L.A. as a "military zone," and to swoop down on citizens and non-citizens alike.

There hadn't been a single act of sabotage in Hollywood, and yet gardeners, grocers, maids, cooks, and college students were all hunted down and herded into camps. Reactionary groups, such as the Native Sons of the Golden West, denounced all Japanese as devils.

"The Native Sons are bullshit artists," Rita muttered one afternoon. "They just want to get rid of the competition. They steal farms and grocery stores from the Japanese. Orsie, why don't you say something? You're on the radio."

The Boy Wonder was perversely quiet. He felt the same way as we did, but once the studios shut down Orson and his Mercury team, he toyed with the idea of running sometime in the future for Senator of Wisconsin, where he was born. He could have talked about the relocation camps on one of his radio shows, and the blind seizure of farms and little shops, but he didn't want to ruin his chances with Roosevelt and all the other pols. Still, he was angered by the cruelty and blood-sucking greed of the Native Sons.

Finally, near the end of a pre-Christmas show at the North Vine studios, he said, "The property of these farmers should be held in escrow, until we can figure out the fairness or unfairness of the matter at hand."

That night, Rita wore the sexiest gown from her Juel Park's collection, which accented her hips and the lyrical leap of her legs. It was a week or so before Christmas, and Rita, the shrimp, and I serenaded Orsie, clutching candles like a party of gremlins.

Who's the man who told the Native Sons to go to hell?
The next Senator from Wisconsin, Sir Orson, Orson Welles

There were repercussions, of course. The Native Sons and their affiliates hit the studios at North Vine with a hurricane of letters and telegrams. Orson nearly lost his sponsor. He had to sign an affidavit never to discuss politics again while he was on the air. And I was at Woodrow Wilson Drive when he got a call from the White

House. It was a kingly call. Orson had to wait until the operator connected him to the President's study on the residential floor. I listened like a worm.

"Yes, F.D.," Orson said in that booming voice of his. "It was an accident. A moment of pique. I promise it won't happen again."

He hung up and didn't say a word.

"Well," Shorty said, "what gives? Who's F.D.?"

"Franklin Delano," Orson replied. "He's contemplating another run and considers me essential to the campaign."

"That's impossible," Shorty said. "No one has ever run for a *fourth* term."

Orson leered at him. "It's wartime. If his party asks him to run, he'll run. And he can't afford any blunders. I'm his voice in California."

"And the camps?" I asked.

"F.D. won't abandon the Japanese who were born in this country. He'll repair the damage—that is, after this *next* campaign."

I preferred the old Orson of *Citizen Kane*, not a flimflam artist who toyed with the notion of entering politics. But I wasn't bewitched by Juel Park's, like Big Red. I fed her as much high art as I could. She knew all about Gauguin and the South Seas. She loved to hear about Dostoyevsky's gambling affliction, and so I would invent detail upon detail: how Dostoyevsky plucked on his beard every time he won or lost a ruble, how Charles Dickens fell into debt and rescued his family from the poorhouse with *A Christmas Carol*, which, I said, he wrote in one sitting.

Orson would roar when Rita recited these tales back to him. "My God, what has Rusty been teaching you? She's an insurrectionist—no, much worse. She'll tear down the sacred temples of Hollywood. The studios will vanish once she takes over as storyteller-in-chief."

"That's good, isn't it?" Rita asked like a declaration of war. "Then I wouldn't have to report to Harry Cohn."

12

IT WAS FINALLY Christmas Eve, and I went out onto the boulevard in my cowgirl corduroys. The Christmas trees were lit with all the white bunting that masked strings of electric bulbs, and there was a quiet glow from the line of shops and beaneries, with holly and silver stars in the windows. Still, I didn't feel much merriment in me. I walked the boulevard with a full load of sadness rumbling in my brain. The Santa medallions stared down at me from the wires. I could have gone to the Cat's Paw, but I wasn't in the mood to dance with some WAC nurse from Wichita.

The manager at Musso's had put a sleigh outside the restaurant filled with pots of eggnog, and his waiters distributed free drinks to people who passed by. The Irish waiter who delivered my drink in a paper cup recognized me.

"Come on in, Rusty. We'll find a table for you near the fire."

"Thanks," I said. "Another time."

I drank the eggnog in one gulp. I could taste the cinnamon and the nutmeg. My head swiveled like a turret. I could have sworn he'd handed me a Mickey Finn. The landscape shifted in front of my eyes like a damn mirage. Byron Brown arrived with his stagecoach.

"Hop aboard, Rusty," he shouted from his driver's seat on the stage, and I climbed the little ladder, sat up front with Byron in his fireman's boots. This time he didn't head for the Hollywood Hills. Byron rode against traffic with his team of pintos that he must have rescued from a glue factory. No one honked at him. There was always bedlam on the boulevard. He leapt up with his reins in one hand and pulled down a Santa medallion from the streetcar wires.

He was disappointed. "It's damn tin," he said, crushing the medallion in his fist and tossing it above the wires. He had passengers, but I didn't see their faces. And it wasn't much of a tour. We could have been on a ride to hell with his team of nags. The shops grew less and less familiar, fading into the distance like burned-out stars. The little doughnut stand was gone. The streetlamps had a cluster of globes, half of them unlit. We moved deeper into the dark.

I wasn't sure where we'd go next. I looked for signs I could recall, little remembrances. Oddly, my favorite bookshop was still standing, with its name in big block letters above the striped awning: PICKWICK BOOKS. Then the letters began to crumble, one by one, until nothing, nothing was left. That's when the first tin shack appeared in the middle of the boulevard. And I saw the barbed wire.

Byron's magic pintos must have manufactured Manzanar on Hollywood Boulevard. But we weren't in the desert. A streetcar ran beside our coach, barely a crease away. The conductor waved to us, but someone must have skinned him alive. I could see every bone and hollow in his face.

"Byron," I asked, like a child, "what's our destination?"

"Ain't none, Miss Rusty. Not tonight."

I leaned hard at a desperate angle, looking for Julie Tanaka. I couldn't recognize a soul, not the owner of the novelty shop on La Brea, where I bought little paper gifts for the street urchins along the boulevard every Christmas and Halloween, not the farmers and their wives who arrived with little trucks of produce and sat in front of their stands on Fairfax, not the calligrapher who stood at the corner of Hollywood and Highland and could write a letter to a soldier or sailor's sweetheart in such a beautiful hand it could make your heart cry.

We entered a vast hollow, as if we were racing across one of Columbia's back lots. I lost my bearings. I must have still been reeling from that Mickey Finn. There were no more streetlamps, no more trolleys, no more tinsel. It was wartime. I worried that I'd never see Julie Tanaka again.

I couldn't imagine a worse damn Christmas for the kid from Kalamazoo.

• TWO •

The Electioneer, 1944–1945

1

THE NOOSE HAD to tighten—and tighten it did.

It wasn't my fault. I worked for Harry Cohn, not the Ophelia Agency, but it was Ophelia that supplied the noose with an ever-tightening knot, though I'd never even been to the agency's offices on North Vine. Harry must have had a sweet deal with Ophelia to arrange such a subtle sleight of hand. I didn't care. I was crazy about Orson and Big Red, and wouldn't have traded jobs with anyone in movieland—yet Harry's arrangement with Ophelia wasn't as solid as it seemed.

Money changed hands in a very mandarin way. Orson—and Big Red—paid me, while I got a bonus from Harry on the sly. But Ophelia also billed Harry for camouflaging my employment. And some dope of an accountant at the studio took Harry's bill from Ophelia and forwarded it to Woodrow Wilson Drive. It might not have mattered, since Orson was always dreaming of some new project, but Shorty served as *his* accountant and uncovered Columbia's folly.

I could tell something had gone awry the moment I left my

jalopy in Orson's garage. Rita was in a mercurial mood, laughing one moment, crying the next. "Wait," she said, "wait until Orsie comes. Oh, my God!" And she pulled on her gorgeous mane of hair, expecting doom to come marching in at any moment.

Orson arrived with Shorty near my quitting time. I hadn't given Rita her usual literature lesson. That's how distraught she was. The Boy Wonder kept waving the notice from Ophelia back and forth like some badge of dishonor.

"Fess up, Rusty. Ophelia is a front. You work for Harry Cohn. You're his spy."

"Yes," I said, "that's true."

And now Orson began to pace. He couldn't subdue the actor in him. "We took you in, adopted you, and you betrayed us."

"I did. But I haven't told that bastard at Columbia anything he couldn't have gotten on his own. I love you both—and the shrimp. My loyalty is to you and Rita."

"Loyalty, she says." And Orson moved toward me with his fists clenched. He swung; I swerved like a bullfighter, and, clumsy as he was, Orson flopped on his ass.

"Don't do that," he said. "I pay you a salary, you know."

He sat there and started to laugh. You couldn't tell what to expect from the Boy Wonder.

"You really are a double agent, aren't you?"

"I'm worse than that, Mr. Welles. I only tell the Janitor what he thinks he wants to hear."

"About Rita—or me?" Orson asked in a somber voice.

"Oh, Big Red. He can't stop thinking about her. So I relate to him exactly what we do—literature lessons. Only I make things up. I weave whatever I want. He hasn't a clue what's going down at Woodrow Wilson Drive."

I had to help the Boy Wonder up, or he might have sat forever on his big ass. But I knew we'd come to an ending of sorts. They'd all be a little guarded around me, and Orson would hide his air of hostility, while Rita remained mute.

So I grabbed my jacket. "I quit."

Orson grimaced. "I have to fire you first."

"Then fire me, Mr. Welles."

Orson's little turned-up nose began to twitch. "You have much more value now that I'm aware of your relation to Harry Cohn. How often do you report to him?"

I also began to twitch. "I won't trade secrets—his or yours."

"Boss," Shorty said, "she's the one who's close to Harry. Forgive me, but the little lady has us by the short hairs."

"Indeed she does," Orson said. "Rita, what should we do? She is your secretary. Shall we fire her in spite of what Shorty says?"

I'd frightened Big Red. I could see the panic in her eyes. "Then I'd have to live without *A Christmas Carol* and Dostoyevsky's gambling debts. . . . Orsie, don't stand there. Tell Rusty that we've rehired her."

"But I haven't fired her, darling," Orson said.

"Rehire her anyway."

2

ORSON CONTRACTED YELLOW jaundice in the middle of a massive War Loan Drive, as he went from city to city across the Southwest and attended one war bond rally after another, accompanied by a trove of Treasury agents there to protect him from supposed saboteurs. He returned to California on the *Super Chief*, with the sallow complexion of a straw man. An ambulance drove him to his new residence on Carmelina Drive in Brentwood—a much bigger house, with a swimming pool and a solarium, where Rita loved to sunbathe in the buff.

Red wouldn't have some old biddy from Cedars of Lebanon look after Orson. She nursed him herself. She cooked, cleaned, fed Orson with her own lovely hands. I wasn't much use. I couldn't even help her find a maid, hard as I tried. All the gals had gone over to the defense plants, and not even the lure of Rita could get them back. They were pulling in wages no one had ever seen until now. . . .

Orson was too sick to have sex. Undeterred, Rita guarded over him like a lioness in her lair. Suddenly she had a dire look. She was scheduled to appear at the naval air cadet base in San Pedro as part of her USO tour, and she didn't want to leave Orsie by himself. So she was sullen.

Orson had a wheelchair whenever he wasn't in bed, and it was Shorty who wheeled him from room to room. "Darling," he sang from his portable chair, "don't be silly. Shorty will drive you to San Pedro, and Dadda will look after me while you're all gone."

Dadda, Orson's former pediatrician, who had been both his mother's paramour and his father's best friend, had moved to Los Angeles once Orson had made his "success" in the movies. It was Dadda who had discovered him in Kenosha, after all, and had declared him a genius. Dadda kept asking Orson for money, even though he had a license to practice in California and had an office in Beverly Hills. He was now also Orson and Shorty's personal physician.

Still, even with Dadda, I couldn't cure Rita's nervousness about her trip to entertain the naval air cadets.

"Darling," Orson said, trying to reassure her, "you'll sing and dance."

The lioness licked her wounds in front of us. "Didn't you hear Harry Cohn? I can't sing."

Orson rolled his eyes like King Lear. "Cohn's an idiot. You have a beautiful voice. And Shorty will do a skit with you. He's always wanted to act."

"Fine," she said, "my own little accomplice. I need a director, dammit."

"And you shall have one," Orson said. He set about preparing several skits and dance numbers for Big Red, with Shorty swirling around her. Orson shouldn't have derided Shorty's acting skills. Shorty could have played Lear's Fool on any stage, with Orson wearing one of his rubber noses and a wig.

In spite of his sallowness, Orson insisted on coming to San Pedro. Rita said it would be suicide, considering the severity of his condition, and Orson had to use all his wiles to convince her otherwise.

"Yes, I feel shitty. But I have my wheelchair." And the moment he saw Dadda arrive, he said, "See! We have our savior. If I'm suffering, Dadda can always dig a needle into my arm."

Dadda was small and natty, with dark eyes and a Roman nose—a lady-killer, if that's the kind you liked. I lured him into the back seat of Shorty's Cadillac. Dadda was a man of terrifying contradictions. He stole from Orson, went after other men's wives, and was something of a bluebeard. Years ago he had courted Mina Elman, the old-maid sister of wealthy violin virtuoso Mischa Elman. Mina fell madly in love with Dadda, who wouldn't marry her unless Mischa paid him a dowry of fifteen thousand dollars—a fortune in 1915. Mischa paid, and Dadda dropped Mina after six months. Yet he worked without payment at the clinic for indigent actors and stuntmen in Hollywood, and drove to Manzanar twice a week to look after patients with pulmonary problems.

"I protest," Dadda said, with his medical bag on his lap. "This man has yellow jaundice. He should be in bed."

"Dadda," Orson said, "Rita is performing for a bunch of cadets. And she can't perform without a director, and I'm the only one available these days. So sit back and enjoy the ride."

I couldn't even recognize movieland in wartime, with anti-aircraft guns on every hill and military transport trucks on most boulevards. We arrived at the end of the streetcar line and rode into the harbor district, with sentries stopping us at every second corner. But we had Big Red in the car with us; they saluted her and urged us on.

There were rolls of barbed wire in front of the naval base. The sentries let us through the gate and several of them accompanied us in a jeep with a siren, as Rita grew more and more agitated. She didn't like sentries gaping at her through little windows.

"I can't sing. My throat is all dry. I lost my voice."

"Darling," Orson said, "we'll give you a chaser of water and whiskey—or lemonade. You'll be fine."

I could make out the markings of a few Grumman Hellcats with little insignias painted below each cockpit; there was a blue devil on one, a clown with green eyes on another, a picture of Betty Grable in the white bathing suit that servicemen loved, and one of Red in a nightgown. I didn't point it out to her. It would only have made her suspicious, as if a fighter plane had somehow captured her identity.

We stopped at a converted warehouse that must have been used as a lecture hall for the naval air cadets. A bunch of naval commanders met us at the door. They were excited to meet Big Red, but she hid her face and marched right past them. They were bewildered by her sullen behavior. They couldn't understand that the most beautiful woman on the planet couldn't bear to be looked at—that's how shy Red had always been.

Orson shrugged as Shorty wheeled him inside. We marched Rita to the dressing room that the commanders had prepared for her, with a vanity table borrowed from the Santa Monica Playhouse. She was wearing a white strapless gown that Orson himself had lifted from Columbia's wardrobe department. Now that he was married to Big Red, he was much more cavalier about his relationship with Harry Cohn, and he came and went as he pleased. But Rita sat shivering in the corner, mute, just as I had imagined she had been when she was locked in the dressing room by her father.

"I can't sing," she whimpered. "I look like a witch."

But the maestro had brought along Rita's makeup kit, and he soothed her with a few strokes of her mascara brush.

"Darling, you're entertaining air cadets, whose lives might be in danger a few months from now. Dare we disappoint them?"

"No, Orsie," Rita said with a faint smile. "We dare not. . . .

Rusty, hold my hand. It will bring me luck. We're always ordered about by men. I'll be the best little soldier I can."

And that's how we exited that dressing room; Shorty wearing some kind of Shakespearean costume that the Boy Wonder had supplied, with a codpiece and a feathered hat; Dadda clutching his medical bag; and me, holding Rita's hand. Shorty wheeled Orson right onto the barren stage of the lecture hall. It did have a five-piece band, cadet clarinetists who were also magicians with the sax and trombone, here to play for Rita.

The auditorium was packed with air cadets in bomber jackets and rough-looking gals in the cadets' own blue blouses. The commanders had explained who they were—women prisoners from the federal correction facility on Terminal Island who had been on good behavior and were promised the chance to see Big Red at the naval air cadet base across the road.

The auditorium exploded as Rita appeared onstage in that first flash of white. Most of the cadets had never been near a movie star, not one like Rita, with such melody in each step she took. Her fear seemed gone, or perhaps it was hidden so deep, as it had been with Eduardo, that she now wore the mask of pleasure. She pranced about the stage in her stilettos. It was Shorty who ran after her with the microphone. But he couldn't keep up with her swaying rhythms, which grew wilder, well beyond Shorty's limited art. She was in her own land of frayed delight that must have preserved her sanity when she had danced with Eduardo. Now, here with us at the naval base, it was as if she were taunting some phantom of a partner, and her dance was a unique kind of composition, her manner of staying alive. It wasn't only Shorty. None of us could keep up with Rita's utter abandonment to the will of her own body. Then she stopped, and returned to us.

"Well," she shouted, with a finger to her lips, "what do we have here today?"

"A bunch of flying bums and their ladies," Shorty said, staring at his codpiece, which was his prize package.

The cadets laughed and shouted, "More, more!"

Then Shorty pranced over to the cadet musicians on stage and whispered something to the bandleader. The band started to play "You'll Never Know," and Rita serenaded the cadets and their commanders and the gals from the federal facility. She sang with a slight waver, as if every note were a parting kiss to the air cadets.

The Janitor must have been crazy to have "ghosts" dub Rita's voice. She should have been on the hit parade.

Rita couldn't sock out a song like Kate Smith, the President's favorite songbird, who weighed over two hundred pounds and whose voice could carry across the entire Hollywood Bowl as she intoned "God Bless America."

But Rita was a whisperer. All her sweetness was in every word. She sang and swayed, enticing the cadet flyboys and penitentiary sweethearts, with Shorty as her sidekick, and Orson sitting near her, like a conductor with an invisible baton, his face growing a ghoulish color in the pallid light of the auditorium. Dadda, with his medical bag, stood ready to rouse him with a vitamin shot.

She did the samba with Shorty, sang "Brazil," one of last year's hits, her hips putting every cadet in a trance with a kind of tele-pathic caress, as if her own limbs were independent creatures.

"Miss Rita," Shorty asked, "remind me what you like best."

"Dancing the samba with you," she said, winking at the cadets, while she twirled her hips and stepped as high as she could in her heels. She was Rita of the red hair. The sad history of her child-hood had gone out of her as she high-stepped on that stage to the sound of a tenor sax, all alone in that wonder of hers.

3

I WAS SUMMONED TO Gower Street like a servant, and it wasn't for our usual Wednesday afternoon séance. The Janitor was all excited. He wanted me to meet Parnell Wilson, who was in charge of all the "A" productions at Columbia, including Rita's films. Parnell was one of Harry Cohn's flamboyant thugs, with a bachelor's degree from Dartmouth. He was very tall, with cruel eyes and a cruel mouth. He ran after every starlet on the lot.

"Rusty," the Janitor said, "Parnell is a big fan of yours. He's been dying to meet ya. He's read all the reviews you did at the Regina."

Parnell pivoted his head toward me. "It's my preferred movie house in Hollywood. I like its quaintness. Go there all the time. Love what you wrote about *Gone With the Wind*. Called it a 'white man's lollapalooza,' didn't you?"

I stared right into his vicious mug.

"In my opinion, Hattie McDaniel and Butterfly McQueen were put there to play a comedy act. But both of them were degraded Black servants in a white household, Mr. Parnell. And there was nothing to laugh at, I guarantee."

The cruelty in him only crept deeper. "Didn't Hattie win an Academy Award, or am I mistaken?"

"Sure," I said, "the men and women at the Academy chuckled at her imitation of a house slave."

"That's unkind," Parnell said. "She's the first girl of her color to win an award of such stature."

"She's a woman, sir," I said. "And all she did was her own style of vaudeville for a white audience. Black folks in every damn movie house understood that."

The son of a bitch turned to the Janitor. "Harry, I think you've hired a viper. I tried to praise her and her mimeographed sheets at the Regina, and look at the reward I get. Is she a commie, a pinko? I never realized we had such radicals at Columbia, except for a few hack writers who sit in their own corner at the canteen."

He wasn't much of a researcher, this cruel-eyed man. "Hattie couldn't even attend the world premiere at the palace on Peachtree Street—in Atlanta. The town's grand marshals wouldn't let her in."

"Well, missy," said Parnell, "I can't account for Peachtree Street. She did attend the Academy Awards at the Cocoanut Grove. I was there. She cried at her acceptance speech and thanked us for our kindness. I remember Hattie's words. 'My heart is too full to tell you how I feel.' "

I slashed Parnell with the razors I hid inside my head. "And she carried that award right back to the segregated table she was assigned—at the Cocoanut Grove, Mr. Wilson. This wasn't Peachtree Street. It was Wilshire Boulevard."

"That's preposterous," Parnell said, with pure hate. "Harry, you were with me, for cryin' out loud. I don't remember any such segregated table."

"I do, Mr. Wilson. It was when I first arrived in Hollywood. I was a waitress at the Grove."

"Enough," said the Janitor. "I brought Parnell here to praise you. Apologize."

I had to tap-dance in my own dark void if I wanted to remain at Columbia. So I curtsied like some damn courtesan. It wasn't hard. I had been doing it half my life in my dealings with men, and sometimes with women, too.

"Forgive me, Mr. Wilson. I hallucinate a lot on an empty stomach. Perhaps Hattie sat with Mr. Gable."

He wasn't fooled. But he didn't care much. I didn't exist for him, except as Regina X, the writer of mimeographed reviews that didn't circulate much beyond the boulevard.

"Harry," he said, "I'll see you at the producers' table." He glowered at me and was gone.

The Janitor held court at his own table in the Columbia canteen. It was sacrosanct. You couldn't claim a chair without an invitation from him. And often you couldn't claim it for very long. He was a fickle creature, that Harry Cohn. And now he turned his fickleness on me.

"Rusty, I think it's time for you to exit Carmelina Drive. We'll prepare a note, pretend it's from the people at Ophelia. We'll say your mother's dying, and we have to break in a new girl as Rita's secretary."

I was silent for a moment. I hadn't been prepared for this move. He was playing checkers on some mythical checkerboard, crowning his own men, while I was left with idle pieces. But I had one weapon—Rita.

"Big Red depends on me," I countered.

"That's the problem. You're too attached. That doesn't make you the best of spies. I don't trust your judgments, Rusty. You roughed up my own private secretary. That's not what I call allegiance."

I had to keep up my tap dance. "Mr. Cohn, Sally Fall ratted on me to Louella. I could have lost my place with Big Red."

Cohn had on his favorite jacket, with leather elbow patches and leather-lined cuffs, from the swankiest store in Bel Air, where he had his very own tailor. All the moguls shopped at Raymond's of Bel Air. They wore hunting jackets in their very own style. No one else could afford Raymond's prices. There were never any off-season sales.

"Sweetheart," said this checker champion with his row of kings. "You already lost your place. I had Ophelia fire you."

"Fuck Ophelia," I said, ready to march out of Cohn's office and whack Sally Fall one more time.

"Wait," he said, watching his king's row of checkers scatter in front of his very own eyes. He was scheming again. I'd made that poor bastard shiver in his pants. He must have worried that I might gab about him to Rita. And she'd begin to rebel at the studio. So he had to reconsider.

"You can have another six months. But don't miss a Wednesday, you hear? You still report to me."

I knew the Janitor's repertoire of tricks. He would have one of the wardrobe girls rat on me to Rita. But I held the last crowning checker. "Harry, have I missed a single Wednesday?"

"Show some respect. Call me Mr. Cohn."

4

I WASN'T WORRIED ABOUT his wardrobe girls. They could tattle
all they wanted. Rita knew that I hadn't come from Ophelia.
I was a Gower Street girl, right off the Columbia lot. No, I was
worried about Orson. There was a real dilemma. I wished he could
stay on Carmelina Drive forever with a touch of jaundice, have
Shorty wheel him around. Big Red was happiest when she had her
Orsie at home with her. The bedroom didn't matter as much while
Orsie was a "prisoner" she could feed and bathe. Rita loved to
wash his hair. It had become a kind of ritual. It took the three of us
to sit him down in the tub, naked as Adam, while Rita wore a Juel
Park's negligée. She would cut his toenails and spend a half hour
shampooing him from his widow's peak to the nape of his neck.
But she didn't have a magic potion that could keep him there.

He recovered.

Now that his yellow complexion was gone, they decided to
go to Tijuana for a week. Orson loved the bullfights. But Tijuana
was where Rita's mother and father had imprisoned her as a child,
locked her in the dressing room at some casino or palace hotel and

gambled away the earnings of little Margarita with the painted black hair. Still, the bullfights excited the Boy Wonder, despite what he knew about her haunted childhood. And he was adamant about teaching Red all the rituals of the ring. So she acquiesced. Shorty drove them across the border and then drove back and served as caretaker at Carmelina Drive, while I was paid my full salary with nothing to do.

So I walked the streets like a tourist in her own town, and something caught my eye on Wilcox. The Tanaka grocery store wasn't boarded up; it was open for business. The Baron was behind the counter slicing cold cuts on a brand-new machine, while Julie was at the cash register. Nothing in the papers or on the radio had told of a mass exodus from the internment camps. The Baron and Julie couldn't have escaped on their own. Manzanar was a little country of barbed wire, wind, and sand.

It was Julie who saw me first, not the Baron, who was a prince of grace, no matter what had been done to him and his daughter. She had an angry edge. Still, I went into the store. She wouldn't even allow me to hug her. It seems that our friendship hadn't survived Manzanar.

"Ah, our little hungry one," the Baron said, and began preparing a Swiss cheese sandwich for me on rye. I loved the crust, and would gnaw at it like a rabbit.

"Baron, I'm so glad to see you—in your old habitat on Wilcox."

"Old habitat," Julie said, looking right past me. "That's quaint. Do you know how hard the Baron had to fight just to get back what belonged to him, or should I show you the case file? He couldn't plead for himself. His English wasn't good enough to fight all the sharks of the Golden West and every other round-eye. I had to plead for him, a citizen of the second class. But how are you, Rusty-san?"

Her politeness was like a chop to the throat. She'd never been my sweetheart. We'd been comrades, Julie and I. But it seems the camp had made her suspicious of all "round-eyes."

Still, I managed to talk her into going to the Regina. We saw a double bill, *Tobacco Road* and *The Shanghai Gesture*, both starring Gene Tierney, and the audience must have recognized me as Regina X, queen of the mimeographed broadsheet and philosopher of Hollywood flicks, because after the films they whistled and called me to the front of the curtain. I wasn't in the mood to entertain. I missed Orsie and Big Red too much.

"It's Gene Tierney's green eyes," I told the movie lovers in their seats. "They haunt you like no other actress. You're stuck in a chill."

"Come on," said a wise guy who helped pack the house every night. "Rusty, how can you tell her eyes are green? Both films were in black-and-white."

"Well," I said, "shame on you, Walter. A green-eyed gal has her own shine. She's like a sleepy cat, wild as hell when she's only half-awake. That's her particular brand of beauty."

That shut him up. "Tell you one thing, though. The war brought in a new kind of hero, the dead-eyed man, like Victor Mature and Dana Andrews."

"What's so dead about their eyes?" asked Myrtle, one of our ushers. She wore purple eye shadow and spent most of her days and nights in the dark.

"They sleepwalk through their performances," I said. "Haven't you noticed? It's as if they're defeated, or they defeat themselves. It's a kind of terror."

"What's Vic Mature afraid of?" asked Myrtle.

"Afraid of? I don't know. Women. War. Life itself."

And I walked out of the Regina with Julie Tanaka. She lived in the back of the grocery store on Wilcox. It was past midnight and the store was still open. The Baron had been waiting for Julie to return. He turned down the shades, locked the front door, and removed the cash box from the register. Then, like the cavalier that he was, he welcomed me into their living quarters. They had a simple kitchen, and one tiny room with a toilet attached. The Baron placed the cash box in a drawer, brewed tea for us, and put little almond cakes on the kitchen table. He didn't bring up Manzanar, but Julie did.

"I couldn't accept your little packages. They searched Father's pockets, interrogated him for hours. What could he tell them, Rusty-san? He does not have your gifts. I had to interpret for him. They searched my pockets, too. And they had rough hands, these round-eyed soldiers."

"Daughter," the Baron said, "you must not speak of such things." He had a wistfulness and a deep anger in his dark eyes. And then he started to laugh. It was a very bitter laugh. But the Baron wasn't bitter about me.

"Rusty, why were we let out of Manzanar? Did you write to the director of the camp?"

"I did, Baron," I confessed.

"And was it on your employer's stationery?" he asked.

"Yes, Baron."

And now his laugh was much less bitter. "Then the puzzle is solved. The director saw 'Rita Hayworth' on the letter and it bothered him. She might mention us in an interview. And after that Manzanar would have reached millions in *Life* magazine. The director would have been in trouble with the generals in Washington. He could not afford so much bad publicity. It was better to release us like two forgotten ghosts."

Julie lashed out. "We did not ask you to interfere, Rusty-san."

The Baron stood there and seemed to mask his anger. "Daughter, is this how you repay a debt? The director could have written to Rita Hayworth, and Rusty might have lost her job."

Any kind of emotion was difficult for the Baron. He bowed and kissed my hand. "Rusty, is this the American way—of gratitude?"

"Baron," I said, "wouldn't you have done the same for me if I had been tossed into some camp?"

"No, Little Daughter. I wouldn't have dared."

It didn't matter. I had realized that Big Red's name would have some effect on the director of the camp. So I'd drafted a letter to him on Rita's letterhead:

Project Director Ralph P. Merritt
Manzanar War Relocation Center
Manzanar, California

Dear Director Merritt:

I am writing you on behalf of my best friend, Julie Tanaka, and her father, the Baron, who I am told are residing at your delightful resort in the desert. Julie and I have been friends since I first arrived in Hollywood. The Baron is an excellent accountant—he keeps his own books—and Julie is superb in chemistry, but she also plays the piano and the violin. Should you ever have the opportunity to hear her play, I would highly recommend it. I am writing you now in the hope that you will do your best to get in touch with Julie, since most of my letters and postcards to her have been returned, with my own miserable penmanship blacked out.

Shall I describe her to you? She's quite cute, almost 5' 1", with a barrette in her hair, which is normally combed back. Could you tell her that she is sorely missed on Hollywood Boulevard? And if there is any way I could visit her suite at your resort or pick her up, could you let me know?

If you wish you can get in touch with me by calling my employer, Miss Rita Hayworth (the actress) at WILSHIRE 4-7743. You can even reverse the charges, because I know that Miss Hayworth would love to hear from you. I would be exceedingly grateful if you could get back to me, and I remain forever in your debt.

Yours truly,
Rusty Redburn
c/o Rita Hayworth, Columbia Pictures

And Mr. Merritt did what camp directors like him do best. He got rid of the problem of Rita's letterhead by removing the Tanakas from Manzanar, probably in the dead of some dry, moonless night. . . .

I left the Baron and Julie standing there and returned to the boulevard. All the traffic lights had gone out. So I had to scramble around and rush across the street. I'd never seen Hollywood so somber. It was autumn, and there wasn't a single light on along the entire boulevard. I could have been in an open grave, with a grass-and-concrete blanket under my toes.

5

SHORTY CALLED ME to Carmelina Drive the very next day. He'd driven Rita and Orson back from Tijuana. I wasn't sure what to expect. But I had my researcher's intuition, born in the basement of the Writers' Building. Big Red didn't talk about bullfights. They were lovers again. I could tell that from the way she danced around Orson. She was a girl who couldn't hide the music in her bones. She flirted with him now that he didn't have a gaunt, yellowish look. She slithered up against his body like a nubile snake. But it was Rita's misfortune that they were in the middle of an election year. President Roosevelt had invited Mr. and Mrs. Welles to the White House for a ceremonial dinner.

At first Rita was delighted, but then she began to grow alarmed. "Orsie, are you sure the President wants to meet me?"

"Of course. And so does the First Lady. F.D. said she was delighted that you might come to the capital."

Big Red was even more confused. "But why would Mrs. Eleanor be the least bit interested in me?"

Orson put on one of his mock faces, like some grand Cossack chieftain. "Isn't it obvious? You're Rita Hayworth."

She never understood her own worth. It was an election year, and FDR was running against the gangbuster, Governor Tom Dewey, who had demolished half the mobs in Manhattan. FDR adored the movie capital, and he would savor having Orson and Hollywood's love goddess at his side. And Eleanor would have relished Rita, too. She liked soft, shy women. But Rita was terrorized by anyone she believed was above her station. She'd always been a little afraid of Orson. That's why I fed her literature and philosophy by the teaspoon. Eleanor spoke with the slow drawl of an aristocrat. And Rita was a girl who had performed on gambling ships. Eleanor's music was in her voice, and in her manner, in her knowledge of the world. And despite my lessons, Rita was no match.

Orson couldn't seem to soothe her until he lured her into the bedroom. And the next morning she would be as morose as ever. "What if Mrs. Eleanor asks me about world events? I can talk about Alice and Humpty Dumpty, but I can't say much about Stalin's mustache."

Orson twisted his head around with a sense of ire. "F.D. doesn't give a hoot about Stalin's mustache. He adores the latest Hollywood gossip. He'll ask you how Greer Garson stubbed her toe on her own Academy Award and where Betty Grable got her stash of silk stockings."

Rita was even more pained. "The only gossip I get is from the wardrobe girls."

"Darling, they'll adore you no matter what you say."

And Orson danced Rita around from room to room, knocking over lamps that got in his way, and all the sweetness returned to her face.

"Oh, Orsie," she said, as he sambaed her into the bedroom and kicked the door closed with one of his outsized shoes. But even with all his patience and resourceful maneuvers, he lost the battle. He couldn't enchant her time after time. The closer it came to leaving for the White House, the more she grew mummified. Her hips froze. The simple ring of the telephone alarmed her, woke her out of that rigid state. Orson clutched her in his arms and tried to rock some kind of melody into her.

One of the White House secretaries was on the line. I knew how important it was for Rita to accompany Orson, to declare herself as a person beside her genius of a husband. Yet she'd rather sit naked in her solarium than groom herself and be greeted by the First Lady. Red was sure she would have been utterly out of place in that patrician world of the President. Nothing I said or did could change her mind.

"Rita, the entire entourage at the White House will cling to you."

"Why?" she asked. "I have nothing to offer."

"Tell them what it was like dancing with Gene Kelly and Fred Astaire."

"I wouldn't know. I just did it. I danced."

Unlike Rita, Orson was curious about everything. He loved to experiment, to play, or he could never have mastered the feat of *Citizen Kane,* no matter how many technical wizards were at his beck and call. He was a showman, a huckster, a magician, a man without fear, while I feared that he would be swallowed up by other worlds and would leave Big Red behind. That's why I packed her suitcase without telling her.

Over the last few months, Orson had become FDR's special envoy, and he enjoyed all the privileges of an envoy, which included his own great silver bird—a Douglas Skytrain to carry him aloft to the capital after several stopovers for fuel. Shorty drove us right up to the boarding ramp of a hidden runway behind the Army air base in San Bernardino, so Rita could give Orsie a goodbye kiss.

Orson scrambled out of the Cadillac with a wretched look on

his face. "Darling, please come. You'll have a grand time at the White House. F.D. will desert Eleanor. He'll show you off to all his aides and all the senators he can find. They're greedy men. They'll want to dance with you half the night. I'll have to fend them off with bottles of champagne. I'll hurl the bottles at their heads. Come with me, darling, *come.*"

Rita was unprepared for his sudden proposal. "Orsie, I—I don't—have a thing—to wear."

He was persistent, as usual, and persuasive. "We'll shop at Garfinckel's, my love. I'll get you a new wardrobe that you can wear at the White House. . . . Please, please come with me."

I could feel the compelling ardor in his big brown eyes. He wanted his beautiful wife with him in Washington.

And that's when I whispered, "Go with him, Red—go!"

I'd put her suitcase in the trunk of the car and I revealed that to her in the sign language we often used when we had something we wanted to hide. Rita stared at me with a vacant smile, as if all feeling, all attention to detail, had been battered out of her. "I can't, Rusty, I can't. I just wouldn't know what to say. Imagine me and Mrs. Eleanor. I never even finished the eighth grade."

Eduardo had plucked her out of school before she was thirteen, and that only deepened her shyness about herself and her ability to maneuver in the world. She distrusted all strangers. Red might have danced around FDR and his wheelchair, but Eleanor was an aristocratic lady who would have seen right through Rita's lack of an education. . . .

Orson kissed Red with a bearish hug, climbed up the ramp—I could sense the disappointment in the hump of his back—and vanished into the Skytrain.

Rita stood on the runway as the propellers whined, and whatever emotion she felt had fled to some country deep within herself, where she couldn't be touched.

6

E VEN WITH ORSON'S all-consuming passion for the bulls,
Rita had still gotten pregnant while she was in Tijuana on
her "honeymoon," as she liked to call it. But Orson couldn't rejoice
with her while he was away. He met ambassadors and other movie
stars at the White House. Cunning as he was, he had Eleanor call
Rita, who was petrified.

"My dear," Mrs. Roosevelt said in that sad patrician voice of
hers that sounded like a musical shiver.

I had to pinch Rita and mouth her words for her, as if she were
a marionette.

"Hello, Mrs. Roosevelt."

"*Dooo* call me Eleanor. Franklin and I are so pleased that you
and Orson will be parents soon. We are so fond of Orson. Franklin
will have to rely on him during the campaign. How lucky we are
to have such an intelligent, vibrant young man on our side. Promise me you will visit us the first opportunity you have."

I pinched Rita again.

"I promise, Mrs. Roosevelt—I mean, Eleanor."

Rita hung up the phone. I scolded her. "You didn't even say goodbye to the First Lady of the United States."

"I was too scared," and she started to cry.

Rita had confidence in the supple slyness of her movements, in the shake of a shoulder, in the jig of her leg. Words couldn't define her or fuel her dreams and desires.

We talked and talked. I gave her lessons in politics, told her how FDR had kept actors and musicians and writers from starving with all the different projects of the New Deal, and how a mogul like Louis B. Mayer despised the White House and had once been chairman of the Republican Party in California.

"Rusty, are you a Democrat?"

"Me? I never vote. I bought a couple of war bonds. But that's my limit."

Seems I'd gotten her animated on the subject.

"Orsie works so hard," she said. "We sold ten million worth of war bonds—together. Rusty, I miss him so much."

He sent her telegrams and flowers, wooed her, but always from afar. He went from the White House to the Waldorf Towers in Manhattan, where he delivered speeches for FDR at Madison Square Garden. He called her, sometimes twice a day, always having a girl at the Waldorf ring in advance as a warning that it was him, and not the Janitor, or some other custodian from Gower Street. Her spine would curl with excitement. He read poetry while the operator listened in, quoted entire speeches from *Hamlet*, and the sounds intoxicated her.

"Orsie, when are ya coming home?"

He always had one more speech to deliver.

He had the same silver bird, the Skytrain that took him everywhere—Denver, Des Moines, Mobile—except home to his pregnant wife. Her eyes began to wander after a while, as if she went whirling about in a dream.

"Rusty, I'd like to dance. I haven't gone dancing in a long time. You can be my beau."

"Your beau?"

"Yeah," she said, punching my arm with a soft fist. "My escort."

I panicked. "You'll have to wear a wig, or everyone will recognize you, and there'll be a riot."

She laughed, as if to tease me. "No one recognizes you if you don't want to be recognized—that's a movie star's little secret. Uncle Harry is too thick to understand. He thinks I need a bodyguard wherever I go. But it's the bodyguard who gives you away."

We didn't even dress for the occasion. She wore her blue jeans and one of Orson's shirts, and I wore my fatigues from a secondhand shop on Sunset. Shorty himself drove us to the Cat's Paw and went inside with us. I doubt that Rita had ever been to a lesbian bar. It was packed that evening with soldiers and sailors and gals from the defense plants. There were also lots of tourists and timid wallflowers who were plucked from a corner by drunken military cops without their armbands or their whistles. The Cat's Paw had risen in the world. It now had its own quartet of jazz musicians, with a bass fiddler who was a maestro of imperfection. It didn't seem to matter much. You had to dance to your own beat, and there were darn few lesbians at a lesbian bar.

I danced with Rita. She didn't hide her mane of red hair in a wartime bonnet. She was right. Not even the bartenders recognized Big Red, even though her dance steps were unmistakably hers, with all the music coming from her hips. I wanted to show her off. But I wasn't delusional. I worked for Rita, and I was paid for every dip I took at the Cat's Paw.

It was Shorty who was the real conqueror, fleet as Fred Astaire. He must have lined up half a dozen beauties. Rita had to curtail some of his conquests.

"Shorty," she shouted into all that cacophony, "behave yourself."

Her cheek was close to mine. I could taste her breath in the heat of the room. She'd had a whiskey sour.

"Rusty, why didn't you ever introduce me to this place?"

"Your husband might disapprove. There are a lot of rowdy sailors."

"Who cares?" she said, beginning to swallow half her words. "Orsie's in Des Moines. He'll never notice."

And that's when I noticed the Janitor's private secretary, Sally Fall, with her crew of sycophants. I expected nothing less than malice from her, though she had to be careful, since Rita was Columbia's prize attraction. So she whispered in a girlfriend's ear; the girlfriend pointed to my dancing partner and shouted above the distant roar of the band with a mordant smile on her pockmarked face, "Hello, hello, there's Rita Hayworth. The love goddess has dropped right into our lap."

That's all it took. The noise and sway on the dance floor turned to bedlam. It wasn't on account of the soldiers and sailors, who maintained their shy decorum. And it had nothing to do with the gals from the defense plants; they adored Rita and would never have intruded upon her privacy. It was the other civilians, those who had come to gawk and parade in a lesbian bar. They grabbed at Rita and ripped her clothes in search of souvenirs.

I couldn't protect Rita on my own. There were just too many of these civilian predators. They nearly scratched my eyes out and managed to pull Rita away from me. I might not have survived that onslaught if it hadn't been for Shorty. He barreled right into the crowd, and I was able to get Rita out of the Cat's Paw in one piece, with Shorty just behind us.

I was the one who was crying; me, who never cried. "I shouldn't have brought you here, I shouldn't. . . ."

It was Rita who calmed me down, Big Red. "It's not your fault. I was invisible, but not invisible enough."

7

I T WAS WHILE Orson was campaigning for FDR that Eduardo
and Volga suddenly appeared. They'd never have come had
Orson been around. He despised them for what they had done to
Big Red. Eduardo was a rooster of a man, light on his toes. Volga
was nearly a head taller than her husband, a sullen beauty with
streaks of gray in her hair. I could imagine how she must have
looked when she had danced in the Follies; that's how exquisite
her posture was—Rita had inherited her mother's broad shoulders,
slim ankles, and long legs. The Cansinos had arrived bearing gifts
for their pregnant daughter: trinkets and toddler toys.

There was something vile about them, and venomous, too. Eduardo required Rita's signature in order to guarantee a rather large
loan. Of course, Rita wrote him a check for the entire amount.
Eduardo hummed to himself, while Volga fidgeted for an instant
or two, her eyes bulging like a bird of prey. I did not like them at
all. And Volga was clever enough to read my disregard.

"Are you Carmen's nurse?" she asked.

"No, Madame Cansino, I'm her private secretary."

"And where is her husband?" she asked in the same venomous tone.

"Campaigning," I said, suddenly Orson's champion.

The bantam rooster cocked his shoulders like a feathered creature. "Shouldn't he be at home with his pregnant wife?"

"Not when he's out on a mission for the President of the United States," I said, as rudely as I could allow myself.

Volga scrutinized me from head to toe. "And what are your obligations to my daughter, Miss Redburn?"

"To keep her well oiled until her husband arrives from the battlefield."

Eduardo seemed perplexed. "What battlefield?"

"That's what politics is, Señor Cansino—a battlefield."

"But I do not see many soldiers at the rallies," he said.

"Look around," I answered. "Sometimes they wear civilian clothes."

Volga began to munch on the chocolate cookies that Rita had prepared. She'd expected her daughter to be alone, so she could continue to prey upon her. She and Eduardo had little to talk about. It was hard to reminisce about memories that were nothing more than a bleak night song. And so they didn't mention Rita's past. But Eduardo sure had Rita's sense of movement. He danced while he talked. It was hard to suppress the desire to strangle him.

"Carmencita, we will be here for the baby," he said in the midst of a tango step; he could have been partnering his own twelve-year-old daughter somewhere in his depraved mind. "We could always move in if the campaigner forgets to come back."

"Why would he forget?" Rita asked.

"Oh," Volga said, "a campaigner could go on to other campaigns."

They clutched at her and kissed her goodbye, but it seemed difficult for them to leave. Volga had a crease of anger near her eyelids, as if she and Eduardo were looking to pick at Rita's bones, to devour their daughter, rob her of whatever independent life she had left. I could almost imagine them remaining here on constant maneuvers.

Finally they did depart. Rita was trembling, and so was I.

"How can you bear the sight of them, Red?"

She had the vacant look in her eyes that she must have had when she was one half of the Dancing Cansinos.

"I suppose your parents were perfect," she said, lashing out a little.

"Not at all," I said. "The first time my father touched me was also the last. I nearly broke his jaw. I had to move in with my mother's sister, Maiden Aunt Fannie. I've been on my own since I was fifteen."

"But you went to college," she said, as if I'd accomplished a miracle.

"Yeah," I said, "a couple of years at Kalamazoo. But the Regina was my bible and my church. Oh, I can write a mean sentence. I've been schooled in all that. That's not what excites me. It's Orson. He breaks all the rules."

Rita smiled at me. "That's what he's good at, breaking rules."

Orson had a high fever while he was in Manhattan, and was laid up at the Waldorf Towers for a week. Rita begged him to return to Carmelina Drive for a rest cure, but as soon as his fever subsided he returned to the road. He campaigned until the very last day of the election, November 7, traveling from precinct to precinct, his voice like the macabre croak of a bullfrog. Still, he couldn't ignore Roosevelt's gray complexion, the slight trembling of his hand.

There were some who feared that Dewey might win. But Governor Tom didn't have a chance. FDR grabbed thirty-six states—it was a landslide. The President's senior aides called his new protégé "Senator Welles." And the "Senator" took the Skytrain back to San Bernardino. He had gained weight as he wandered through the hinterland for FDR. He looked a bit like Frankenstein's disheveled monster, shambling along on his flat feet. He'd also agreed to write a column for the *New York Post*, Orson Welles' Almanac, meant to predict America's political future.

Meanwhile, Rita, looking like a goddess with slightly swollen cheeks, was eight months pregnant. She'd dance with her belly in her hands. I'd never seen her more content. Orson usurped her solarium, and used it as his office and his study. He wandered around in his slippers, searching for topics. His first attempts at writing a column were abysmal. His sentences were as feckless and shoddy as Frankenstein's flat feet.

"Orsie," I said, "you're neglecting your wife."

He seemed pitiful to me in that solarium. "Well," he said, in his bullfrog's voice, "I have a column to deliver. I keep delaying the deadline."

"I'll help you write it—if you pay a bit more attention to Big Red."

"A deal," he said, and went in search of Rita, while I pulled out all the little extra strings of his prose until he had a coherent argument. I saved all the anecdotes that deepened his argument and cut out the rest. He was an adapter, I realized. He could take Conrad's *Heart of Darkness* and adapt it for the radio, just as he had adapted *The War of the Worlds*. The original script of *Kane* hadn't been his. He'd seized Herman Mankiewicz's screenplay, torn it apart, and made it touch upon his own life as much as Hearst's. He, too, had been ripped from his mother and father. He, too, had had an inheritance, even if Dadda had held on to most of his money. His real genius was in cannibalizing another person's material and swallowing it whole, whether it was Shakespeare, Mank, or H. G. Wells. He overwhelmed us onscreen because he wasn't really playing William Randolph Hearst, he was playing Orson in a putty nose. . . .

He looked after Rita while I rewrote his drivel. And soon we had the very first column of Orson Welles' Almanac.

"Astounding," he whispered, as he squinted at my revisions, word for word. "I hereby dub you as my deputy."

"Never mind," I muttered, "just be nice to Big Red."

And that he did. In December, she was admitted to Saint John's of Santa Monica, a hospital renowned for its privacy from celebrity seekers. Of course, all the women on the maternity ward realized it was Rita Hayworth who was wheeled in, under a covey of blankets and sheets. They whispered among themselves with their own enchantment, as their bodies began to sway. . . .

I was among the first to peek at the little red, wrinkled seven-pound girl, born with Orson's slightly ominous look. Rita called her Rebecca, or Becky, after the kindhearted Jewish maiden who cares for the wounded Ivanhoe in Sir Walter Scott's novel.

The Boy Wonder barely held Rebecca in his arms. I was the one who rocked Becky in her cradle, who changed her diapers, and powdered her bum while Rita was bedridden.

Rita stared at me from her pillowcase, numb as she was. "You're so kind, Rusty."

I wasn't kind. After a couple of weeks, I haunted the tattoo shop hidden behind the tobacconist on the Santa Monica Pier, across from the abandoned Hippodrome and its wrecked carousel. When I first arrived in California, I rode those wooden horses day and night. I made love like mad on one of those rottenly shellacked horses with Ginnie, the gal who ran the Hippodrome booth. But that's a tale I don't often tell.

The tattoo artist's name was also Ginnie. Her needle was rather sharp. I wasn't much of a sentimentalist. But I had a wrinkled red baby etched into the rippling skin of my upper thigh. I didn't want that baby attached to a heart or a bow or a wooden horse. But while the baby rose out of the drops of blood on my skin, I must have tumbled into the dream of a dream. I could hear the music of the old carousel as the wooden horses went around and around on the ratchets of its magnificent wheel. And I imagined myself riding a wooden pony across the pier. Folks had to scatter. I had Rita's daughter, Becky, on my back. She clung to me with her little fingers. I was on some kind of mission I couldn't recall. It must have already been wartime, since I saw an antiaircraft battery and a sergeant sitting in his saddle. And then I rode past Eduardo dancing on the pier with Rita, who couldn't have been more than twelve. The pony wouldn't stop. But I did catch the masked smile on Rita's face. She could have been a waxed doll. Her eyelids fluttered. She wore a pound of paint. And when I arrived at the end of the pier, I no longer had a wrinkled red baby on my back. . . .

8

ALL THE TROUBLE started with the inaugural lunch. The Senator without a Senate seat was invited to the lunch along with Rita, and then to a private chat with FDR and the First Lady on the second floor of the White House, away from all the clamor. Orson and Rita accepted the invitation, though she wasn't fully recovered from the ordeal of Becky's birth. She'd just risen out of a week in bed. And as they were about to depart for the air base in San Bernardino, Rita suddenly decided that it might be too stressful to fly. The real reason was Red's crippling fear of her own unworthiness and her terror of the unknown. She was frightened of Eleanor's patrician manner and preferred the company of beauticians. She felt much safer with them.

I knew what the after-echo would be like. It was the second invitation from the White House that she had run away from, and I felt that this time it would be fatal. I tried to convince her to accompany Orson.

"Red, you have to go."

"I can't," she said.

"You'll lose him. He's a wanderer by nature. And it would be best if you wandered with him once in a while."

But she couldn't be reasoned with. And he left for the San Bernardino airstrip alone. He wanted her at the White House. He'd counted on it. He liked to have her on his arm, as *his* first lady. I could sense his melancholy—and hers. She must have thought in her wildness that he wouldn't leave her and little Rebecca.

But he did.

He didn't even kiss Becky goodbye.

"You'll come right back after the inauguration," she muttered. But the limousine was already gone. I didn't need a fortune-teller from the pier to chart his journey. He went from Washington to the Waldorf. He toured several states, lecturing against Fascism, while he followed the radio circuit. Meanwhile, Volga fell out of Rita's life. It wasn't a spat. Something seemed terribly wrong with Volga. She was incoherent at times. Her skin had yellow spots and she couldn't get out of bed.

Rita visited her with Shorty, held her hand. Doctors were called in—quacks, really. They grabbed Rita's money and gave her little bits of advice. Rita managed to locate Orson, who had Dadda Bernstein examine Volga. She had a ruptured appendix, and was rushed to Saint John's. Rita paid all the bills, and her mother had a private suite at the hospital of the stars.

I was confused when Volga asked for me.

There were roses and violets surrounding her hospital bed. Volga seemed entombed by all the flowers. She was paler than pale. Her mouth was very dry, and I fed her sips of water.

"You don't like me, do you?"

"This isn't the right time to like or dislike," I said in as neutral a tone as I could summon.

"Oh, but it is," she said, as I wiped her forehead with a towel that I had dipped in a bucket of ice water.

She grew slightly delirious, and I wanted to call the doctor on station, but she gripped my hand, clenched it like a claw.

"I could not stop him . . . I could not. She never cried, not once. I might have done something . . . if she had cried."

"But she wasn't a crier, Mrs. Cansino. She kept it all in. It was the only world she had, dancing in the ballroom."

Volga turned quiet. She fell into a very deep gloom as she lay dying, a mother who had lost Big Red. Her eyes had that same dullness that Rita often had. Mother and daughter had suffered from temper tantrums that soon turned into a zombie-like withdrawal. Volga was forty-seven years old. She'd been an alcoholic half her life.

Rita came into the room wearing slippers, a child's despair on her face. I don't believe that Volga recognized her. After twenty minutes or so an intern arrived and pronounced Volga dead. Dadda would diagnose the cause of death as acute peritonitis. But that was a clinical reading at best. I would venture to say that Volga died by degrees. The alcohol must have numbed her a bit. How could she have borne it whenever Eduardo danced with Carmen as husband and wife? It had to eat away, one dance step at a time. A daughter she had sacrificed for her husband's sake. Was she the shadow dancer in that whole affair?

I drove Rita back to Carmelina Drive in Shorty's Cadillac, with the wooden blocks on the pedals. I didn't utter a word, didn't console her. She sat up front with me, her head on my shoulder. I could feel her cheek. It was ice-cold.

9

ORSON DIDN'T FLY in for Volga's funeral. He should have, for Rita, at least. But he was busy fighting Fascism on the radio and in town halls. He talked about Europe as a broken continent, a torn continent, caught in political intrigue, with Nazis rising out of the rubble, madmen dreaming of a Fourth Reich. Some were captured with medals in their pockets, others escaped to Buenos Aires or elsewhere. "We must follow them into their shadow land and crush them," the electioneer insisted. "Crush them, I say." He sounded like Charles Foster Kane.

He and Rita had become the most revered couple in America, after the President and the First Lady; a lot of it was on Rita's account, though Orson did have his followers, thanks to the President—and the liberation of Paris. Parisians had lived under Nazi rule for over four years, existing on turnips and rutabagas, while German officers dined on caviar at Maxim's, with the likes of Coco Chanel. As the bedraggled Boche marched out of Paris, the city broke into a tumultuous parade. I watched it all in the newsreels at the Regina, girls sitting on American tanks, like little marshals of war. Other girls, collaborators, often as young as twelve, with shaved heads, were spat upon and flung about like rag dolls in that feverish dance of victory. I didn't know their sins. But I pitied them. Perhaps I was thrusting my own girlhood in rural Illinois upon their shaved heads. And I would have liberated them myself. . . .

Certain French critics stumbled upon a print of *Citizen Kane* now that Paris was no longer part of Greater Germany. And somehow, my own mimeographed articles on *Kane*, written for revivals at the Regina, began to appear in French periodicals, under my nom de plume, Regina X. One or two renegades agreed with me that Hawks and Ford and a few others had a kind of *accidental* greatness, within the studio system, but Welles was an outlaw and would always be one.

The outlaw returned to us several weeks after Volga's funeral. He found Eduardo living in the library, and he was furious.

"That rooster," he declaimed.

"Orsie," Rita said, with a fire I had rarely seen in her, "you haven't kissed me yet."

He took her in his arms and kissed her until she blushed and turned slightly blue in the face. She caught her breath and told him, "I can't kick Papa out. He's in mourning. He misses my mother. But he's promised to move to Miami."

Orson returned to his column after a night with Rita. I had to rescue him again and again. He was a marvelous speaker, but his rhythms didn't transfer to the page. Orson Welles' Almanac wasn't gathering much momentum. The *Post* was bleeding money on the column's syndication rights. Paper after paper was dropping Orson Welles, particularly in the South and the Midwest, where his ideas were too radical. He had the nerve to ask us to share our wealth with other nations.

And then, that April, FDR died of a cerebral hemorrhage at the Little White House in Warm Springs, and so much of what he stood for died with him. Suddenly the New Deal was under attack. Congress and the FBI went after Communists in the film industry while the Soviet Union was still on our side. Writers, actors, and directors were called out, and films that had supported the Soviets, such as *Mission to Moscow* and *Counter-Attack*, were vilified. The FBI interviewed Orson and Rita right after the Germans surrendered in June. Two agents arrived with newly fashioned ballpoint pens and scribbled line after line in their ledgers about every petition Orson had ever signed.

I watched them scribble. They couldn't take their eyes off Rita.

"Welles," one of them asked, "did you attend a rally for Stalin held at Gilmore Field in 1943?"

"Indeed I did," the electioneer said with deviltry in his eyes. "The President asked me to speak. Should I have disobeyed FDR?"

It didn't really matter. Rita wore a cloak of invincibility as America's love goddess, and the FBI left Orsie alone.

Meanwhile, Eduardo was still living in the little library I had prepared for Rita. He went around wearing a blanket in June, still with that dancing step, just like Rita's. Orson didn't even nod to him at the breakfast table.

"Am I an outcast?" Eduardo asked. "Then I'll pack—this morning."

"Papa, stay," Rita said. She appealed to Orson. "Orsie, tell Eduardo that he's welcome."

Orson rose above the kitchen table in his silk pajamas. "Yes, darling, Eduardo is welcome—if you say so."

He left the table with a slice of Russian coffee cake from the Farmers Market and one of the President's coffee mugs and trod into the solarium. But all his political ambitions had evaporated—without FDR. He was now the Senator of nothing at all. Yet he was still electioneering, as if he were running for some mysterious Senate seat . . .

There was a curious shift among the moguls. The electioneer

had wandered into a studio tent and wasn't cast out—he was Rita's fellah, after all. Producer Sam Spiegel had found a vehicle for him to act in and direct, though he would have third billing, after Edward G. Robinson and Loretta Young. It was *The Stranger*, a spy thriller about a Nazi war criminal, Franz Kindler, who escapes to Argentina. After being hounded by agents of the Allied War Crimes Commission, Franz changes his identity, and ends up as Charles Rankin, a history professor at the Harper School for Boys in a small Connecticut town. Orson didn't wear one of his putty noses, but he did have a mustache, and he was far too heavy, so he received diet shots in his buttocks right on the set. Often he didn't return home until after midnight.

Rita cried all day long. That didn't stop her from tossing priceless Baccarat bottles of Shalimar at him. Despite the wafts of vanilla coming from the shattered crystal of her favorite perfume, she could smell the heat and musk of another woman on his clothes. She was right most of the time. The electioneer had been dallying with other women while he was at the Waldorf, and he continued to dally, so he and Rita now had separate bedrooms at the house on Carmelina Drive.

Eduardo was bewildered by the arrangement. "I don't understand," he muttered. "A husband and wife should be a husband and wife."

Soon the Boy Wonder hardly came home at all. He moved into Shirley Temple's former bungalow at the Goldwyn studios, where *The Stranger* was about to be shot. Perry Ferguson, who had been production chief for *Citizen Kane*, designed a mythic town square with a Gothic clock in its bell tower. Clocks, it seems, had been Kindler's great passion, and he meant to repair the clock in the tower. . . .

Orson asked me to help him revise the script. But it made little sense that a stranger such as Kindler would land in Harper,

Connecticut, as a history professor at a boys' school and become engaged to the town beauty, Mary Longstreet, the daughter of a Supreme Court justice, played by Loretta Young, while "the stranger" hid his real identity, all within months after the war. And the only clue to that identity was his love of clocks.

I changed what I could, and kept whatever hokum was left. Orson asked Rita—*begged* is more accurate—if he could borrow me as his script girl on the film.

"I'll pay her salary, darling, and you can have her back before the end of the shoot."

Rita glared at him. "Don't you *darling* me. You can borrow Rusty three days a week."

"A deal," Orson said. "Shall we shake on it?"

"Shut up."

She went into her bedroom and I ran after her.

"Red, I don't have to go with Orsie. He can always find another script girl. I'll stay with you."

"No," she muttered, her face dug into a pillow. "You'll learn a lot. And what could you ever learn from me?"

10

INSPECTOR WILSON, PLAYED by Edward G. Robinson, has a clever plan. He will have one of Kindler's former henchmen, Konrad Meineke, help him track the ex–Nazi officer. That crumpled little man in a crumpled coat, Meineke, played by Konstantin Shayne, a minor actor who had studied at the Moscow Art Theatre—a nobody in the moguls' eyes—steals every scene he is in. We first meet Meineke in Argentina, as he uncovers Kindler's whereabouts and new identity. Meineke remains in the shadows, as if we were watching a German Impressionist classic, such as *M*, a movie made fourteen years earlier, where the underworld chases Peter Lorre, a child murderer. Meineke is a murderer of a different kind. But he's on a new mission, to locate Kindler and convert him to the teachings of God, "the All High." He arrives in Harper on the very day that Kindler—Charles Rankin—is set to marry Loretta Young.

Kindler/Welles is horrified to meet this rumpled man out of his past, someone who can identify him as a Nazi mass murderer. He sends Meineke off into the woods behind the boys' school for another rendezvous. The contrast between the two men is striking. Kindler is a shuffling giant in prep school tweeds, and Meineke is a tiny man with a religious fervor in his eyes, as he wanders in and out of the shadows.

Repent, Meineke says, *there's still time*, while Kindler dreams of a Fourth Reich, just like the fanatics I'd witnessed at the Regina in the March of Time. Kindler strangles Meineke, covers him in leaves and dirt, but there's no point of view in the shot; the camera remains neutral, like the rest of the film until the very end when Kindler is impaled by the sword of a Gothic angel in the bell tower; all of this done without Welles' singular touch, as if he were directing in a fugue state.

The oddest thing about the film is Kindler/Welles' relationship with his bride, Mary Longstreet/Loretta Young. She's blinded by his aura, or perhaps by the gift of marriage. Even when she discovers that he's a Nazi fugitive, a master of the death camps, she's still his bride, faithful to the half-mad look in his eyes. It's only at the very end of the film when she's alone in the bell tower with Kindler that we hear her say that she's come to kill him, as if she's rising out of a nightmare. But we return to the village below, and her haunted marriage fades from the film. . . .

Yes, I was Orson's script girl, and yes, I had a marvelous time watching him bustle about in the director's chair. But Orson had a super-cutter standing right behind him, Ernest Nims, a hatchet man put there to watch his every move and to safeguard the film's narrative flow. The darkness was suddenly much less dark without Orson's usual flair.

Orson liked to call himself a "king actor," one who could hold an audience in a hypnotic spell. He was a king actor in *Kane*, where his performance had such energy and appeal that he could have carried the entire cast. And what could have been a magnificent manhunt in *The Stranger* became pure melodrama, with the king actor thrust into a cardboard landscape. He was much too large, much too baroque, to appear in such a pedestrian film, so that every gesture of his seemed out of proportion. It was as if he were removing *M* from Berlin, with its cast of gangsters, and shuffling it into a fanciful Connecticut town. And he didn't have his usual Mercury Players to rely on. He was stripped bare, with the super-cutter right behind him.

He was a pariah again, the man who couldn't even make a spy film with much punch. *The Stranger* was forgotten before it was released.

But his disappointment at Goldwyn was nothing compared to the trouble he had at home. It wasn't only the crying fits. Rita attacked him one night with a kitchen knife. His litany of liaisons seemed to make her more and more mad, and she imagined him in love affairs that never happened, with other script girls and makeup artists. Orson was frightened of her rages, and I had to talk her down from her mad plateaus. She stared at me like a magnificent witch with a red mane.

"Traitor, you've been sucking him off."

"Where?" I asked.

"On the set."

"Have I ever shown an interest in your husband, Rita?"

She was articulate all of a sudden. "Haven't you called him a genius at least a hundred times, the master of modern cinema? And what is that damn French word?"

"*Maître.*"

"Well?" she asked.

"I still can't bear his body odor. Rita, I'm not that fond of men."

"I don't believe you."

Somehow, I got the knife out of her hand. The worst of it was that he ignored Becky. He wasn't a good father at all. An over-grown child himself, he didn't have the instincts to play with another child. Shorty was much more attentive, and so was Eduardo, until Rita sent him off to Miami with a train ticket and a thousand dollars in cash.

Eduardo was distraught. "But I am of use to you, Carmencita. I watch after the little girl."

"And if you stay here, I might murder you in your sleep."

It only confounded him more. "You are not a murderess, child."

She answered him as briskly as a lifelong partner in a vaudeville act.

"Oh, yes, Papa, yes, I am."

Eduardo left within the hour, like the vagabond he was. She kicked Shorty out, too, then Orson, though I'd swear she was still in love with him. She conferred with her lawyer and her agents, and decided on a divorce. She didn't want a dime of alimony, and he didn't have much more than that. Once again, Orson was barred from the Columbia lot. He moved in with Shorty. Both of them inhabited a tiny bungalow behind another bungalow on La Brea. And I wondered if I would get the hatchet, too.

"You can stay," she said. "I haven't finished with my education yet."

She was fine at the studio, where she was now working on *Gilda,* a romantic thriller that took place right after the war in Buenos Aires, a beehive for Nazi agents. *Gilda* starred Rita as a femme fatale with her famous dancing walk, and Glenn Ford as a past lover she had come to hate. That's all I knew, since I was never on the set with her. She was always punctual, an automaton with a glaze in her eyes. I soon realized that Red had begun to drink at home. At first there were tiny sips, and then she collected bottles of gin and rye whiskey. She would have a bitter laugh as she gulped the rye, like a lady pirate with red hair. I had to rouse her from bed or she would have missed every call at the studio. Often I soaked her head in the sink.

"You're not Rusty," she said with that same bitter laugh, "you're Harry Cohn's cop."

I couldn't get her to stop drinking, so I measured the gulps she took. I stayed with her most of the time, put her to bed, and sometimes slept beside her. I got her ready before five a.m. when the chauffeur from the studio appeared at the door.

"I miss Orsie," she blurted.

"But you kicked him out."

"I can still miss him. It's not a crime."

And off to the studio she went, vamped by hairdressers and makeup artists, who must have told her about Orsie's current love affair with Judy Garland. They were cruel, just as Orson had been cruel to them, not allowing a single one of these girls near Carmelina Drive—they weren't dignified enough for him. Now they followed Rita everywhere, like a bunch of harpies.

"Tell me," Rita muttered, with rye whiskey in her nostrils, "does he fuck her twice a night, or do they have a threesome with the Tin Man?"

"Red, I wouldn't know. Judy Garland isn't in my circle of friends."

"You don't have any friends. You're a freak with a tattoo on your ass."

She whipped her shoulders back and forth like a wounded deer.

"I didn't mean it, Rusty. I'm the freak."

"You're not a freak. You just happen to have married the most self-absorbed man in the world."

The trouble was that she couldn't make up her mind about anything. She'd invite Orson to dinner, then disinvite him in the same breath, after a slug of gin.

Orson wasn't empty-handed. He envisioned a stage version of *Around the World in Eighty Days*. It was one more attempt to recapture his past, like the circuses he'd seen in his childhood, or his visit to Houdini's dressing room in Chicago. *Kane* itself was afloat in magic tricks. That's why *The Stranger* hurt so much. It was devoid of magic. Yet I had promised Orsie to present it at the Regina.

The movie house was mobbed. The lines snaked around Hollywood Boulevard. I hated to send people away. We broke every fire rule in the book. The projectionist and the entire staff could have been arrested by the county fire marshals. I would have had to spend a weekend at the women's prison farm near Tehachapi. But still they came. The Regina wasn't like Grauman's Chinese, with its endless feast of grand openings—there were searchlights again on the boulevard now that the war was over and we didn't have to fear enemy fire. But the Regina had its own vault of memory. *Kane* had never disappeared from our psyches, even if it was so hard to find another print.

I didn't introduce *The Stranger*, or utter a word about Welles. We showed the film all the way through without a single comment. There was a deathly silence in the theater, as if we all fell into Kindler's own dream of a Fourth Reich. No one clapped. The lights were snapped on. Orson sat there in the first row. He wouldn't climb up onto the stage with me. I would have preferred a dialogue with the master. But he left me flat, exposed to all the Jacobins, those incorruptible believers in high art.

"What do we have here?" I asked.

"*Hollywood*," came back at me in a bitter chant.

"Regina X," asked one of my staunchest followers, "did you work on this film?"

"Yes, I was one of the script girls."

And that's when Orson climbed onto the stage with me; he'd gained fifty pounds since the end of the shoot, and no longer had Kindler's sleek look or his groomed mustache.

He didn't offer a single excuse, or put the blame on Ernest Nims. He paced back and forth. "I couldn't inhabit Kindler, and not because of the enormity of the crime." He stared at us. "I like killers. . . . I didn't search hard enough. I couldn't find his depths. I seized *Kane*. I owned it. I owned nothing here. I couldn't crawl under Kindler's skin."

"You went Hollywood," said one of his biggest fans.

"Worse. I couldn't even master their own shit. I failed, you see. The film never jelled. . . . I was afraid. I didn't direct. I dug graves."

The discarded electioneer climbed down and left the theater in his usual shambling gait, as if he had nowhere else to go beyond the Regina's front door.

· THREE ·

Gilda, 1946

1

YOU FIRST SEE her head rising out of the bottom of the screen, like a gallant jack-in-the-box with her mane of red hair, defiant, playful—in black-and-white. It seemed utterly original, unique, until I remembered where I had seen such playfulness before, in Orson's Wonder Show for servicemen on Cahuenga Boulevard, where she rises ghostlike out of a box and dances with Gilda's audacity. She was Gilda before Gilda was ever born. But no one, not Harry Cohn, not the Publicity Department at Columbia, not Louella Parsons, nor Hollywood itself, would realize that Gilda, the femme fatale who never stands still, would become a worldwide phenomenon, the "bombshell of bombshells." When she danced "Put the Blame on Mame," about a mythical temptress who causes earthquakes, fires, and floods, every one of Gilda's moves had a planetary pull. An atomic atoll would be named after Gilda. GIs stationed in Europe would write her stacks of love letters, with marriage proposals, of course, and lucky dollar bills. For a moment, in 1946, there was no other star; no one could compete with Mame, who did a striptease just by taking off a glove. Women across the county—housewives, vixens, bobby soxers, widows, even other femmes fatales—went to the movie houses and watched the film six or seven times, glued to Gilda, utterly bewitched.

Cohn, the penny pincher, had never had such a success. He and his star were wanted everywhere. But Rita preferred to stay at home with Rebecca. I fielded all her interviews and appearances. Red wouldn't speak to anyone without me at her side. Hollywood reporters played up to Gilda's new press attaché—Rusty Redburn, the kid from Kalamazoo. Louella called six times in one afternoon.

"Rusty, I'll run you out of town."

"That's your privilege, sweetheart."

I was getting my revenge for what she had done to Orson and *Kane*, how she had sabotaged the reception of the film on behalf of Hearst, and nearly drove Orson out of Hollywood.

Gilda had become far more important than a vitriolic lady with wattles and a booth at the Brown Derby. Now it was Lolly Parsons who needed Gilda, and Gilda needed no one at all.

"Louella, dear, when there's a scoop to be had, you'll have it. Meanwhile, you'll have to wait in line."

Cohn was eager to capitalize on *Gilda* and have her get to work on another film. But *Gilda* had captured a kind of postwar trauma and malaise; her curious sexuality, lethargic and wild from moment to moment, couldn't be captured again. She herself was having a series of love affairs. Singer-actor Tony Martin, a curly-haired Lothario, was the man of the month. But he didn't have Orson's swaggering brilliance. And Rita was aware that I didn't have much respect for either Tony's talent or his intellect.

"If you aren't nice to him," she said, "you'll be out on your skinny ass."

"Fine," I said, "but tell me, Gilda, dear, how many interviews have you done without me?"

"I'll learn," she said. "I've had a good teacher. And I can't be Gilda forever."

That was the problem. I wished that she could. Gilda had all the heartbreak of her childhood, the loneliness, the abuse. She had desolation in her eyeballs. Her brazenness was a weapon, a shield. But Cohn didn't understand Gilda at all. He couldn't read much beyond ticket sales. Big Red had caught a moment in history, and that moment would soon be gone.

2

ILLFUL AS SHE was, Red wouldn't sign the divorce papers. And she stopped answering Tony Martin's phone calls. "Isn't that what you wanted?" she asked.

I didn't say a word. And then we both heard a curious rumor that Harry Cohn, who never spent a dime he didn't need to spend, had invested in *Around the World in Eighty Days*, a Broadway show that never got to Broadway; it was filled with Orson's love of mechanical devices and live animals that couldn't coexist on the stage—elephants riding in locomotives, tigers captaining carousels, and other insanities, such as wild pigs that soiled customers in the front rows and natives of the Wild West who shot arrows into the audience, while acrobats hung from the rafters dressed as skeletons; it all reminded me and Red of the Mercury Wonder Show spinning out of control, as the stagehands rebelled at having to work twenty hours at a time, actors vanished in the midst of rehearsals, and costumes always managed to arrive in the wrong town. But Orson, in a desperate search for cash, agreed to direct a thriller for Harry without any pay if he could borrow twenty-five thousand bucks.

Harry saw a singular investment. He could flaunt the Boy Wonder as part of Columbia's stable of directors. The film was about a femme fatale, hopefully another Mame who could dance the hoochy-coo. It had no title as yet. And no cast.

I told Rita: "Jump at it, Red. There won't be a second chance."

"But Orsie hasn't asked. And no one has talked about the deal."

Rita was petrified.

"Let's go to the Janitor," I said.

We didn't make an appointment. We simply strode into his suite. Everyone stared at Rita. Even Sally Fall, Cohn's personal assistant, was mesmerized by Gilda. We entered the Janitor's private office. He had to be careful with Rita now. She was a bigger star than his studio had ever produced. One of Gilda's yawns could send Columbia's New York bankers running to the toilet. She hadn't been to his office in years.

The Janitor snarled at me. "Rusty, why did you bring her?"

"It was my idea," Rita said. "I hear Orson is making a film for you."

The Janitor laughed in his Sulka shirt.

"Come on. It's a programmer, a 'B' pic. I'm paying the guy peanuts, for God's sake."

Big Red wasn't coy with him. "I'm told there's a part for me."

The Janitor slapped his sides like the vaudevillian that he once was. "Rusty, did you put her up to this?"

"Yes, I did, boss. She wants to work with the Boy Wonder."

The Janitor smiled. "Welles is a clown. He couldn't even get his props to Broadway. He was laughed right off the stage. How can I trust my biggest asset with him?"

"Simple," I said. "Give him Gilda. And line him up in an 'A' production."

The Janitor pressed one of the buttons on his phone. "Tell Parnell to drag his sorry fat ass in here."

We'd have to deal with that cruel-eyed man, master of Columbia's 'A' productions. I could sniff trouble the moment he sauntered into the office in his saddle shoes. He smirked at Rita, didn't even bother to say hello. I understood that little exchange. Eddie Judson must have pimped Rita off to Parnell on more than one occasion.

"What's the matter, boss?" he asked.

"Laugh at this. That property Orson asked us to buy. You remember the name?"

"Yeah, one of those Inner Sanctum mysteries, *If I Die Before I Wake*. We got it for a song."

"Well," said Cohn, "Gilda, dear, wants to act in that Inner Sanctum."

"Harry," Parnell said, "we've budgeted the film. There isn't one 'A' list star. It's a programmer, like Charlie Chan. There's no room for Rita, and the role isn't right."

But Gilda was in full possession now. "Parnell, what do I have to do to get that role—sit in your lap? Like the last time?"

The Janitor didn't like to hear about any of his prize producers who had slept with Rita when she had rejected all his overtures.

"Harry," Parnell said, "New York wouldn't want to risk Rita on Orson Welles."

"Yeah," Cohn said, "how can I convince the Columbia Board?"

Rita sambaed over to Harry. "Tell them to put the blame on Mame, boys. Gilda will work with Orson, or she won't work at all."

Then she kissed Parnell in front of Cohn and sambaed out of the office, while I followed in her footsteps.

3

RITA MOVED WITH Rebecca into a ranch house on Rocking-ham Road, at the foot of the Santa Monica Mountains. The furniture was all hand-carved, at one of the studio's own shops. It was like living in a museum, with posters of Gilda on the walls, dancing the hoochy-coo. Gilda was the real motif of Rockingham Road. She could dance on the tiles, sunbathe in the solarium that was hidden between several panels and walls. She glided through the house in her bare feet, like a Sioux warrior. Gilda was beholden to no one—but Orson Welles. . . .

He returned from Manhattan without his elephants and acrobats, his show in ruins, without a penny in his pocket, and was back in Shorty's bungalow at La Brea. So she invited him to dinner with Shorty—Shorty was essential.

Orsie arrived in rumpled clothes. His fingernails were dirty. His eyes were bloodshot. One of his shoes had a missing sole. He wouldn't tell Rita about his situation, but it seems that he and Shorty were about to be evicted from their bungalow.

Doing her damnedest to please the maestro, Rita lit a Cuban

cigar for Orsie. She fed him meat loaf and mashed potatoes, the meal he loved best, and had me open a bottle of Napa Valley wine. She had to serve him three portions of potatoes.

Then she attacked. "I want to be in your new film—for Columbia."

"Darling," he said, "it's not *Gilda*. The role is too small."

"Then," she said, as she danced around the table, "make it bigger."

"Jesus, am I being ambushed in the middle of a meal?"

"Yes," she thundered.

"But I could shoot it in thirty days—in New York. It's a simple caper about a poor slob who gets framed. There's a murderess in the film. She doesn't dance and she doesn't sing."

"Perfect," Rita said. "I'll take the part."

"I'll have to revise the whole novel—pull most of it out of Manhattan."

"When can you begin?"

"Well," he said, examining his dirty fingernails like an inspector general. "Shorty and I . . ."

"You can both move in here. I'll have the master bedroom redone. Orsie, the bed isn't big enough for your feet."

It didn't matter who courted her. She still loved this brilliant oaf with the dirty nails. She'd loved no other man. Yet Orson had moved on. I could read the tale in his darting eyes. The deep warmth was gone. He would remain with her while they worked on the new film. He would cherish her out of politeness, yet part of him would be absent. He was a dynamiter, in his films and in his relationships.

But Gilda was no ordinary girl. She could conjure up an earthquake around Orson, keep him at Rockingham Road. For the moment he was helpless against Mame.

FOUR

The Lady from Shanghai, 1946–1947

1

I T WAS THE flimsiest of melodramas, *If I Die Before I Wake*, with a fall guy as the hero. Orson chose the book for Harry Cohn because it had the kind of linear plot that would excite a studio boss. He scrapped most of the novel and moved the locale to Mexico, Sausalito, and San Francisco, where he would be as far from Harry and his henchmen as he could get. Meanwhile, Orson had to write the scenario in Rita's new house. She got rid of all her gin bottles and swore she wouldn't guzzle—not while she was preparing for a part.

It was pure magic to have Orson at Rockingham Road, shuffling around in his silk pajamas, while Red wore his favorite negligée from Juel Park's. Orson was amazed. Rita had given him more prestige and firepower at Columbia than he ever could have imagined. This time he didn't have a super-cutter to watch his every move. Welles worked alone. He would not only act and direct Rita, he would also produce.

He had to change the personality of his own part. A king actor like Orson Welles couldn't play a cipher and a victim, and so the fall guy became "Black Irish" Michael O'Hara, a seaman and gallant rogue who had fought on the Republican side during the Spanish Civil War and had once killed a man—he'd strangled a Franco spy with his bare hands. Orson wasn't always attentive to his brogue, and it was rare to find a seaman with such jowls, but Michael O'Hara was still a kingly role.

Now he had to attend to Rita. And he did give her plenty of style. She was Elsa, the wife of Arthur Bannister, America's greatest criminal lawyer. Elsa Bannister was born in Chifu, the world's most wicked city after Macao. Her parents were both White Russians who had escaped Stalin and the revolution and fled to China. Elsa had ended up in Shanghai, perhaps as a gambler or a high-priced courtesan. We're never told the details. But we do have the title for the untitled film: *The Lady from Shanghai*—picked by Orson himself.

Bannister, it seems, has blackmailed her into marrying him. He holds all the secrets. He's played by Everett Sloane, who was "Bernstein" in *Kane*, and a member of Orson's original team, the Mercury Players, that went out with him to Hollywood. Bannister has *two* mangled legs in *The Lady from Shanghai* and walks with a pair of crisscrossing canes. Everett Sloane had to wear very tight braces, and his legs hurt with every step he took.

"It's supposed to hurt," Orson said. "We want to feel that pain on the screen."

"I won't stand for it," Sloane said. "I'll quit."

Orson growled at him. "Ev, it's been four years since your last part, Ev—four years—and this is the role of your life. You won't quit. I'll call Cohn and have him double your salary. 'Harry,' I'll say, 'we can't have Everett Sloane crying on the set all the time. He needs compensation for allowing us to torture him.' Will that do, Ev?"

But Rita was the real problem. Orson didn't want his mysterious Lady from Shanghai to be a stand-in for Gilda, the femme fatale with a heart of gold. So he had Helen Hunt, the hairstylist at Columbia who had helped turn Rita into a colossal star, clip off her red mane and dye what was left in topaz, a fancier platinum blond.

Orson had sixteen photographers celebrate Rita's uncrowning as a redhead.

LOVE GODDESS RESTYLED TO PLAY MYSTERIOUS VAMP FROM CHINA'S WICKED COAST

Some fans rebelled immediately; they didn't want their favorite star's hair shorn like a female Samson. And when Harry Cohn first read about Rita in the Hollywood rags he raged for a week. He wanted to fire every one of his producers and the entire Publicity Department. But he couldn't admit that he was the last to learn about Rita, and he couldn't afford to have a shouting war in public over Columbia's most lavish production of the year. Instead, he had his chauffeur drive him to Rockingham Road.

"I'm ruined," he cried once Shorty let him through the door. "The studio will never recover from the damage of that haircut."

He didn't have much of an audience. He had to skulk around until Rita and Orson came out of the master bedroom, both in silk pajamas.

He railed at Orson. "Clever, ain't ya? I'll never hire a director again who's one of the film's stars. You can't fire him. He's bulletproof—like Batman."

"It's not too late, Harry," Orson said in his silks. "We can scrap the film."

"How?" Harry asked. "You already cut her hair. She's Elsa Bannister now . . . a murderess. I have to have my head examined."

"Harry," Rita said, "I don't want to play Gilda for the rest of my life."

"What do you know?" the Janitor asked with a surge of self-pity. "Gilda is your meal ticket. We market you again and again, even as a bald blond."

"I'm not bald," Rita said, caressing her new coiffure. "It's a feather bob."

Harry turned to Orson. "Genius, does our bobbed beauty sing in your film?"

"No," Orson said.

"She has to sing. That's final."

"Yeah," Rita said, "with my usual ghost, Anita Ellis."

"That's final. Or this ship doesn't sail."

"Harry," Rita said, without missing a beat, "the ship has already sailed. It's your biggest number of the year. I can bow out, and Orson can do a quickie for you. He can play Charlie Chan."

"Nix," Cohn said, "you'll always be my Big Red, even with your bob. . . . Is there any food in this house? I'm starving."

We all sat down to a breakfast of pancakes. Cohn devoured an entire stack, with a full decanter of maple syrup. Suddenly he felt in command again.

"Genius, make Red a murderess we can never forget. I'm counting on you. We love her and hate her in her new bob. We can't take our eyes off Rita. That's the kind of picture I want. Pass the maple syrup, please."

2

I WAS SUCKERED ONTO the set. Orson knew I couldn't resist
the squall inside his head. He would be the sole master of his
tiny kingdom at Columbia, at least while *The Lady from Shanghai*
was being shot. I heard him gab with Glenn Anders, an actor who
hadn't worked in years. Anders had been a Broadway star during
the silent era. Orson wanted him for Grisby, Bannister's conniving
partner. He didn't bother with agents. He discovered that Anders
was living on the dole in Tallulah Bankhead's Manhattan apartment. I managed to get him on the line.

Orson picked up the phone. "Glennie, darling, we need you—
tomorrow. . . . Yes, it's a new film. Never mind the part. You play
a lunatic. Ask Tallulah to lend you the fare. You'll have a contract
the moment you arrive. I swear on John Barrymore's grave."

Meanwhile, he had the craftsmen at the Columbia Prop Department build him the beginnings of an abandoned fun house and a
hall of mirrors with over a thousand pieces of glass—the mirror
maze alone cost sixty grand, but the Accounting Department didn't
question him. He was producer and director of the show. Orson

didn't have to depend on the craftsmen for everything. He, Shorty, and I climbed onto the walls of this castle—the fun house—and Orson, who'd been an artist manqué all his life, painted bizarre, mutilated bodies and faces of courtesans and clowns on the walls, while Shorty held the paint can like a magician's apprentice, and I wiped the drippings with turpentine and a rag.

He was working on a particularly gruesome face with a lopsided mouth when he chuckled. "Doesn't that look like Harry Cohn?"

"No, I said. "It looks more like his lady vampire, Viola Lawrence."

Viola was the first female cutter in Hollywood history, and she worked for Cohn as his film editor. She would cut Orson to ribbons, mutilate his film for the sake of continuity. And whatever dreamscape he had in mind would be gone. But he was a stubborn son of a bitch and wouldn't listen to a word I said. He didn't know Viola as I did.

"Rusty, she won't be coming with us to Acapulco, and she won't be on the set."

I was amazed at his naïveté. Columbia was a little empire of butcher boys and butcher girls, like Vi. And still he believed in the sanctity of his art—our Renaissance prince.

He smiled at me while he attacked with his paintbrush. "This time we have our own little family—you, me, Rita, Shorty, and Everett Sloane."

"Sloane is about to quit," I said. "The braces are killing him."

"He'll lament throughout the shoot. He'll make us miserable, but he won't quit. He can't bear giving up a part. . . . And don't forget Glennie Anders. You'll have to pick him up at the airport. California never agreed with him. He's like a little boy lost in an orange grove."

Hollywood had lost its orange groves years ago, but that didn't seem to matter to Orson, who had to stop painting gargoyles and get back to his script. The shoot would begin tomorrow. So we climbed down from that papier-mâché dream world of an abandoned fun house that the Prop Department had half built and returned to Rockingham Road with our brushes, paint cans, turpentine, and rags.

The fun house was where Orson decided to end the film; the blond murderess intended to trap her fall guy, poor Michael O'Hara, hide him forever in a fanciful hall of mirrors. . . .

3

HE APPEARED ON the set in a black cape, while Shorty held a bowl of hot water and shaved him with a barber's pearl-handled razor. The master had no time for the trifles of human existence. He was sitting on a crane, preparing his next shot, when I arrived from the airport with Glenn Anders, who had enormous, startling eyes and the thickened face of an alcoholic. Still, I liked his bug-eyed eccentricity. He was nervous about his role. I could tell.

Orson descended from the sky until his big flat feet were in Anders' face.

"Glennie, dear, do us a favor? Do you see that stretcher?" And a stretcher suddenly appeared with a spanking-white sheet and a studio cop as the stretcher bearer. "Well, wrap yourself in the sheet like a good little boy, shut your eyes, and play dead."

And that's exactly what Anders did, but before the camera began to roll, a clerk from the Contract Department arrived with a sheath of papers. "Sign here, please, and there."

Anders signed without perusing a word, then folded his feet, and played dead. He did it all in one take. Anders didn't know it yet, but his character, Grisby, was preparing to stage his own death in order to collect some sort of diabolic insurance. And his plan was to pay Michael O'Hara—Orson—to "murder" him. The plan would go afoul, of course. . . .

Meanwhile, Orson was still in his director's chair.

"Wonderful, Glennie," he purred like a monstrous kitten.

"But I squinted. I'm sure of it."

Orson laughed. "That will only add to the luster of the scene. You're a fabulous corpse."

I drove Anders to the Hollywood Hotel and returned to the set. Orson was now shooting the first scene of *The Lady from Shanghai*, an encounter in New York's Central Park, where he had to direct Rita and himself. There was no sunlight in the studio, no real sense of the sky, so this scene had the muted look of a fairy tale stuck in a moment of time. Rita was wearing a white polka-dot dress in a hansom cab. She was magnificent in her new coiffure, but she didn't have the spontaneous warmth of Gilda. She was an utterly different creature here, a siren seeking out lads like Michael O'Hara to lure into her spider's web. He had on a sailor's pea jacket, and talked in a Black Irish brogue. He invented a name for her—Rosalie, out of the same misbegotten fairy tale. He guesses at her wicked past in Chifu, the queen of gambling dens, and saves her from being robbed—or raped—by three roughs.

Rita is riveting as a mysterious blonde. It's Orson who troubles us, his brogue a little too thick. But there's another reason why the carriage ride is so static. The trees are as fraudulent as the sky. They stand on rollers, and are pushed about by prop men to give us the sense that the hansom cab is moving across the nonexistent space of a nonexistent Central Park.

The next scene was shot in the sailors' hiring hall, where we meet Arthur Bannister—Sloane, Everett Sloane—with his twisted legs and dancing canes. Every one of his moves is masterful, like a stuttering ballet. Michael, the would-be novelist, is sitting at a typewriter when Bannister arrives. Michael's "Rosalie" turns out to be Elsa Bannister, the crippled man's wife. And Bannister wants to hire Michael to accompany him and Elsa on a cruise from Manhattan to San Francisco via the Panama Canal and Mexican waters. Bannister had his own yacht, the *Circe*. He invites Michael and a few of his fellow sailors to have a drink with him at a waterfront dive. Bannister gets drunk, and the sailors have to haul him out of there. We warm to Michael, feel a kind of compassion for him as his brogue softens. And we move out of a static fairy tale and into a narrative with all the magic of Everett Sloane and his dancing sticks. . . .

4

A MOTLEY CREW OF thirty-six actors, clerks, and technicians arrived at a private airstrip in Pasadena, where a chartered Douglas DC-3 sat surrounded by a virtual hurricane of Hollywood reporters, since *The Lady from Shanghai* starred Big Red, movieland's own atomic bomb. The plane ride to Acapulco was a gift from Harry Cohn, I presume. But it backfired. Big Red would hardly greet the reporters. She was morose. Her child had to be left behind on Rockingham Road with a nurse. And it ripped at Rita that she couldn't take little Rebecca on such an arduous journey.

A reporter stuck his microphone in her face and asked, "Rita, how does it feel to be the number-one star in the world?"

There was a long silence, almost apocalyptic, it seemed. "It feels, it feels—like a ball of thunder."

The press corps was perplexed. But I did my own adagio. "Rita can feel some of that atomic pull," I said and hurried her onto the craft.

She did not see herself as a love goddess. Nor did Rita see herself as much of a wife. She and Orson were always within proximity of one another, but they never touched. Yes, they would occupy the same bedroom at Acapulco's Hotel Casablanca for appearance's sake—director and star, husband and wife. But I suspect it was a kind of camouflage. . . .

The plane landed on another private airstrip, without a single journalist to greet the circus of actors and technicians that belonged to *The Lady from Shanghai*. We were on a plateau at the side of a mountain somewhere and were met by a contingent of soldiers in armored trucks. The soldiers were all dressed in jungle-green. With them was a general who carried a *bandolera* of roses and a silver jug for La Señora Rita Hayworth. The jug was for washing her feet in the morning.

This welcoming party was the general's own idea. The landing strip belonged to him. There were no bandits within five hundred miles of Acapulco, he said. I assumed he wanted *mañana* money, some kind of payoff for his protection. I whispered in the ear of the clerk from the Accounting Department who had accompanied us. His Spanish was better than mine. I told him to offer the general five hundred clams a week out of our budget for "incidentals."

He did.

For a moment, I worried the general would have the clerk shot. It seems we'd offended him. He didn't want any payment other than to accompany La Señora to the Hotel Casablanca, which sat on its own cliff, and to have dinner with the maestro and Rita in honor of the film that was to be shot in Acapulco, *his* backyard.

His men loaded our tons of equipment in their steel canisters and crates onto the armored trucks, while the general, who was nearly as tall as Orson, offered the *bandolera* of roses and the silver jug to Rita, doffed his military cap, and said in English that was twice as musical and sonorous as mine, "Señora, you have given me the greatest of pleasures with your glove dance in *Gilda*, and I would be a brute with the manners of a tree monkey or a wild pig if I did not repay that pleasure with a small token of kindness from me and my men."

He had to stoop, as Orson might have done, to kiss her on the cheek, and then Rita, Shorty, Everett Sloane, Glenn Anders, the maestro, and I climbed into the general's armored truck and he himself drove us down the winding roads of the mountain without taking his foot off the gas pedal. The descent was very steep. The first glint of the water nearly blinded us. We had to clamp a hand over our eyes to catch the unchartered sweep of the bay. Orson must have known that Acapulco was an undiscovered paradise, with mile upon mile of beaches—I preferred the Santa Monica Pier. The slightly sweetened aroma of cleanliness was toxic to me.

5

THE HOTEL CASABLANCA was like an ocean liner condemned to dry land. It even rocked a bit in the wind, and had
decks rather than terraces, while I lived in a "cabin" that faced the
trash barrels, with a porthole the size of a pea. The general's men
escorted Rita and Orson to a dining room that looked and felt like
a sinister dreamscape, with the mountains tilting right into our lap
at a precipitous angle and the twilight waters of the bay disappearing into the darkness and leaving a desert of sand.

The guest of honor wasn't the general, but Señor Errol Flynn,
whose celebrated yacht, the *Zaca*, sat in Acapulco waters like a
commandant. It had a memorable past. The *Zaca* had been used
by the Navy during the war to rescue the crews of planes that had
fallen out of the sky. Flynn looked as if he himself had fallen from
the same sky. He wasn't even forty, yet he had sunken cheeks and
flinty, yellowish green eyes. His film career had plummeted. Yet
even in his decline, Flynn was still the most popular male star at
the Regina. He sat there in a yachtsman's blue jacket, the master
and captain of the *Zaca*. Damn him, that's why we were all in

Acapulco. Orson had decided to rent the *Zaca* from Errol for fifteen hundred dollars a day—it would be our *Circe*. But we couldn't have this rapier-nosed yacht with its magnificent white wooden hull without Errol, who would remain as captain and guard the sanctity of his tub—his schooner, as he called it. He'd become a cocaine addict in Acapulco, was also a hopeless alcoholic married to actress Nora Eddington, who was eight and a half months pregnant at the time. But I think he loved the *Zaca* more than his wife.

We were seated near the bar—Errol, Nora, the general, Big Red, Orson, and myself. Nora was leaving for Los Angeles tomorrow to have her baby where Rita had had hers, at Saint John's of Santa Monica. The captain of the *Zaca* wasn't accompanying her. He wouldn't license Orson to shoot *The Lady from Shanghai* without him on board. He was demonic in all matters concerning his boat. He would have howled at every scratch the cameramen made.

Nora was twenty-two at the time, and had her own sultry look. I liked her instantly. She reminded me of a sphinx with long legs and a ribbon in her red hair.

We drank a toast, Irish whiskey all around—I gave Rita permission to gulp the whiskey with a nod of my head.

The general saluted Rita. "To your great success, La Señora, and may the *Zaca* bring you all the luck in the world."

I had red snapper and roasted potatoes. The general had squid.

6

THE *ZACA* LOOKED like a magnificent swordfish that could
vault through the water without fins. She was a perfect
replica of the yacht Orson needed. Our problem wasn't the yacht.
Our problem was Errol Flynn. Nora had departed for California
and he had no one to needle, no one to jab. He was drunk all
the time. He flung hammers and marlinspikes at members of his
own crew. He interfered with our cameramen. It was impossible
to shoot around him, yet our contract insisted that we had to shoot
with him around. So Orson had to joust with Errol while he was
directing a scene.

"Flynnie, we'll cut you up and feed you to the sharks. Who
would notice? Who would care?"

"Play, is that what you want? Well, come on, old chap," Errol
said with a spike in either hand. "I'm captain of this ship. I want a
woman in my bed, and Nora isn't here. Well, Orson, supply one if
you expect to shoot on board the *Zaca*. Rita, will you volunteer?"

Orson swung at Errol and nearly fell overboard. Errol laughed
gallantly, like Captain Blood. But he still had yellowish green eyes.

Rita walked up to him, brushed against the spikes. "Behave," she said, "or I *will* feed you to the sharks."

Errol dug the spikes under his belt and clapped his hands. "Congratulations, Orson. You've raised a tigress. I'll bet she'll be sensational in this part, your lady from Shanghai."

"Why didn't you take Nora to the hospital?" Rita asked. "She's your wife, isn't she?"

"No need," Errol said. "Bless Nora. She's already got another chap. My marriages never last. What about you, dearest one? I'm told there's trouble in your own little paradise."

Rita slapped his face, and that's when Errol grew surly. Shorty tackled him before he had a chance to strike her back. He sat there, then clambered to his feet, squinted into the blinding sun, and went sulking below to his cabin.

7

H E WAS BOSUN and first mate of the *Zaca*. His name was
Nando. He must have been nineteen. Errol had found him
on the beach when he had his first yacht, the *Sirocco*; the boy was
an orphan who seemed to have no lineage at all. He learned much
faster than any of Errol's other louts. He was climbing the ratlines
at eleven, with a rigging knife between his teeth, tarring ropes
that had begun to rot, often ripping his hands as he moved among
the ratlines. He was the boat's helmsman at thirteen, and marked
the bells of every second or third watch. The other crew members
despised him because Nando did all the work and exposed them as
lazy louts. But they were also frightened of him, of his litheness, of
his agility on the ratlines, of the rigging knife in his mouth.

I was struck by his sheer beauty, by his grace on the *Zaca*. Nando
never wore shoes. He could peel an apple with that rigging knife
between his toes. He had no hips. He was built like a tomboy, with
ropes of muscle rippling under his dark skin. Rita looked at Nando
in a secretive manner. I'm sure she desired him, locked as she was in
a marriage where her husband's prick had wandered away. Orson

was devoted to her on the set. His eyes never strayed. And she was devoted to the sinister power of his direction. But that wasn't a marriage; it was no more than a movie pact.

Yet it was painful. Nando had been with Errol for almost ten years, had watched stars come and go. And Rita was just another actress to him. He didn't look at her once. I was flattered by the way his dark eyes wandered in my direction with undeclared desire. I spoke first.

"Nando, I'm not that fond of men."

He laughed, and it was a hearty sound, like a sudden burst of wind, without a trace of deviousness. "Miss Rusty, neither am I."

I hadn't fondled a boy since I was fourteen. I'm not sure I would have known what to do.

"And you're like a case of poison ivy. My employer, Big Red, is kind of stuck on you. Can't you tell?"

"She'll recover."

"But she could also kick my ass," I said.

He laughed again, with that same windswept sound.

"Do I have your permission to court you, Miss Rusty?"

"It doesn't seem like you need anyone's permission."

Still, we couldn't make love under a tattered sail. We were in the middle of a shoot. He lived on the *Zaca*, and I lived on land, in the hills of Acapulco; I left the *Zaca* with the rest of the company after each day's wrap. Rita never even mentioned Nando, but that rapport we'd had soon deteriorated. She snapped at me.

"Your head's in a cloud. We never read. I will forget all of Dostoyevsky's gambling debts."

"But whenever I try another book, you say you have to rehearse and don't have the time."

"Rusty, I'll make the time."

And then she ran to the terrace with a fevered glint in her eye. She had the director she always wanted, but he was like a bloated whale in his director's chair. She broke her promise. She began to drink when the weather was bad and we couldn't shoot on the *Zaca*. She would stumble down to the Casablanca's bar in her sandals and a flimsy robe and flirt with sea captains from cargo ships. I caught her with one particular captain. He had a swaggering eye and was clutching Rita's rump while they danced in the lounge. It was none of my business.

"You're adorable," the captain said.

"So are you," she slurred.

"I'll capture you, dearie. You can be my cargo. I'll take you to Tahiti."

"No," she said, "I'll capture you."

She was Rita on the loose, Rita running wild in her feathered bob. And she would sabotage our stay in Acapulco. I swung the captain around, and sent him packing with a swift kick.

She stood there, fuming. "Rusty, you have no right to interfere. I can tell Orson to banish you from the *Zaca*. Then you won't have that pathetic sailor of yours, who looks like a girl. Does he wear lipstick when he's riding high in the sails?"

I seized her by the collar and dragged her back upstairs to the royal suite as if she were a puppet from Orson's childhood of tricks. How on earth could I wash away her unhappiness? She wanted a husband who would make love to every one of her limbs, and all she had at the moment was a Buddha in bed, brilliant, yes, adoring in the reflection of the camera's eye, but indifferent to her as a woman.

"Look at me—the Janitor's right. I'm bald."

"You are not," I said. "You're just not Gilda, and you'll never be Gilda again. You're Elsa Bannister, and you have a demonic touch. Murder is your vehicle, not a glove. Do you want to have a Harry Cohn production tattooed on your ass for the rest of your life?"

"Then what should I do?" she muttered, with bourbon on her breath.

"Be Elsa Bannister. Play the murderess. Scheme—plot. You'll never have another chance. Orson won't last at Columbia. He doesn't believe in the little gods of continuity. He sculpts. His camera lives in the shadows. He'll bathe you in light and dark, caress you and seduce, with his own version of Gilda's glove. Viola will have a shit fit. So what? You'll still be that murderess from the coast of China."

She stared at me for a very long time. It wasn't a drunken stare. She didn't totter, didn't sway. "Rusty, that murderess might murder you. You've gone over to Orson's side."

"Yes," I said, with a taste of bitterness. "On a Rita Hayworth flick. I didn't abandon you. I never would."

I was startled by my own bravura—and deviousness. I was part of Orson's crew. I had palpitations in his presence. He worked by sheer instinct, instinct alone. He had an eagle's eye as he looked into the lens. No detail was too small for him not to notice. He sculpted, painted with each glimmer of light. He caught the *mood* of Rita's cheekbones, surrounded her with disturbing depths. He didn't rely on close-ups, like other directors at Columbia and MGM. He clawed at his characters, trapped them in an ever-deepening field. There were no clusters. Each character was isolated, as in *Kane*, each had his or her own austere kingdom, her own paucity of space. And Orson excited me as no other director could.

8

ORSON AND RITA both had sinus attacks, and Orson's were crippling. Often he had to direct on his knees, with a hand over one eye, and position the camera between groans. It was Nando, my Nando, who had the only cure. He would massage Orson's forehead with his lovely hands. I'd watch the ripples in his back as he worked on Orson, and I would mimic the path of his hands in my own mind. But Errol grew possessive of Nando, his first mate, would give him chores to do, send him up to the crow's nest to see if any "hostiles" were around.

Yes, there was an occasional pirate or two. But they weren't locals. No, these were Hollywood refugees, crippled stuntmen who had come to Acapulco for one purpose and one purpose alone: to prey upon the rich yacht owners of Mexico's Riviera. Many of these stuntmen had worked with Errol, and would never have marauded the *Zaca*. Yet Nando, at Errol's command, had to race across the ratlines and scour the sea with his spyglass for these stuntmen in their speed launches, while Errol sat in his deck chair with a bottle of bourbon and pillbox of cocaine and pestered Orson any way he could.

That wasn't the worst of it. Errol would disappear for days, and we weren't permitted to film unless he was on board. That gave me a chance, during one of these disappearances, to visit the *other* Acapulco, the rat-infested streets near the Zócalo, the main square, Acapulco's "downtown," far from the Riviera and its white sand. These streets were filled with ice-cream parlors and movie theaters, most of them as small as the Regina, or smaller, and I would wind through an afternoon in one of these palaces, with a soft cone in my fist and a swashbuckler on the screen, staring at some fourth-rate Errol Flynn. . . .

The real Errol returned the next day with a long-stemmed beauty from Idaho who advertised herself as twenty-one, but couldn't have been much older than eighteen. She had a driver's license, so Orson, our own particular sheriff, couldn't badger the ship's captain. Errol called her Kitten, and Kitten she was. I could tell that she was a runaway. Errol must have found her on the beach.

It angered me, this latest liaison. She was a teenager, despite the sultriness of her moves.

Errol caught me looking at Kitten. "Stay out of my affairs."

But I couldn't. I got to know her while Errol was in his cabin, dead asleep after a wallop of coke. Kitten wasn't secretive at all. She had never gotten past the sixth grade. She'd been living in Hollywood, until some high roller brought her to Acapulco. Rita was even more incensed than I was. She saw glimmers of her own past in the girl's vulnerability beneath her brazen mask.

Errol ate with us at the Casablanca with Kitten cradled in his lap. By then the coke had destroyed whatever green he had left in his eyes. Captain Blood would have looked like a ghoul in Technicolor. His face was lined. He fell asleep at the table.

"Run," I said to Kitten. "We'll get you a plane ticket."

She smiled, and that's when I realized that we'd misread her maneuvers. "My three saviors," she said. "What would you like to do, darlings? Summon a marshal from San Diego and have him deliver me to some runaway center for overripe girls, where I could be raped every night? I admire Uncle Errol. He's been my hero ever since he played Robin Hood. He doesn't love me, and I don't love him. He has a wife. He doesn't need another one."

"And what will happen after Nora returns?" I asked.

"I'll find another uncle," she said, "and another. Uncles aren't hard to find."

Kitten had defeated us. Our moral compass made no sense to her. She was Errol's bedmate on board the *Zaca*. Their simple pact was much more reliable than anything we had to offer. She shook Uncle Errol awake and led him upstairs to his suite.

"Good night, old chaps," he said. "Good night, good night."

9

WE REACHED A kind of equilibrium after that, a rough-edged peace, like an endless seesaw. We'd arrive in the early light on a speed launch with Orson's camera wrapped in several blankets, like a huge mechanical baby. *Our* Bannister, Everett Sloane, kept whining about the braces he had to wear. No one listened. It was Rita's morning. She had to swim toward a large rock in a one-piece black bathing suit that fit her with the same provocative glory as Gilda's glove, in the movie that had defined her.

Nando had spent an entire afternoon scraping off a pestilence of rare poisonous barnacles from that rock with his rigging knife. And now he swam beneath her with a spear, to protect her from sharks. Orson worked all afternoon, pacing back and forth on the deck, to frame his *Circe* in the water and on that rock. He was relentless. "Again," he said. "No, it's not a wrap."

It never was. He'd have shot until dawn if we hadn't dragged him off the *Zaca*. I was always miserable every time we had to leave Nando with that madman Flynn. I would have loved to smuggle him onto our launch. But he wouldn't have left the madman alone, wouldn't have abandoned the movie star who plucked him off the beach when the boy with luminous dark skin was living on rotten pieces of passion fruit. Yes, Errol was hard on him, but Nando had risen from cabin boy to first mate. It was Nando who ran the *Zaca*, not that snorter of cocaine in his king's chair.

I dreamt of strangling Errol in his sleep. He sat with his bottle of bourbon and did his best to undermine Orson. He was earning thousands in rental money from Columbia, yet he still wanted to shipwreck *The Lady from Shanghai*. It was Orson's movie, not his—Orson was the master here, the chief conjurer, and that irked Errol. There was a meanness in him that belied his heroic aura as a movie star. He was on constant battle alert with Orson's crew. He kicked over the camera once, and sent the dolly spinning out of control. Nando had to lunge at the dolly and rescue it from hopping overboard.

Errol was furious with him. "You little prick, I'll dock your pay if you ever do that again."

But Nando was never servile, even if he owed his existence to Errol. "Cap, it's time for a snooze."

He'd tap Errol lightly on the chin—Nando had enormous knuckles from all his dancing on the ratlines—and carry him below to his quarters with Kitten at his side. And that's how we'd continue *and* complete the day's shoot.

Errol was a fickle son of a bitch. His mood could change overnight. At times he let us film and film without an instant of sabotage. And he invited me to remain on board the *Zaca* after one difficult day's shoot. Rita could hardly refuse his request.

I couldn't call it a honeymoon with Nando. I'd never been married. Besides, it was much better than that. Our bodies touched all the time; it's as if one glided right off the other, as if we were on the ratlines, looking at the sea, like a maddening mirage that shifted from moment to moment, or we lay entwined in Nando's tiny cabin, or I was at the wheel, without a stitch of clothes, and marked the beginning or the end of a watch.

The other crew members were jealous of this sudden burst of romance. They'd never seen Nando with a woman. They would have been trounced had they ever dared attack. Besides, it would have been a sort of mutiny. Nando was their first mate. He taught me as many nautical terms as he could. But it wasn't an education that I was after. I wanted to ride the sails of that wind-jammer with him, and have my own medallion of ripped hands, just like Nando.

And I did, I did.

Our lovemaking was nobody's business. It didn't last. How could it? We had our last day of shooting on the *Zaca*. I couldn't even give Nando a proper goodbye kiss in front of the entire cast. I fondled his curly black hair and his narrow torso that reminded me of a hermaphrodite with a sailor's tattoos. His lips swelled like a jungle flower. We did rub each other's ripped hands.

10

ORSON HAD ANOTHER five days of shooting around Acapulco, in the jungles north of the Riviera. He had dreamt up a picnic scene on the banks of a shallow river filled with crocs. Birds screamed at us, mosquitoes bit us to pieces and swarmed around the arc lamps, leaving us in the land of midnight. The general, who accompanied us into the jungle, attacked the mosquitoes with a spray gun that was as big as any cannon, and suddenly we had some light.

Elsa, Arthur Bannister, and Grisby sit on the riverbank like drunken conquerors with murder on their mind, and ask Black Irish O'Hara to join them. But Michael demurs. He compares the threesome to a band of sharks at the far end of the world that falls into an eating frenzy and devours other sharks, then one another, and finally themselves, until the ocean is pink with blood. Michael's tale sounded a bit morbid and melodramatic to me no matter how well he told it. Besides, I was thinking of Nando in the midst of the shoot, of his lean, sculpted body, his long silences, his acrobatic leaps among the ratlines, his lizard-like tongue along the

ribs of my spine, the screams I had to stifle or I would have woken
the entire crew.

We returned to Acapulco swollen with mosquito bites. Orson
had a sudden urge to screen his own raw footage, and so I taxied
downtown and bargained with the owner of that tiny movie palace
near the Zócalo; I paid two crisp hundred-dollar bills to shut him
up, and we had his palace with its fifty seats for an entire day and
night. Shorty served as the projectionist, and we wandered into the
theater one by one.

The theater wasn't refrigerated, of course, and we baked in that
little box as we sat in the dark. But what I saw on that rumpled
screen felt like a snake tunneling through my insides, as if I were
about to give birth to some kind of hydra. Orson was shrewd to
rent the *Zaca*, no matter how tyrannical its captain had become.
The tension Errol had caused was compressed into every shot.
Orson captured the agony of Bannister's leg braces in the malice
and hidden terror around his eyes. The looniness of Glenn Anders
was evident in his half smile.

Rita was sad and subdued in her role as a siren; her psyche was
somewhere else, in some other film. She didn't glide like Gilda;
she was both tense and languid, as if her movements were misplaced. She was a murderess with little to gain. She loved Michael,
and loved him not. Orson had zeroed in on her current state. She
was a woman who had lost every rudder, every gauge. She had
a husband who wasn't cruel, but had still become a stranger the
moment he stopped directing her. She was caught in a maze, like
a child in the maelstrom of a silent scream. And then there was
Black Irish O'Hara, the knight-errant who had fallen into the
siren's lap, despite his fable about the mischievous sharks at the end
of the world.

The farther Orson moved from Hollywood, the less of Hollywood there was on the screen. His wide-angle lens had turned the

Zaca into a deep pocket that was like a floating mortuary chapel filled with ghosts rather than a yacht with a fo'c'sle and a captain's quarters. These were like the ghosts that I could recall from *Kane*, characters filled with fury. Welles was like no other director I had ever written about. John Ford had his heroes, gunslingers from the painted hills of Wyoming, or wherever he shot. And Welles, he had his gargoyles.

11

WE SPENT A miserable Christmas in San Francisco, shooting inside a Mandarin theater in Chinatown, one of Elsa/
Rita's hideouts after she left the China coast. Michael is on trial,
having been accused of murdering Grisby. Somehow, he escapes
from the judge's chambers, moving as swift as Mercury on his flat
feet. He hides in the Mandarin theater with Elsa until the cops
arrive. And he ends up in an abandoned amusement park. But the
interior of this fun house was on the Columbia lot, so we had to
return to Hollywood.

I was at the studio most of the time, working on the final scenes
of the film—in the fun house with its enormous slide and its dragon's head, and the maze of mirrors at the bottom of the slide, where
Bannister and his wife are transformed into fragments of glass. No
one but Orson could have invented that maze, the shattering of a
person's persona right on the screen.

John Ford had wonderful shoot-outs, sure, but never in a hall
of mirrors, where each figure was replicated over and over again.
And as Bannister shoots at Elsa, he's also shooting at himself. It

was more daring than anything Welles had done in *Kane*, a kind of manifesto that the screen itself was fragmented, that we were all creatures of glass. Only the Boy Wonder could ever have delivered that, and at Columbia, a studio that insisted on nothing less than complete continuity.

We had Rita on our side, and she was still the hottest property in movieland, so I didn't fret at first. But I knew there would be a reckoning. Despondent, I went to Schwab's, something I had never done on my own before. I sat at the counter with starlets and unemployed screenwriters, who were part of movieland's under-privileged class. I looked in the mirror, and I must have been in a daze. All I saw were grotesque masks of Harry Cohn, brittle noses and leering mouths—I must have entered the Janitor's private fun house. But I wasn't a magician, like Orson Welles. Nothing I could ever do would make Harry shatter into shards of glass.

• FIVE •

Rough Cut, 1947

1

THE BOY WONDER worked within his own storm, preparing a rough cut of *The Lady from Shanghai* for Harry Cohn. I sat with him in one of the cutting rooms at Columbia, watched him and his crew cut and splice, cut and splice. "Rusty, a film is nothing more than a ribbon with a dream inscribed on it," Orson loved to recite. He worked on that ribbon day and night. He exhausted an entire team of us. "No, we'll save that," he said, as the ribbon went into the Moviola machine. His eye was sharper than ours. Where we saw fragments, he saw a melody in every stitch.

Then, perversely, he'd shout, "Cut, cut, cut."

Orson had to juggle, since Harry Cohn had Columbia's star cutter on his side. Viola had already worked with Big Red, had revealed every vantage of her face and hair in *Cover Girl*. Yet Orson didn't trust her. She was Harry Cohn's hand-picked executioner who recut many a director's film. So Orson couldn't risk sending Viola his rough cut. He dumped his rushes on her instead, the raw footage he had shot day after day.

The next afternoon, Cohn summoned Orson and Rita to his

office, and Rita asked me to come along. Cohn's secretaries were all aflutter as we entered the inner sanctum. Viola stood in front of the Janitor's desk. She had a formidable air about her. Viola wore dark glasses, since her eyes were sensitive to sunlight. She had a silk scarf knotted tightly around her neck. Vi was taller than Cohn in her pumps. She had scars on her hands from all the splicing she had done. She sniffed with one nostril as if something foul had entered Cohn's quarters.

"Who is this female?" she asked with a twist of her mouth.

Viola had met me in Rita's company more than once. She'd been to my discussions at the Regina and had read my broadsides. And still she had to show her authority in front of the boss.

"Rusty works for me," Rita said.

"And she's been a valuable assistant on the film," Orson said with a scowl.

Viola curtsied in her dark glasses. "I know who Rusty is. I treasure her articles. I'm fond of Regina X. But *why* is she here?"

"Because," Rita said, penetrating Viola's dark glasses with a fierce look, "I asked her to come."

Viola was sullen for a second as she glanced at Cohn. But he didn't support his star cutter. She smiled and curtsied again. "Then you have my apologies, Regina X, and my permission to stay."

"She doesn't need your permission," Rita said to the cutter who could have ruined her career.

"Stop with this gab," Cohn said from behind his desk. Viola had long been a legend in movie circles. She'd started in the silent era as a messenger at Vitagraph in Brooklyn at the age of eleven, dressed as a boy. But she migrated toward the cutters' table, memorized every splice each cutter made. She asked questions, poked around, confident enough now to get rid of her disguise. Soon she sat at their table and joined their ranks as an assistant cutter before she was fifteen. She moved to Hollywood in 1917, and became

Cohn's chief cutter at Columbia by the time she was thirty. No one but Harry could get in Viola's way, and often Harry himself didn't succeed. Vi was sacrosanct at her table. . . .

She removed her dark glasses for a moment. She had pendulous bags under her eyes and the pallid, sunless face of someone who had worked in cutting rooms all her life. She put on her glasses again and suddenly seemed invincible. She clapped her scarred hands.

"Bravo, Welles. The mirror scene is magnificent, at least as much as I can make of it. And the shots on the *Zaca* are a poem. The moments in the jungle are delicious. How did you manage to set up your camera among the crocodiles? The aquarium took my breath away, with the barracudas in the background. But . . ."

She stopped right there—it was like a hammer blow, and was meant to be.

Orson masked his own chagrin. "By your leave, Vi, pray tell us how I have sinned."

That's what I liked about him. He flourished in the face of danger, flew right in.

"How have I sinned?" he asked again in the Shadow's voice.

"Close-ups, my dear," Viola said. "I couldn't find a single close-up of Rita, and I looked *everywhere* with my magnifying glass. She may be your femme fatale, but she is the star of the film."

"Close-ups would rip apart continuity. Vi, you of all people ought to know that."

"You needn't lecture me," she whispered into the profundo of his voice, belittling all his bravura. "It's *beauty* we're talking about, Welles. And we cannot find it if Rita is hidden somewhere in your wide-angle murals."

"Murals?" Orson asked with a deeper scowl.

"Yes, you like to paint on the screen. You are a painter first and foremost."

Orson closed one eye, which had swelled up during the shoot

in Acapulco when he was bitten by a bug. "Vi, are you suggesting that my shots are static?"

She turned toward Cohn in her dark glasses, as if we all were gusts of wind that had wandered into the room. But she was still addressing Orson. "I never said that. Your murals are most alive. But we can't have Rita as part of a fresco, one more face on the wall. We need more close-ups if we are going to introduce her as a blonde. The public has to be alerted."

Orson stared into the void of those dark glasses. "But surely she's identifiable."

"Yes," said Viola. "And lovely in a hard-bitten way. But this is a Rita Hayworth film, and you'd never know it."

"I thought the film was directed by Orson Welles," Orson had to insist, his voice beginning to crack.

Viola had cut him to pieces, as she would have done on the cutting room floor.

"Oh, Orson," Viola said, "you are such a child. Harry borrowed your genius, but the film belongs to Rita, and you shouldn't forget that."

"And neither should you," Rita said, joining the battle. She wasn't concerned about Viola's concern over the rushes, nor was she concerned about her career. She'd rather be with her baby on Rockingham Road. "If you want your close-ups, Vi, you'll have to ask my husband's permission."

"That's absurd," Viola said. "You, my dear, are Mr. Cohn's employee, even if you receive a portion of the profits. He can have you fired."

"Then," said Rita with all the misanthropic flair of a femme fatale, "let him fire me."

Cohn looked as if a stick were suddenly up his ass; he had invested over two million in *The Lady from Shanghai*, and he couldn't afford to watch all that cash wash away. "Wait a minute. Vi, remember, you work for me. Ask the genius's permission about the close-ups."

"I won't," she said. "I'd rather die."

The Janitor had one of his famous fits. He must have practiced variations of this fit every morning in front of his mirror. His eyeballs bulged. His arms flailed. "Die, die, die, Viola, but on somebody else's time. We have a picture to finish."

"I could move all my stuff to David's lot."

She meant David O. Selznick, the driving force behind *Gone With the Wind*. I was beginning to enjoy myself, even though I could feel Orson's pain, and Rita's, too. I would have loved to see Harry and Viola claw at each other on the Columbia lot.

"Go—go with David; you'll work on one picture every six years. He doesn't even have his own cutting room, for chrissake. You'll ask the genius's permission, and the genius will give it, right, Rita?"

"She'll have to ask," Rita said.

Viola sighed, coughed into her fist, and said in a slow, deliberate voice, "Orson, dear Orson, I believe *Shanghai* would benefit from a few close-ups of our luscious star. Would you be willing to work them into your rough cut?"

Orson's warrior-eye went like a periscope from Harry to Viola to Rita and back before he said, "Yes, Viola, dear—I would be willing, just for you."

2

WE DIDN'T HAVE room for a replica of the *Zaca* on our
own lot; so Orson commandeered the Columbia ranch
in Brentwood, where studio craftsmen rebuilt an abandoned
yacht, painted *Circe* along its bow, and floated the yacht in a gigan-
tic tub hoisted onto a series of rockers; that tub was meant to be
the Pacific Ocean. There was a crisis afoot, and Orson had to
override his delusion of grandeur in Harry Cohn's Hollywood;
he was clever enough to realize that ignoring Viola would have
gotten him banned from Gower Street again without a single reel
of *Shanghai*.

Reluctant, he still wrote additional dialogue for Rita, who was
magnificent in what she revealed and what she did not. I stood
opposite her, off-camera, and fed Rita her lines. I could feel her
psyche unravel with every word. Elsa Bannister was that starved
child within her, a shriek that traveled inward and rewarded her
with a sad, silent mask. Rita may not have been a murderess, but
otherwise she was Elsa, with a shriek right under the surface. And
with that shriek came bottle after bottle of whiskey and gin. She

guzzled night and day when she wasn't on the set, prowling from room to room, like some wildcat with her face on fire. Whiskey didn't give her what she really wanted, the rub of Orson against her body. And I lacked Orson's timbre, Orson's roguish smile. I couldn't amuse or mollify Red. She was hollowed out, like a broken toy. And all her loveliness didn't matter. She didn't have the resources to soothe herself. . . .

It wasn't until we shot at the Columbia ranch that Orson realized the swamp he was in. He would lose *The Lady from Shanghai* if he couldn't get past Viola and her own fury to cut whatever she could. He stitched the close-ups of Rita into the rough cut. But he wouldn't screen his version in any of the Columbia screening rooms. There were too many of Viola's spies around. He decided to screen his cut at the Regina after midnight. We'd had three different cinematographers because of the long shoot on location; none of them were present. It was just Orson, Rita, Everett Sloane, Glenn Anders, and half a dozen loyal members of the crew, with Shorty serving as projectionist.

Orson's rough cut was a daunting 155 minutes. It wasn't Rita's film. Beautiful as she was in her blond cut, she remained hidden somewhere in the tapestry. It was Black Irish O'Hara's tale; he was the narrator—all the action flowed through him. He was in almost every scene, every shot. The film was *Alice in Wonderland* with a very different kind of Alice. The Alice we all knew was obstinate and blessed with a flurry of movements and words. She danced and skipped along, a match for everyone she met in the rabbit hole, whether she shrank or grew into a giant, or encountered the Mad Hatter and the Queen of Hearts. And she was only seven. But Michael was *our* Alice here, and glued as I was to every minute of Orson's rough cut, I found it hard to believe in Michael O'Hara's naïveté. He's sucked into a whirlpool like a sleepwalker. Yet we continue to follow him. Glenn Anders, as Bannister's partner Grisby, would have made a marvelous Mad Hatter. The camera dotes on his lump of a face, shot at steep angles, so he constantly seems on the verge of falling out of the screen. His plan to have Michael confess to a murder that isn't supposed to take place is insidious. Grisby dies, and Michael, with the signed confession, is charged with murder.

Here the plot wanders off into unknown territory. Have Elsa, her crippled husband, and his insane partner all conspired to murder one another to collect some mysterious insurance, and use Black Irish as the fall guy? Not even the Mad Hatter could have made sense of such a scheme. But we're still enthralled by the hypnotic spell of the camera. It seems to close in around us, capture us, and deposit us in a world of precipitous angles. *The Lady from Shanghai* was an exercise in angst; terror lay under the masts in the Acapulco harbor; it hovered over the aquarium scene in San Francisco, where Michael and Elsa meet, with the sea animals caged behind them, magnified and capturing most of the light; it was in the abandoned amusement park, where Michael goes to hide from the police; he's catapulted through the mouth of a cardboard dragon that could have swallowed a whale; and he's caught in the magic mirror maze, where Rita and Everett Sloane shoot at each other's multiple reflections, until our own sanity is at stake.

"Well," Orson said, after the screening. "What's the verdict?"

Rita was silent, and so were the others, but I had to raise my hand, like a sophomore at Kalamazoo. Weren't we all sophomores around Welles, with the jarring melodies he introduced in every shot?

"Ah," Orson muttered, "our own Regina X."

"*Maître*," I said, "now is not the time to get cute. Viola will do her best to slaughter us, and you know that."

His lower lip curled with anger—he had to lash out. "Rita, darling, what do you think?"

She sat there frozen. She would never contradict Orson, even if their marriage had fallen apart. "It's your film, Papa." That's what she called him now that all their intimacy had flown away.

He stared me down, as if we had become combatants in that little theater. "Rusty, what do you suggest I do to please Viola?"

"Cut," I said.

"Where?"

"I'm not a cutter, boss. But I clocked the amusement park scene. It's too long."

I understood Orson's intent. It was where the lady from Shanghai means to get rid of Michael O'Hara. Like Circe, she had to "kill" her sailor.

"Jesus," he said, clasping his hands. "You helped me paint all the props. Michael goes from mask to mask, to mutilated torsos, as he rides down the chute. We need that sense of shock. It prepares us for the magic mirrors. I gave Viola her close-ups of Rita. That's all I'm prepared to give."

You didn't have to be a genius like Orson to understand the damage he had done—to Rita, himself, and the film—through his willfulness. He sent the rough cut to Columbia. He waited and waited, and didn't hear a word from Harry or Viola. The tension at Rockingham Road continued to mount. Orson worked on other projects, chased one wild scheme after another, smoked his Cuban cigars, ignored Rita most of the time, and slept on the living room couch. He behaved like a big, oafish child. He was a child. He moved with Shorty to a beach house in Santa Monica at the beginning of May, and barely kissed Rita goodbye.

I got to Shorty while he was packing up all the scatter of Orson's different projects.

"Doesn't Orson realize how much weaker we are when we're all apart?"

Shorty shrugged. "Rusty, the boss is spent. He can't function here. He cares for Rita, but you know what love is like between married couples—an elegant rag with rents in it."

An elegant rag with rents in it.

I hugged Shorty and away he went.

It didn't matter how many times we called; still no news from Columbia, not a morsel.

Then Orson showed up at my hotel in a rumpled white suit. We sat in the lobby with all the wraiths who had once been stars of the silent screen; their streaks of white powder made them look like animated cadavers in a cartoon. Orson ordered oysters and a bottle of white wine from the dining room and charged it to my bill, of course.

He ate his oysters with a sucking sound.

"Don't hate me," Orson said after a sip of wine.

"I don't hate you," I said.

"You'll tell me that no other filmmaker has my talent."

"It takes more than talent to do what you've done. But you should have been attentive to your own daughter."

He sucked on a fat Pacific oyster, and he gave me a horrid look. "I've always been a monster with children."

"That's a pathetic excuse."

"It's Rita. You hate me because you think I abandoned her."

"You did."

He was playing Falstaff now, with a bit of swagger. "She's the one who threw me out of her bed."

"Rita was much too kind. I would have hired an executioner to cut off your cock."

"Darling," he croaked, "it's already been done. Viola had me canned."

"But she wouldn't dare. Rita would. . . ."

"Has the vampire lady been in touch with Rita? Divide and conquer. That's her method—and her motto."

And then he started to cry. This giant of a man with his enormous flat feet sat there blubbering like a baby. I didn't know how to soothe him. I tried. I hovered over Orson and grasped his Buddha's body in my arms.

"Rusty, I am no longer in possession of *The Lady from Shanghai*. I should have listened to you at the Regina and cut before Viola had her chance."

"It wouldn't have mattered, Orson. You would have clashed however little or much you cut of the film. She's a cutter. That's what she lives for. But whoever she hires, she can't have any additional footage shot without Rita's consent."

"Rita's consent," he muttered to himself, "Rita's consent." He wiggled free of my embrace and wandered out of the Hollywood Hotel, while the wraiths from the silent screen stared at Orson, revealing their ravaged, sunken faces. . . .

3

RITA FILED FOR divorce. But I no longer recognized her as Rita. I saw her as a forlorn Circe in a feather bob. She couldn't change that style or let her hair grow out until she heard from Cohn. And still we waited, even after Orson's demise as producer-director of *The Lady from Shanghai*. Then the call came. We weren't summoned to Harry Cohn's suite. It was Viola who called.

"Rita, dear, it would be a delight if you could come to my office. And do bring Rusty."

Viola didn't mention Orson's final cut, didn't mention him at all. I drove Red to Gower Street and parked in the Columbia garage across from the Janitor's office. Viola had an entire floor in the Administration Building, filled with cutting rooms and conference tables; she herself had a tiny office compared to Cohn's. But the studio couldn't function without her team of cutters; it would have come to a halt. There were curled snips of celluloid everywhere; these snips clung to our shoes, snaked across the carpets, collected like little mountains under the conference tables.

The doors of the cutting rooms were always left open. The

cutters sat hunched over their Moviolas. It reminded me a little of the Writers' Building at Columbia, where the writers sat in their cubbyholes with their Remingtons and clattered away; they had to produce a certain number of pages every week or they would have been fired. And so the clatter was constant. They existed in a state of unrelieved panic. That's what Cohn wanted, and that's what he got. He fired half of them in spite of the clatter. So there were always new writers on the lot, half of them arriving from the East after a success on Broadway or the glamour of a Book of the Month Club selection. A good number of these newcomers would also be fired after six months. But the cutters endured. Viola was loyal to every single one.

Her office was meant to be small. But it was Viola's and Viola's alone. It was decorated with posters from the films she was proudest of: *Only Angels Have Wings* (with Rita in a small part), *The Lone Wolf Takes a Chance, Here Comes Mr. Jordan, My Sister Eileen,* and *Cover Girl* (with Rita as the star). Viola neglected to include *Queen Kelly*, which she had recut at Gloria Swanson's command. Viola had helped ruin Erich von Stroheim's career. Von Stroheim had been as innovative as Orson, but in the silent era. Born in Vienna, the son of a Jewish hatmaker, he arrived in America in 1909 and passed himself off as a prince. The prince went to work as a traveling salesman and landed in Hollywood. He clashed with producers from the beginning of his career. The original print of his masterwork, *Greed*, was ten hours long. It was cut and cut again to a version that was less than three hours; the denouement in Death Valley was among the most spectacular scenes ever shot, with a renegade dentist who is about to die alone in the desert; the film was still unmarketable. Nevertheless, Gloria Swanson hired him to write and direct *Queen Kelly*, about a nun who becomes the mistress of a brothel. Swanson despised the footage she saw and removed Von Stroheim from the set. Another director was brought in; scenes were reshot. And Viola recut *Queen Kelly*. The film was never released in the United States.

Von Stroheim was considered an outlaw in Hollywood after *Queen Kelly*; no studio would hire him to direct another film. And I was concerned that Orson would suffer a similar fate. So I attacked before she said a word.

"Why did you have Orson pulled?" I asked.

"Oh, Harry can't bear the sight of him. Both of us were baffled by his cut. Harry said he would pay a thousand dollars to anyone who could tell him what the hell the film was about."

And the Janitor insisted that Rita sing a siren's song in the film on board the *Circe*. He decided to use a maudlin ballad, "Please Don't Kiss Me," and his strategy was to have this ballad played again and again as a leitmotif to lighten the mood. Of course, Rita was stuck with her current vocal ghost, Anita Ellis, and not a word she herself had sung on camera would make it into the film.

"Will Orson direct?" Rita asked, wandering out for a moment from under that deep sadness of hers.

"That's impossible," Viola said.

"Nothing's impossible," Rita said. "Harry will have to rehire him—for that one scene."

"Rusty," Viola said, "will you reason with her? Rita owns twenty-five percent of the profits. If she refuses, Harry will close down the shop, and she'll never see a cent. Trust me, dear. I've seen him do that before. Be careful, very careful."

Rita danced across that tiny room, creating a whirlwind of celluloid. "Tough. It's Orson, or nothing at all."

And we marched out of Viola's office, arm in arm.

4

W E RETURNED TO the Columbia ranch in Brentwood, Rita
and I. The yacht had already been disabled, and had to be
repaired by the studio craftsmen, with *Circe* repainted along its
bow. Orson arrived late on the set with Shorty at his side. He was
wearing the same filthy white suit he had worn at the Hollywood
Hotel. He had the odor of defeat about him, sweat and grime. He
talked to no one, not even members of his own crew. He shot Rita
as she sang "Please Don't Kiss Me" in a voice that was much sexier
than her ghost's. Then Orson said, "That's a wrap," and without a
word to Big Red or a wink to me, he was gone.

I had to find something to distract Rita, break her somber
mood. So we walked over to the model town where Columbia's
"B" westerns were shot: *Bullets for Bandits, Both Barrels Blazing*, etc.
It was a cardboard city, with dust and sand surrounding a papier-
mâché saloon, hotel, jailhouse, dry goods store, and coffin-maker's
shop, each with a missing wall. It could have been Abilene, Dodge
City, or some other tin-star wonderland that existed in a movie-
goer's mind. There were mirrors everywhere, to reflect the blaze

of the sun and duplicate the shoddy storefronts, make them seem larger, so that you had an illusion of an illusion, like Orson's mirror maze in *The Lady from Shanghai.*

The wooden sidewalks were real enough, cut from the poorest lumber, laden with rusty nails, and overrun with waves of sand coming from wind machines. We left our carved initials in the planks of wood, cowgirls of a different era.

5

VIOLA AND HER insidious army of butchers cut the film to eighty-seven minutes. Much of the angst was gone. Orson wasn't permitted to shock us. Most of the amusement park sequence had been cut, its reminder of mutilation and madness now in tatters. Black Irish still narrated the film, but in Viola's version it felt more like a decorative jar of paste than a point of view. Harry Cohn's film of the year had been reduced to a "B" production, with the studio's biggest star hiding behind her feather bob. Viola had plundered almost *everything* in the film except the magic mirror maze. Here Orson's editing was too subtle and complex, even for Viola's cutters. They couldn't touch the sequence, couldn't rip it asunder. The repeated images of Bannister's twisting canes embodied the disorientation that Orson had been seeking. There was nothing remotely like it. Yet that artful shatter of glass couldn't compel Cohn. We sat in his screening room on velvet cushions, Rita, Harry, Viola, and I. He was furious ten minutes into the film, and his fury grew and grew.

"Lights," he said, after the final sequence in all the shattered glass. "I don't want to sit in the dark."

The lights went on. "We'll burn it," he said.

"Harry," Viola said, "you can't mean that. It's a perfectly decent little thriller."

"*Decent*," Cohn said, "what's decent about it? We have a schmuck for a hero, and a heroine who's hidden in the shadows. She's Gilda, for God's sake. And I have to squint to find her. We'll burn it. That's the only solution."

"I like every minute of it, Harry" Rita said, draped on her velvet cushion. "And my lawyers will sue the shit out of you if you burn this film."

"Okay, big shot, we'll bury it."

"What does that mean?" Big Red asked with a furrowed brow.

"We'll delay distribution. We'll put you in another film as soon as your hair grows back and you stop looking like a butch warden at the women's farm. We'll make a real Rita Hayworth film, where you can dance and sing. Audiences are dying for their favorite redhead, not this piece of crap."

Viola perused the Janitor from behind her dark glasses. "Harry, you've gone too far. My girls cut Orson's extravagances, and now we have a whodunit that can stand alone."

Stand alone.

I wanted to dig under her glasses and blind the bitch. She tore the heart out of Orson's film and left us with a skeleton that dangled at every limb. Yet I still had to admire Viola and her cutters. She was a seamstress as much as a cutter, and the film, I had to admit, did have its own strange, dreamlike continuity. But Cohn continued to fulminate.

"Stand alone with an ending like that? The schmuck walks out into the sunset and leaves Elsa the Bald, the one character we care about, to die in all that dust."

"I'm not bald," Rita said. And we stormed out of the screening room, with its lights sculpted as seashells hooked into the cream-colored walls.

• SIX •

At the Regina, 1947–1949

1

ENTOMBED BY HER own cascade of empty rye and gin bottles, Rita couldn't stop guzzling. No one needed her on the set right now. Her bald pate had to disappear before Harry could cast her in his new adventure, *The Loves of Carmen*, which his accountants and production chiefs had already predicted would gross twice as much as *Gilda*. But she wasn't Gilda anymore, and it had nothing to do with the color of her cropped hair. That vital dancing step of hers had fallen asleep. Her liveliness would return for an instant whenever the telephone rang, and it was peculiar, because she'd always been anxious about telephones, since the number-one star in the world felt she had nothing to say.

"Is that Orsie?" she'd ask in her deep whisper.

"No," I said. "It's Vi. She's worried about you."

"Too bad. Tell her I'm in the middle of *War and Peace*, and I can't interrupt my reading schedule."

We hadn't read a book together in half a year. I made my excuses to Vi, while Rita grew worse between great gulps of gin.

And like clockwork, she'd ride down off Rockingham Road in

her maroon Alfa Romeo, a gift from that miser Harry Cohn, who had to cozen up to his biggest star until she was Red Rita again. She went to a bar on the Strip and returned with some lowlife, a replica of her first husband, Eddie Judson, a real snake-in-the-grass. She was drawn to such lowlifes; they seemed to mirror the way she perceived her own lack of worth. They mooched off her, grabbed whatever money they could, and the moment she tired of them, I was tasked with throwing them out.

But one of these snakes was shrewder than the rest. He was a Hollywood type, a born grifter. I'd seen him before. He might have once lived at my hotel. His name was Marvin Marsh. He had a gray mustache. He advertised himself as a haberdashery sales-man. He didn't have Orson's flat feet. He could dance the tango and the hoochy-coo with Big Red. I have to admit—this low-life had mastered all the steps. Red woke from her slumber with Marve around. They went dancing at the Cocoanut Grove—armed with her petty cash. Marve never seemed to have much pocket money. Rita had to give him an allowance. I was the one who wrote the checks.

He wanted to romance me, too, the son of a bitch, but he noticed the blizzard in my eyeballs.

"Be good to Rita, Marve, or I swear you won't live long enough to regret it."

I wasn't of much value while Rita was with Marve. Rebecca now had her own nurse. But I was still commander of Rita's check-book. I had to sign the bills for all her booze. At least she had a man in her bed, even if he was a grifter. I refused to give him extra pocket money. Marve had one refrain. And he was crafty as hell.

"Gimme gimme, or I'll get you fired."

I played deaf to that diabolic son of a bitch. I should have real-ized how gullible Rita was.

"Rusty," she said, "give my *fiancé* whatever he wants."

Soon her "fiancé" had a closetful of clothes—Sulka shirts, like Harry Cohn, and custom suits from Hershel's on Rodeo Drive. I wouldn't have minded all the pillage if Marve had really been nice to Red, but they had drunken brawls that I had to break up. Yet I was the one who got scolded.

"Don't you interfere," she intoned, with whiskey on her tongue. "You work for me, remember?"

"I remember."

Rita sobered up for a moment and had me write a check with my name on it—for five thousand dollars, almost as much as I earned in a year.

"Red, what the hell is this?"

"Severance pay," she said. "No, call it a bonus—for all the Shakespeare you shared with me, so Orson wouldn't think I was a dummy."

I crumpled the check, but she uncrumpled it and dug it into my fist. "You earned that, Rusty. Hey, remind me of that killer of kings who ruled over England's purse."

"Cromwell," I said, "Oliver Cromwell."

"That's him," she said. "You're my Oliver Cromwell."

It felt like a wicked slap. "Rita, how many kings have I killed?"

"None I can name. But you're interfering with my love life. You shouldn't have been stingy with Marve. You made him feel small."

I didn't even defend myself, didn't tell Rita that Marve had been robbing her blind. She wouldn't have listened. I packed whatever stuff I had—my lipstick, my book bag, my pencil sharpener, but I left her all my classics.

It didn't seem to matter how devoted I had been, not while she had that tango dancer in his Sulka shirts and suits from Rodeo Drive that were charged to her account. He didn't last, of course. I read about him in one of Louella's columns. Rita dropped Marve for another grifter. I wanted to call her, but somehow I couldn't. Pride, I suppose, got in the way.

I found out from Louella that Cohn was sending the love goddess on a four-month tour of Europe, where she could represent Columbia Pictures as a goodwill ambassador. Cohn was sacrificing his own personal assistant, Sally Fall, who would accompany Rita as some kind of companion-cum-secretary. Sally was a much better spy for Columbia than I could ever be. I kept staring at that crumpled check. Finally I deposited it at Wells Fargo. I deserved every penny, but it still felt like an act of betrayal. I went to Musso's and drank myself into oblivion.

2

WAKING OUT OF my stupor, I ran with the wind.
I bought out my other partners with Big Red's five
grand and gained full control of the Regina. I knew I would have
to work my ass off at impossible hours. I rarely rented from distributors. I'd buy a print long after it made the rounds from Manhattan's Radio City Music Hall to theaters in Anchorage—Alaska was
always the last stop. There was no such creature as a revival house.
We were the dregs of the trade, second- and third-run theaters.
But I had most of what I loved in my vault. And I got it at a bar-
gain rate. There was little value in second runs of a film, unless it
was a classic, like *Bambi* or *Gone With the Wind*, which the studios
would hold back for several years and then rerun at a movie palace
in Wichita or Des Moines. But the Regina could survive without
Bambi when we had *Citizen Kane*.

We did have a candy counter, but no one to collect the cash.
It would have been much too expensive to hire a counterman. So
we kept a basket on top of the counter filled with pennies, nickels,
and dimes. We had a very limited repertoire—Jujubes, Chiclets,

and Almond Joys, with a price tag affixed to every item. Customers reached into the basket and collected their own change. I doubt that anyone ever stole from that basket, because we had a particular clientele—*cinephiles*, as French critics began to call us, people who were passionate about films and kept away from the first-run houses, because they weren't that fond of the typical studio fare.

We did need a cashier, since customers could walk into the Regina right in the middle of *Scarface*, and someone had to collect the tickets and keep a tally, or the government would have run us out of business, my accountant declared. And I had to have a small battery of ushers on call, to seat customers with the help of a flashlight, since very few arrived at the beginning of a film. I couldn't afford to supply the ushers with uniforms.

And then there were the projectionists. They had their own strict cabal. I had to bring them coffee at a certain hour, a snack at another. The equipment at the Regina wasn't in perfect order, and there were breakdowns several times a week. I had to pay these prima donnas for the extra hours it took to rethread a reel, and because the nitrate prints were highly flammable, there was a very strict regimen about who could be hired. I had to treat them like magicians.

Money was leaking out of my pocket right and left, with payoffs to fire marshals and union bosses, and a big slice of overtime to the projectionists, and I could imagine myself in a couple of months as a beggar with a movie house on the boulevard. And then there was a rap on the door of my tiny office behind the cashier's booth.

I figured it was a bill collector or a fire marshal wanting his due, so I played dumb. But the rapping continued, and I heard a familiar growl.

"Rusty, open up."

I recognized the voice of Orson's valet. I hadn't seen Shorty in months. He still had that smooth, angelic face that could drive Hollywood women delirious. But he'd lost some of his sweet temperament.

"Shorty, what's the matter? Did the Boy Wonder fire you?"

"Not a chance," Shorty said, turning indignant at the mere mention that Orson might have let him go. "The boss wanted me to follow him to Europe, where he's making a flick. He's moved all his operations over there. Fed up with Hollywood, he says. But Europe isn't my style."

"Have you ever been overseas?"

"Nah" he said. "It's filled with countesses and dukes."

"That's nonsense," I told him. "I'd kill, I really would, to get to Paris. It's where they have film clubs almost on every boulevard."

It's the French who really loved the Boy Wonder, and recognized him as the genius behind *Citizen Kane*, not as a Hollywood gun for hire. That still left me with Shorty Chivallo, unhinged and unemployed. Yet it was Shorty who came up with a solution. He offered to be my usher. I wouldn't have to hire anyone else. He would take every shift.

"That's impossible," I said. "And I can't pay you much."

"Pay me?" Shorty said. "I'll get to see every film."

"And the Regina is too poor to provide you with a uniform."

"Means nothing," Shorty said.

He came to the Regina that same afternoon looking like the fabled Philip Morris call boy in a black pillbox hat, a red jacket with gold buttons and epaulettes, piped trousers, and white gloves. I didn't even have to supply him with a flashlight. And he did work every single shift, seven days a week. So did I.

He wouldn't accept a salary.

"Shorty, my accountant won't tolerate that. It's bad for the books."

"Well, I'll take a small chunk of the profits."

"There are no profits." And I told him about the fire marshals . . . and the projectionists who behaved like divas. He made a few calls from the telephone in the lobby, dropping dime after dime into the slot while he whispered into the receiver.

The fire marshals never visited me again and the projectionists stopped asking for overtime whenever there was a blackout on the screen that had to be fixed. I never asked Shorty whom he had called. He must have had "gonnegtions" somewhere, like Jay Gatsby.

We began showing a profit two weeks after Shorty arrived at the Regina. We still had discussions after the screening of a film and I still wrote my broadsheets. We waited and waited, and still not a word from Harry Cohn about the release of *The Lady from Shanghai*. I did get a cryptic note from Big Red while she was away, without so much as a greeting or a word of goodbye.

It's a nightmare.
People clutch at me wherever I go.
I can't leave my hotel.

The letter was postmarked from Paris. But it didn't carry a return address. I wrote to her in care of Columbia Pictures and, of course, I never got a reply. Evidently, the love goddess couldn't escape her fans no matter where she went. There was a storm of publicity the moment she got back to America. I called Rockingham Road several times. Sally Fall was Rita's permanent secretary now.

"I'm so sorry, but Miss Hayworth is much too busy."

Finally, I did hear from Big Red. It was another cryptic note, mailed to the Regina.

I miss Dostoyevsky.

Rita, I learned, was filming *The Loves of Carmen* in the mountains near Lone Pine, California, with her co-star from *Gilda*, Glenn

Ford, who was handsome in an invisible sort of way. Carmen had a full crop of red hair as far as I could tell from the movie posters. The distributors must have assured Cohn that the film would be a bonanza, because he released *The Lady from Shanghai* that June, fifteen months after we had the final cut. But he buried the film, as he had promised, buried it at the bottom half of a double bill, just like a "B" western made at the Columbia ranch.

It disappeared within a week.

Harry considered that a successful coup. Now no one would recall Rita as a murderous blonde in a feather bob. For once, I didn't wait for the film to arrive in Anchorage. I exercised the Regina's distribution rights and got a print of *Shanghai* the second it was available. I rented a hundred sandwich boards and hired as many unemployed stuntmen as I could to advertise the world premiere of Orson's film at the Hollywood Regina, within walking distance of Gower Street and the Columbia regime.

We had to turn away hundreds at our premiere because of the fire code. I kept looking for Big Red in the audience, wishing she might arrive in a veil to preserve her mystery. But Big Red wasn't there.

We had a famine at the Regina, as the entire candy counter emptied within minutes. I didn't even have a Jujube to suck on. I wouldn't deprive a paying customer of a seat, so I stood in the aisle, defying the fire code. I fell right into the deep shadows of the film. It was a fairy tale, a flawed one. I had a terrifying premonition. Viola hadn't been the real wrecker. She had tried to minimize Orson's fundamental urge as a filmmaker—to experiment, to shock, to play. The first shock was to clip Rita's hair, to erase her as a redhead. Was there a hint of spite in that desire to destroy Gilda and the image that had helped make her America's love goddess? Yet Rita was the one and only ace he had in his battle with Cohn. Rita's fans might have accepted her as Gilda's wandering ghost, a ghost with red hair, and it wouldn't have mattered how the story strayed.

There was a much deeper matter, though: his portrayal of Michael O'Hara. That dynamiter, Orson Welles, had not looked hard enough into his own mirror. We needed a knight-errant—or a cynical detective like Sam Spade—and not a Black Irish sailor who was scoffed at as "Mr. Poet." And yet I loved the film, even with Viola's cuts; the audacity of its design, the idea of mirrors within mirrors, culminating in the abandoned fun house, where the fabric of the film, like the characters themselves, was made of glass.

I'd never seen anything remotely like it before. Yes, Chaplin had used a magic mirror sequence in *The Circus*, but that was 1928. Charlie hides from the cops and has a hard time finding his hat in the maze. It's a masterful comic trope. It doesn't spell disaster. Little is at stake. But the multiple mirrors in *Shanghai* duplicate the illusion inside Michael O'Hara's head. Orson himself is the illusionist. Every frame splinters our perception of what is on the screen. The screen behaves like a battered eyeball—it splits as O'Hara/Welles finds himself inside and outside the maze. The blond Circe—Rita—who has brought him here either intends to kill him or run away with him into the sunrise. Then we hear the terrible squeal of her husband's canes and his image multiplies in the mirrors. Arthur Bannister has arrived. Her plot to murder him—Everett Sloane—has misfired. And like Circe, he's armed with a gun. We glimpse his sadness for a moment. He's still in love with his blond wife. Killing her, he says, is like killing himself.

Arthur and Circe point their guns at each other. But they're already part of Orson's grotesque panoply. Their images multiply. We hear pistol shots. The mirrors shatter, one by one. Arthur drops out of the frame. Circe, too. They've both found their targets, despite the multiple mirrors. Arthur is dead. His wife crawls

out of the mirror maze. She will also die soon. O'Hara himself isn't
unscathed. He's been hit in the hand by a stray bullet, showing us
that he's also caught in the maze. And he walks through the turn-
stile of the fun house, leaving Circe to her fate.

Not even Vi, with all her tools, could crack the magic material
of this scene. It's the best of Welles, the moment when he makes
us doubt our own existence, our sense of the real, as if we're stuck
there forever in those shards of glass. . . .

There was utter silence at the end of the screening. I climbed
onto the stage. The audience started to clap. They wanted my wis-
dom, my clarity. I had none.

"Regina X! Regina X!"

"Children," I said, "I cannot help you here. I have no key to
turn, nothing. I can't even tell you if the film is a failure or not."

A voice shot back from the audience. "Regina X, you invited
us here. Dammit, you're our muse. The film is a maze—a
magic mirror."

"Ah," I said, "we are confused and lost. And then we walk out
into the sunshine, with Black Irish. No, I feel swindled."

"And why," asked another member of the audience, "why can't
Welles be a swindler?"

"Because," I said, "a swindle is incomplete."

"And where did he fail?" asked a third member.

"Oh, God," I shouted into the audience, "it's better than the
pap we've been fed this year. But I expected more, the same magnificent puzzle as *Kane*."

"Shame on you," said that first voice. I recognized where the
voice came from—Mark Wyle, a celebrated professor of literature at
UCLA who'd started a film and theater department and had snuck
a course on Hollywood classics into the curriculum. He was around
fifty, with a paunch and a white beard that made him look like a sat-
urnine Santa. He was one of the faithful who read all my broadsides.

"Did you want the maestro to repeat himself?"

"Yes!" I shouted, wandering across the stage like Lady Hamlet stepping out of a tin box. "There's a hollowness at the heart of the film. The camerawork is remarkable. But the characters begin to blur. They scheme and scheme, and what are they scheming for?"

Wyle stood up and clapped his hands with not a hint of sarcasm. "Poor Regina. Plot has never been the maestro's strong point. But he gives us moments that no other director could ever have dreamed . . . in Hollywood."

"Still," I said, "I have the right to put his feet to the fire."

We had a few more give-and-takes, but neither one of us could convince the other. It was well past midnight and Shorty began to send me signals with his flashlight. So I said, "This is a wrap," and people began to shuffle toward the exits like slumbering snakes. That's when I noticed Viola. *She* was the one in a veil. She'd put on her dark glasses now that the lights had been turned on.

"Bravo, Rusty," she said. "I felt the same hollowness that you felt—from the first. The man cannot tell a story. But he *wounds* us with every shot. We're held in his sway."

"Why did you come here?" I asked. "To rejoice over the master you made invisible?"

"Don't be silly. I always come to your openings."

"This one felt like a wake," I said.

"No matter," she said. "I'm still here. And the maestro will always have you to defend him, will always have his Regina X. That's worth a lot."

And she left with all the others. I felt a sudden chill as I faced row upon row of empty seats. I didn't want the shrimp to see me cry.

"What's the matter, beautiful?" Shorty asked.

"Flatterer," I said, as he wiped my eyes with an usher's pristine white handkerchief.

"Rusty, we struck gold. We could shove back the rear curtain and add twenty seats. You're a genius. With *Shanghai*, we'll have packed houses for a month."

"We'd still be presiding at a wake."

Shorty knew what I meant. It had nothing to do with Viola and her cutters, or Harry Cohn. With Rita behind him, Orson had his first and last chance to break through the barrier of Hollywood and pack houses across America. *The Lady from Shanghai* should have resurrected Orson, but Orson only did what a dynamiter could do. And I feared for Rita. The role of Elsa had tested her depths as an actress rather than a love goddess, but how many in the audience had recognized that? They wanted Gilda, and they got an assassin. She was a series of masks, some soft, some cruel, some as hard as metal, until the mirror scene when she dominates the film. Orson almost disappears as he responds to Rita's own frailty, her splintered selves. He'd created a femme fatale we'd never seen before—a blond assassin with a dead whirlwind in her eyes, as if her absence only increased her presence on the screen. No matter how many Carmens the Janitor found for her in movieland's version of Cordova and Seville, she would never be Circe again—or Gilda.

3

RELEASED THAT AUGUST, *The Loves of Carmen* was Columbia's biggest hit of the year. Rita plays a spitfire who destroys
the life of a Spanish dragoon. Poor Glenn Ford seems like a colic
baby in her arms. I didn't love the film. Once again Rita had fiery
red hair, and she wore fanciful peasant costumes designed by Jean
Louis. But her acting was stilted and did not match the mood of a
gypsy seductress who worked at a cigarette factory, though one of
Orson's nicknames for Rita was "Gypsy." She was much too modern and vital for such a silly cartoon of a historical romance.

Rita's fans weren't bothered by all the fakery. What they
objected to was all the publicity around Rita's new beau, Prince
Aly Khan, a twice-married Pakistani playboy millionaire. Rita had
met him that May during a hurried trip to the Côte d'Azur, where
she was as shy and reclusive as ever. She was staying at the Hôtel
du Cap, a blinding white and gray mansion perched on a bluff
overlooking the Mediterranean. Rita had to arrive with a bundle
of cash, since the hotel wouldn't accept checks, not even from Big
Red. Shorty had written to tell her that Orson might be coming

to Antibes in a desperate search of funds for *Othello*. The French Riviera had become a choice vacation spa for moguls and movie stars, and Darryl Zanuck, head of 20th Century Fox, happened to be staying at the hotel. The Boy Wonder put on one of his best performances, at least that was the legend attached to his visit. Orson went down on his knees in the hotel patio while Zanuck was having breakfast and kissed the tongues of his shoes. Zanuck was so embarrassed that he grabbed a telephone from a waiter, called Fox's chief executive in Rome, and had him transfer $85,000 worth of lire to the account of Orson Welles. Orson sat down at Zanuck's breakfast table and demolished a dozen croissants with a bearish smile. When he realized that Rita was at the same hotel, he invited her to dinner.

His ass was as big as an elephant's, and Rita wondered how he could play the Moor in *Othello*. She loved him nonetheless. They dined at a local restaurant, where he devoured three roast chickens and drank two bottles of Chablis, according to one of my very best sources. They danced at a boîte in back of the restaurant, and patrons clapped when the big bear gave her a midnight kiss. I won't talk about their lovemaking. All I could learn was that he stayed with Rita in her suite and left before she woke. Rita was puzzled, but she shouldn't have been. He was returning to Rome and his great obsession, the financing of *Othello*, while she was hoping to patch up their marriage if she could. But fate bumped her on the head.

On the Côte there happened to be someone else who was haunted by her, almost bewitched—Aly, who had watched *Gilda* again and again in one of his private screening rooms, and dreamt of her tempestuous dance with and without the glove. He had his servants seek her out, follow sad-eyed Rita on her walks along the beach. He sent her roses anonymously, without a clue. Then he revealed himself in a note slipped under her door.

Might I have one dance, only one, with Gilda,
at your earliest convenience?
Your admirer, Aly Khan

He was Prince Aly, eldest son of the Aga Khan, the richest man in the world. This mattered little to Rita, little at all. He had a dozen mistresses, each with her own room in one of his villas, town houses, or racehorse stud farms. He'd never chased after a woman in his life, and here he was chasing Rita, or at least her cinematic ghost. He invited her to soirees. Gilda declined. So he, Prince Aly, had to beg international hostess Elsa Maxwell on his behalf. Elsa was a notorious busybody, and she happened to be in residence on the Riviera. She was another toad with wattles, like Lolly Parsons, but much more clever. She invited Rita to a party at a salon in Cannes without telling her that the prince would be there.

"Dearest Rita," she supposedly said, "you must come, or my reputation will be ruined."

Rita arrived late in a white dress that hugged her hips. She stood in a corner, as shy as ever, until Aly appeared in white slacks and a white shirt open at the collar.

"Now," he asked, "may I have this dance?"

She danced with him, her hips swiveling like a tornado. When the music stopped, she returned to her corner. Ali pursued her like a rampant tiger.

"Didn't you demand just one dance, my little Aly?"

"I lied."

He managed to crawl under her cloak of reclusiveness, and their romance began to flower a bit while she still mourned the Boy Wonder with his elephant's ass, and she with the saddest eyes in history.

In all fairness, Aly wasn't a typical playboy. Serving as a captain in *our* Seventh Army, he took part in Operation Dragoon, the Allied landing in the south of France in August 1944. That still didn't endear him to some of Rita's fan clubs, with their prudish ardor. Rita's divorce hadn't gone through yet, and she remained Mrs. Orson Welles—at least for the moment. These same unforgiving fans worshipped *Carmen* and saw the film many times.

I rather liked Captain Aly Khan, with his widow's peak that made him look like a handsome Count Dracula. There were tales about Captain Aly in the international press because of his affair with the love goddess. "The captain, he was a good Joe," said one corporal. "Strange fellah," said a lieutenant. "He was a sharpshooter, our own Wild Bill. Never saw anyone who could handle a Colt or a carbine like him. I watched him draw a bead on a Kraut colonel, whack him through the eye at a hundred paces. Never met anything like it at a Wild West jamboree."

And so a legend grew around Rita and this playboy from the Seventh Army. They lived at Aly's villa right on the Mediterranean, the Château l'Horizon—in separate suites, said the *Hollywood Reporter*—when she wasn't in the middle of a shoot. Cohn's publicity hounds bled whatever they could from this "royal romance." They now referred to Big Red as Princess Rita. Some of her fans were outraged.

Still, I got cryptic notes from her. Still, she didn't want me to get in touch. The notes were hand-delivered to the Regina by Sally Fall or one of her lackeys.

> *I can't bear being on a horse*
> *I'd rather have a steak at Musso's*
> *Don't write*

But Rita was photographed in a riding habit, on the back of a palomino, and Prince Aly on his prize horse Thunder. She was always docile at the beginning of a romance, even if she hated to ride horses.

And where was Orson in this trio? "I wish her all the happiness in the world," he was supposed to have said, with a slightly sour face from a villa in Venice.

We knew that Orson was working on *Othello*, acting in second-rate films, demanding exorbitant fees, so that he could play the Moor in his own production, and one of the films he worked on was Carol Reed's *The Third Man*, a thriller that took place in occupied Vienna. It was hardly second-rate. In fact, Reed's direction seemed inspired by Welles, particularly the scenes in which Welles appeared.

The film had an odd configuration. Orson was the star of *The Third Man*, yet we first encounter him in the second half of the film, and he has less than twenty minutes of screen time. He plays Harry Lime, an American who operates on the black market. He steals penicillin from a Viennese hospital, waters it down, and sells it back to the sick at exorbitant prices. Some of these patients suffer horrible deaths. But Harry thrives, while he lives in the Russian Zone. The Brits and Americans can't get their hands on Harry Lime.

He fakes his own death. But he's invited an old school chum of his, Holly Martins, a writer of pulp westerns, to Vienna on the very day of his own orchestrated death. Jo Cotton plays him to perfection. Cotton had always been close to Welles. He was once part of the Mercury Players, and had appeared in both *Ambersons* and *Kane*.

In *The Third Man*, Holly is a kind of woodenhead. He falls in love with Lime's girlfriend, Anna Schmidt, played by Italian star Alida Valli, one of the rare actresses in the world who could *almost* rival Rita's beauty. Anna's a Czech, living illegally in the British Zone with papers forged by Harry and his friends.

Orson's entrance is even more remarkable than Rita's in *Gilda*, with her head rising onto the screen out of nowhere. The dead man, Harry Lime, appears in the darkened doorway of the house where he had lived . . . at least the man might be Harry. A cat climbs down the stairs and rubs up against the man's stippled leather shoes. Then a light shines from a window above the doorway. Holly is standing across the street, where Lime was supposed to have been run over by a car driven by his chauffeur. We catch our first glimpse of Lime in the eerie light. He's smiling. It's Orson without one of his false noses. He runs off, into the sewers that will bring him back to the Russian Zone.

It's Anna who understands him best. "He's a child," Anna claims. It's the world that has grown up around Harry Lime. She might as well have been describing Orsie. In interviews, after his appearance in *The Third Man* had made him an international movie star, he would claim how despicable Lime was, how foreign to his own nature. But this was flapdoodle, as Huck Finn, one of my favorite bad boys, would opine. Orsie was playing himself, another bad boy, rather than a naïve sailor with a brogue. He'd always been a bad boy; that's why he was so convincing in *The Third Man*. He was a bad boy when he made his *War of the Worlds* broadcast, hoping he would shock half the nation and pull listeners away from another network that featured Edgar Bergen, a ventriloquist, and his prize dummy in a monocle, Charlie McCarthy, who was as popular as the President. He was a bad boy when he made *Citizen Kane*, trying to unsettle Hearst, bait him, really, like an infant matador. He was a bad boy as soon as he went to Brazil and shot week after week of footage that could never fit into an RKO film. And he was the same bad boy when he took Columbia's star redhead, had her hair shorn, and made her into a morbid, almost timid, blond murderess, just to spite the Janitor.

A few months after *The Third Man* was released, Harry Lime called me collect at the Regina. "Rusty, darling, you must come to Venice. I'm surrounded by imbeciles. I can't work on *Othello* without you."

I didn't believe a word. Yet I was still tempted. That's the kind of seductive voice he had. I wanted to join his mad quest. But I wasn't going to run off and abandon Shorty.

"Orson, I can't. I'll lose the Regina."

"What's your little nutshell compared to a new production?"

That hurt. "We've been showing *The Lady from Shanghai* on and off for almost a year. The crowds are phenomenal."

I heard him groan. "Viola's massacre, you mean. If you can't come, you must send us fifty thousand dollars at once, or we'll lose all our costumes."

"Orson, where would I get that kind of money? It's hard enough to keep the theater stocked with toilet paper."

"Darling," he said, "you could kill—or steal."

I offered to send him the last five hundred I had at Wells Fargo for a zero-point-one percent ownership in Orson's production of *Othello*, directed by and starring Orson Welles.

I guess I wasn't the adventurer I might have been. I preferred our nutshell, where Shorty and I were the kings of whatever little space we could command.

I didn't dare give the phone to Shorty, or we would have had to put a lien on the movie house and then lose it all.

The bungalow behind the Regina was part of our property, and we'd been renting it out to help meet our costs, but after our tenants left, Shorty and I decided to move in. I'd been living at the Hollywood Hotel for ten years, and I was sick of the ghosts in the lobby. D. W. Griffith had suffered a cerebral hemorrhage while sitting in his favorite chair in the lobby and nobody had bothered to notice. The night porter had found him with his eyes ablaze, his body all stiff. He might have been dead for a week. The whole of Hollywood mourned him, but he hadn't made a film in seventeen years. And without D.W. sitting in his favorite chair, it was much easier to move out of my roomette at the Hollywood Hotel.

4

*T*HE *THIRD MAN* was shown at half the movie palaces in Hollywood, and it made little sense to have a belated premiere at the Regina. As much as I admired *The Third Man* and its screenplay by British novelist Graham Greene, the film wasn't directed by Orson. The "Harry Lime" theme, played on a zither, became an instant success. Its haunting tones, with a hint of danger, would soon follow Orson everywhere. He couldn't enter a restaurant without being serenaded by Harry Lime's theme song.

Fans wrote and begged me for a screening. Still, I resisted. Others could comment on Graham Greene's words. I cared about the images, and those didn't belong to Orson, even if he did overpower the film with his presence. And then Viola Lawrence sent me a note. She lamented not having a lively discussion of the film, and she offered to lead one herself if we ever had a screening. How could I resist? For once I wouldn't have to play Regina X.

Of course, Shorty capitalized on the event. He got a recording of that zither tune, with its relentless pounding rhythm, and had it played on a loudspeaker in the lobby. And so we had Harry Lime with us an entire week before we ever showed the film.

We were mobbed at our premiere, even though I'm certain that almost everyone in the audience had seen the film at one of the Hollywood palaces. Viola wouldn't allow us to advertise her presence, and she insisted that I go up with her onto the stage after the screening. She arrived in her dark glasses and a black leather jacket, looking like a dominatrix. We watched the film—watched Harry Lime, I mean. Everyone else was a blur, either enemies or allies of Harry Lime, like chess pieces built around him. His best friend (if Lime ever had a friend) was Jo Cotton, with his neutral eyes and mouth that are half-forgotten the moment he departs from the screen. Even his name (in the film), Holly Martins, has a forgettable ring. Only Anna remains with us—the beautiful Alida Valli—because Lime loves her, in his own misbegotten way. And if we attach ourselves to her, it's always as a remnant of him.

The audience was stunned to see Viola up on the stage with Rusty Redburn rather than Regina X. She began to pace in her pumps. She wouldn't allow me to introduce her.

"My children," she said, as if the entire audience were part of her cutting team, "what happens after Lime makes his entrance in the doorway?"

"The film gets a shot of adrenaline," answered one of our regulars.

"Exactly," Viola said. "But how and why?"

"Carol Reed, almost subconsciously, adopts Welles' own visual style," said our precious film professor from UCLA.

"Exactly," said Vi. "The shots are more angled, more violent, more *Wellesian*, as if we've been woken out of a sleepy narrative. It's Vienna, a divided city, with wrecked buildings, looming like stage props. Harry Lime rises up from the sewers if he has to go into one of the Allied sectors, where he's a wanted man—until he fakes his death. And it's Holly Martins, the writer of pulp fiction, who first uncovers Harry's plot to play dead."

"But doesn't Graham Greene add something to the film?" asked another one of our regulars, who must have recognized Viola as Columbia's chief cutter.

"Yes—and no," said Vi. "Greene invented the character, but Welles *incarnates* him. Greene's words do enchant us, children, but the structure of Welles' face enchants us even more."

And Vi summoned up that marvelous scene on Vienna's iconic Ferris wheel that only Greene could have created, with Lime and Holly Martins, who has told the police that Harry is still alive. "For a moment, Lime considers hurling Holly out the unlocked door of the passenger car into the void below. Harry has a vicious, playful tone as Vienna's king of the black market. We can *feel* Harry's violence. Then he digs his tongue into his jaw and turns playful again. The monster has changed his mind. Holly might still be useful to him. We've never seen Welles *wear* a character in this way, grab at his genitals, in a manner of speaking, full of a puckish fury. Lime is indifferent to the world; so is Welles. Both bathe in immorality. Lime is who Welles has become—a monster with pluck and charm."

Vi clapped her hands, and the séance was done. Ah, if only she had been as kind to Orson in *The Lady from Shanghai*. But I didn't quibble with Vi. The audience was delighted with her. She wouldn't have dinner with Shorty and me at Musso's. Nor would she answer any questions once she left the stage.

She'd accomplished what she wanted and was gone in a wisp. She'd given us her own cutter's song.

• SEVEN •

Princess Rita, 1951–1952

1

*C*ALL HER *MARGARITA*.

She didn't want to be a princess, but she was a princess nonetheless. No one cared that the name Margarita Carmen Cansino was written on the marriage certificate at the little *mairie* on a hill near Antibes. She'd abandoned Hollywood, sold her little house on Rockingham Road. She never really wanted to be a movie star. She would have preferred to stay home in her blue jeans as somebody's wife, somebody who would make love to her day and night. But she couldn't escape Gilda's shadow at the prince's château. She was Princess Rita now, both to the servants and to Aly's endless array of guests. He'd wooed her, but the love goddess wasn't enough for a prince who couldn't bear to be alone. He would often have three Persian millionaires accompany him wherever he went so that he could play bridge with them well into the night. Rita fumed. If she tossed an ashtray at him in front of his guests, he looked upon it with alacrity. The prince was proud of his new possession, Princess Rita with her tantrums.

It was a ghost marriage. The farther she moved from Gower

Street and Harry Cohn, the more of a movie star she became in
Aly's little universe. She got along well with Aly's father, the Aga
Khan, spiritual leader of the Ismaili sect of a hundred fifty million
Muslims worldwide. The Aga had once been a playboy and a bon
vivant, like Aly, but he was much too ill now, and much too wise.
He had a weak heart and walked with a cane. He enjoyed Rita,
and not the shadow of Gilda she had to wear. He was touched
by her kindness and her simple tastes. Diamond necklaces meant
nothing to her. And diamonds had most often been the Aga's way.
He would appease a former mistress or wife with some bibelot that
was worth a fortune. But he couldn't dangle a bibelot in front of
the princess.

"My dear Margarita, why do you look so sad?"

She couldn't tell the Aga about his son's infidelities, the mistresses who suddenly appeared at L'Horizon and disappeared into a
secret closet seconds later, or the models Aly danced with at nightclubs in front of Rita, or the prince's hunting companions who
mocked the attempts she made to speak French. She was fluent in
Spanish, but she couldn't seem to capture the flow of the prince's
preferred language at L'Horizon.

"Your Highness," she said, "I am hopeless. I have had tutor
after tutor, and I still can't speak a word of French."

"A trifle," said the Aga, who never traveled without his own
chef, even to restaurants on the Riviera, or to L'Horizon, where he
had his own quarters, separate from his son's.

They were eating chicken kebab with jeweled rice, sprinkled
with crushed almonds and orange peel, and served with pita bread
and mint tea. The Aga also had a lamb chop with Dijon mustard
and mashed potatoes, but Rita stuck with the jeweled rice.

"Aly's friends imitate me all the time."

"I have a simple solution, my dear. We will have their heads
cut off."

Rita had presented him with a grandchild, Princess Yasmin, born at a clinic in Lausanne; he adored Yasmin beyond any measure of paradise; she was the first and only grandchild the Aga had. He would have destroyed whole nations for the right to see her, and the Aga was not a warlike man. He washed his hands in a little bowl that a servant brought with a silk napkin.

"Do you remember when we first met? I did not want my son to marry a movie star. I was adamant. But when I saw you, Margarita, how unpretentious, with such a lovely pounce, like a ballerina— and I am very fond of ballerinas—I realized that you were much too good for my son. Yes, he breeds horses, he hunts, he plays bridge like a champion, but he has no inner passion. His pose is the pose of a prince. He was once a worthy soldier. That I admit. But I worry that you will leave him and run back to Hollywood, and I will lose Yasmin. That loss will be fatal to me."

He spoke in a soft, rapturous voice, as if he were reciting a psalm, but it still sounded like a threat. Rita wasn't frightened of Aly, she would later tell me. But she was frightened of this sick, soft-spoken man, the Aga Khan, as much as she loved him—he could have destroyed her in a second, he had such sway. She didn't love Aly; he'd been tender while he courted her, as devoted as a crafty child with a treasured toy—Gilda. She was on display in her ice-blue wedding dress, her dress that cost thousands and was later mass-produced and marketed at Macy's.

"Your Highness, Aly is what he is. He cannot change."

"You must call me Father, little one," said the Aga Khan. "I will bend Aly to my own will, like a warrior's bow. I am not—and have never been—a man who likes to fail."

He kissed her hands and retired to his quarters at L'Horizon, where the sea washed under his windows.

Aly tossed out his mistresses, danced with Rita and Rita alone at nightclubs in Cannes, did not crawl out of bed in the middle of the night to meet a model he had discovered at the roulette tables in Deauville.

But that didn't really help Rita's situation as a princess on display. No matter how hard she tried, she could not be the chatelaine of Aly's château. She sat at the dinner table without uttering a word. She winced when one of the servants called her Your Highness.

"I'm Margarita."

It was only when the Aga arrived that she livened a bit. She would appear in a pearl-white Dior jacket and rolled-up blue jeans and sit next to the Aga, hiding the scent of alcohol—she'd been drinking bourbon in her bedroom out of the bottle. Aly sat with his male companions, who seemed to Rita like jackals, signaling among themselves with their fingers and babbling in French.

The Aga pounded the marble table with his tiny fist. "Silence!" he said. "Messieurs and Madams, we will speak English here in honor of our hostess, Margarita."

Rita saw a flurry of bitter faces, and then a jackal's smile.

"*Naturalement,* Your Highness," said the young Count Charles, one of Aly's bridge partners and a frequent companion to bordellos in Paris, London, and Wales, where the count had a couple of family castles and stud farms. He was blond and muscular, and winced like Popeye on several occasions. Rita had to slap the young count in the hallways of the château to keep his hands from wandering across her behind. He had slept with nearly all the maids at L'Horizon.

"But we were only welcoming the princess, Your Highness. After all, we are in France."

"Welcome her in English," said the Aga. "Monsieur le Conte, pretend you're in Wales."

That jackal's smile spread across his face. "We speak Welsh in Wales, sire—at least at my castle."

"We are in Aly's castle now," said the Aga. "And your rudeness is intolerable."

Aly whispered to the young count, who tossed his napkin in the air and left the table.

"Margarita, dear," said the Aga, "you must be our Scheherazade and tell us about that exotic place—Hollywood. Surely you must have one tale."

Rita was petrified. She never mingled with the stars. She pursed her lips, and bubbles flew from her mouth.

"Darling," Aly said, trying to rescue Rita from her own muteness and mortification, "Father loves *The Lady from Shanghai*. He says you were enchanting as a blonde. He has watched the mirror scene many times. How did Orson get you to play in it, among all the mirrors?" He paused to scratch his chin. "Of course, I could invite the Boy Wonder to L'Horizon and ask him."

"No," said the Aga. "I want to hear it from Margarita's mouth."

"I stood there," she said, "with a gun in my hand, a studio gun, a prop. There were cameras on both sides of the mirror wall. And Orson whispered in my ear, 'I don't want even a touch of emotion. You're in a dream. Your eyes are blank. Shoot the gun.' So I shot and shot."

2

W<small>E WERE SHOWING</small> the rough cut of *Othello* that Orson had sent us when I got the call. At first I didn't recognize her voice. She whispered into the phone like a frightened child. I wasn't very polite. I had to ponder the logistics of Orson's *Othello*. He filmed wherever he could find money. That's why the costumes and the faces never matched.

"Who the hell is this?"

She was silent. And then she whimpered, "It's me, Rusty— Big Red."

She wasn't calling from the Riviera, I knew that. She had broken from Aly, sailed from Le Havre on the luxury liner *De Grasse*, where she never once emerged from her cabin, or so the papers reported. She arrived in Manhattan at the beginning of April, with half the world's press swooning to greet her. It was the royal fairy tale of the year—the end of Princess Rita's reign.

"Red, where are you?"

She was on the lake, she said. What lake? She had rented a big white house on the eastern shore of Lake Tahoe. Rita was establishing a six-week residence in Nevada so that she could file for divorce. Somehow, she had managed to escape all the journalists so far.

She had to see me at once.

I smiled to myself. This was the woman who had broken all contact with me except for a few cryptic notes.

"What's so urgent?"

She began to cry, and that whipping, hysterical sound made me realize how much I still loved her. I missed that magnificent glide of hers, the princess who could dance on air.

"Rusty, it's a matter of life and death."

Tahoe was hundreds of miles away, on the route to Manzanar, the camp where Julie Tanaka had been interned with the Baron. I didn't want to leave the Regina in Shorty's care; he would have had to become ticket-taker, usher, and pinch hitter for the projectionist. Besides, he missed Big Red as much as I did. So we shut the Regina and put up a sign:

CLOSED FOR CIRCUMSTANCES UNSEEN

We took off in Shorty's Cadillac. We stuck to the side roads— the scenic route, with its bald cow pastures, its abandoned farms, an occasional haunted house on a hill, and half a dozen dead ends, which finally led us right to Manzanar. The camp was shuttered with barbed wire, but we saw row after row of barracks, surrounded by mesquite, flagless flag posts, signs that warned us to keep away from government property, packs of wild dogs that roamed the interior of the camp looking for rats. We saw the bare walls of Manzanar High School, which every teenager in the camp had attended, as well as the Administration Building and the barracks where soldiers and guards had bivouacked, with a bald eagle on the front door. I swear to God, it looked like a set on the Columbia ranch. . . .

"You know," I said, "history has a way of kicking you in the ass."

"What do ya mean, Rusty?"

"Dammit, it's all gone, as if Manzanar never existed and no one was ever here, except the rats and the mice and the mesquite, and that bald eagle on the door."

I had lost my good friend Julie Tanaka because of this ghost camp. It didn't matter how hard I had plotted in Julie's behalf. I was just another "round-eye" to her. She and the Baron had abandoned their little grocery and disappeared from Hollywood. She was in Santa Clara somewhere. I'm sure I'll never see her again.

Shorty drove like a maniac with his wooden pedals. I counted all the Burma-Shave signboards at the side of the road, opposite cow pastures and gas stations. There were over two dozen, some of them nailed to trees. Each signboard had its own dialogue, telling riders, male and female, how smooth it was to shave with Burma-Shave, promising us all A MILLION DOLLAR FACE.

Rita's house was more like a bunker, with bars on every window, and a guard standing outside who could have come from central casting, with his sunglasses and black suit. The bunker didn't seem to belong at the side of a lake with a forest at the far shore, and the quiet melody of the water, like the lingering echo of a guitar pluck, and the flocks of birds with their distant chatter that blended into the silence of the lake. . . .

Rita welcomed us right at the door. She wasn't wearing makeup, and though she clearly suffered from a lack of sleep, she hadn't lost that chiseled beauty. My eye could catch what the camera caught—a softness coupled with defiance that made her so unusual on the screen. She was wearing one of Orson's white shirts and rolled-up blue jeans. She hugged both me and the shrimp.

"Rusty, I was so mean to you last time, when I made you write your own retirement check, like a death warrant, on account of that silly man. What was his name again?"

"Marvin," I muttered. "Marvin Marsh." That goddamn grifter who liked to dance!

"Well, I'm greedy. I want our friendship back."

I could feel a twist of anger in my eyebrows. The hurt was still there. I'd shut the movie house and come to Tahoe the moment she had beckoned. I figured that was all the loyalty I had left. I was wrong. It was as if I'd been condemned to a windless tunnel without her: I was a movie-house mistress who devoured Jujubes and lived in the dark.

Rita talked about her life at L'Horizon, about the fondness she had for the Aga Khan, about his gentleness toward her; about Aly's rampant infidelities despite what he had promised his father. He was carrying on affairs with Joan Fontaine and Gene Tierney, the girl with the luminous green eyes, while Rita raged at L'Horizon.

Despite all his villas and stud farms, Aly did not have any real wealth of his own. He lived on a strict allowance from the Aga. Whatever deals Rita had with Columbia were on hiatus. The Janitor wasn't an idiot. He couldn't suspend a princess. He capitalized on all her publicity, waiting for her to return to movieland. Meanwhile, Aly spent all *her* money, the three-hundred-thousand-dollar pot she had brought with her to the château. She had to borrow twenty-five thousand from her manager just to help her pay the rent at Tahoe.

I gave her whatever cash I had on hand and Shorty wrote her a check for five hundred dollars.

"You're an angel," she said, dancing with Shorty across her rented living room. Then she sat down on a sofa with tattered cushions and crooked legs and started to cry. She was worried about kidnappers.

"Stay where you are," Shorty said. "And get rid of the gunsel. I could sniff him a mile away. I'll send you a bodyguard. And have him stay with you inside the house. You don't have to advertise."

3

S HORTY AND I took turns driving—damn him and his
wooden pedals—and rode through the night, with the sound
of crickets in our ears and the distant blaze of headlights. I had to
reopen the Regina.

Shorty was worried. "They can come at her through the lake—
in a speedboat. She must have a pile of jewelry in the house."

"*They*," I shouted into the wind, "who the hell are *they*?"

"It don't matter. Keep driving."

I let him off on Sunset. It was six o'clock in the morning.
He was back in his usher's uniform by six p.m. And I realized
that he had more than mob "gonnegtions." He was part of some
mythical gang that had moved from the Lower East Side to the
vanished orange groves of Hollywood. Being Orson's valet had
only been a hobby, or a cover. That's why he couldn't move
to Europe with Orson. Whatever mob he was connected with
would have broken his bones. And that's why he had money to
invest in the Regina. For all I knew, the little second-run house
we had on Hollywood Boulevard could have been fronted by a

band of assassins. But no one interfered, no one glanced at our books except Shorty himself.

"You're a mobster," I said between showings of *Destry Rides Again*, my favorite western, about a deputy sheriff (Jimmy Stewart), a born gunslinger who refuses to wear a gun. "That's why you couldn't go to Europe with Orson. You never left whatever gang you were in."

He stared at me with his gorgeous gray eyes. "Does it really matter, Miss Rusty? I watched *Citizen Kane* and I was hooked for life. I wanted to be near his mind. I was in a rotten mood for days when I couldn't go with him."

"Then it had nothing to do with countesses and dukes."

He smiled that angelic smile of his. "If I had to give up Orson," he said, "then my best bet was you."

"Why?" I asked. "I don't have his genius. I could never have created that mirror scene in a million years. I'm not even as gifted as Vi."

"You have your gifts, Miss Rusty. And I always wanted to work in a movie house."

"As an usher, for Christ's sake? That's a job for a juvenile."

He had me jumping through one hoop after another. Shorty was the ultimate mirror maze—fracture him, and he would come right back at you as another figure of glass, like Rita in *The Lady from Shanghai*.

"But I can watch movies day and night. And I get to wear my own uniform."

"Yeah, as the Phillip Morris call boy of the Regina, epaulettes and all."

"Ah, he said, "the important thing is that Rita is safe."

I growled at him. "How safe, Mr. Fancy pants? What do ya mean?"

He ruffled the gold buttons on his usher's blouse. "No hoods, big time or little, would dare come at Rita and her daughters by land or by the lake. I hired the local sheriff and his men to guard the house."

Shorty hadn't lied to me about his past. He'd just carved out his own little piece of the truth. I started to do a little detective work of my own. I learned that he was part owner of the Cocoanut Grove, under a slightly different name. But I stopped right there. Whatever else he did was none of my business. I would never find a more faithful usher than Shorty Chivallo.

He wasn't shy about his accomplishments. He had half a million stacked away at an Eastern brokerage house, mostly in General Electric stock.

"Then why haven't you put money in *Othello*?"

He stared into my eyes like Destry, the gunslinger without a gun. "I've given him a nickel here and there." Now he ruffled his chest, a rooster in his domain. "Rusty, I'm not the Red Cross. I'm an investor, and he's a bad investment. Didn't you call him a dynamiter in one of your broadsides, Miss Regina X? He'd have destroyed theater if he hadn't gone out to Hollywood. And he'd have destroyed Hollywood if the moguls had given him half a chance. That's why I like him so much."

And he told me about all the meanderings of his life.

Shorty had grown up on Forsyth Street in lower Manhattan, the son of a sad-eyed Jewish mother and an Italian father who was a shoemaker on Canal. The other kids taunted him at school.

"Shorty, Shorty, shut your eyes and say goodbye!"

They pummeled him, stood him on his head, and kicked him across the street. His mother had to wipe his bloody mouth at the kitchen sink.

She gave him one of his father's awls from the shoemaker's shop. She was a cunning general.

"Be smart," she said. "Pick the biggest, fattest bully. Don't talk fresh. But take the awl and wound him, wound him softly. That way they won't expel you, and no one will bother you again."

He did wound the biggest bully, digging the awl into the flesh of his calf.

"Next time," Shorty said, "I'll stab you in the heart."

His classmates shivered around Shorty and left him alone.

Several years later he fell in with a bad crowd and used his nimbleness to his advantage for a while. He flitted through factory windows for a gang of safecrackers. He had more brains and mustard than any of his masters. But his own gang ratted on him and he was sent to Sing Sing. He was restless, longing for something to believe in. He rummaged through the library, discovered long articles on Orson Welles. He had enough cash to bribe the warden into renting a renegade print of *Citizen Kane*. He sat there and watched *Kane* moment by moment, and realized that Welles himself had all the imaginative powers of a first-class criminal mind.

Shorty was soon anointed one of the underkings of Frank Costello's mob. He planned robberies while he was in the clink. No one could read the blueprint of a bank or a jewelry store like Shorty Chivallo. He planned more than a dozen heists from his cell. He had his own stockbroker in the clink, his own barber, his own masseur. No one pestered him in the showers. He was celibate, lived like a monk.

He ran to California the moment he was released, though he still kept his mob ties, still planned heists. It excited him to be near Orson, to learn whatever he could from Orson's criminal mind. It amused him to play the role of valet. And when he discovered how certain men had abused Rita, he plotted his vengeance the way his mother would. One guy had his arm broken, another had his house destroyed in a forest fire, a third had his margin account manipulated until he was penniless. It pained Shorty when Orson cheated on Big Red, and he watched after her like a nighthawk.

He couldn't follow Orson to Europe. Otherwise, Shorty might have been excommunicated from his own church of crime, dumped into a garbage barrel, and rolled into the sea. He lived in despair without Orson. That's when he bought into the Regina, became an usher, where he could plan heists while he walked up and down the aisle with his flashlight. . . .

4

EVENTUALLY RITA DID file for divorce. She moved into a Spanish-style ranch house on North Alpine Drive in Beverly Hills. She was back at Columbia because she had so little money. Harry Cohn had a film for her, *Affair in Trinidad*, with her favorite co-star, Glenn Ford. The trouble was he didn't have a script and didn't seem to care. He knew that any film with Rita's name above the title would be a bonanza, as long as she wasn't robbed of her red hair.

Rita suddenly began to stall about the divorce proceedings, not long after returning to Columbia. The Aga Khan had suffered a heart attack. And, of course, he sent the prince as his emissary. Aly began to court his estranged wife. He sent her wildflowers and Persian poems in translation. He was just another lost, abandoned lover in Hollywood, where he had no stud farms and couldn't afford to be seen with another movie star. Hesitant at first, Rita warmed to Aly and went dancing with him at the Cocoanut Grove. She smuggled Aly into North Alpine Drive. Reporters lost sight of him en route.

Rita hated Hollywood, hated *Affair in Trinidad*, hated Harry Cohn. Aly had already returned to Europe, and after she had finished postproduction, she traveled to New York with her children on the *Super Chief*, boarded the ocean liner *United States,* wearing a scarf as a mask, and arrived in Le Havre. Aly, the penitent husband, wasn't at dockside to greet her. He'd sent his trusted valet, Tutti, who accompanied her to Aly's house in Neuilly, a plush suburb of Paris.

"Princess Rita," Tutti said in a voice soft as silk, "Master was detained. And he is so sorry. But he has urgent business in Cannes."

The house in Neuilly was packed with guests. Count Charles was there, observing Rita with lecherous brows.

"Count," Rita said, "if you touch my ass again, I'll knock you down the fucking stairs and you can forget about tomorrow."

Arriving in a wheelchair, the Aga visited Rita that night. He was far more chivalrous than his son.

"Margarita," the Aga said, breathing into an oxygen mask, "you cannot imagine what pleasure it gives an old man to see you again. But I had hoped to see you without such sad eyes."

"Sire," she said, "I'm afraid they've always been sad, ever since I was a child."

The Aga removed his mask for a moment. "And why?"

Rita stared into some void. "I was robbed of my girlhood, forced to dance in casinos and on gambling ships when I was twelve."

The Aga began to cry. "But that is a terrible thing. Not to be a girl among other girls. I only wish that I could wish it all away."

She kissed him between his puckered eyebrows and caressed his cane. "Sire, I am not so sad now—I cherish your gift."

The Aga was confused. "But I have given you none, daughter," he said. "I have come with empty hands. Remember," he said slyly, "no jewels."

"But your kindness is a jewel," she said.

The Aga laughed, baring his brittle teeth. "I am humbled. I have a poet as a daughter-in-law, and a son who is a both a scoundrel and a fool. Why is he not here?"

With that, the Aga's head drooped, and he fell asleep in his wheelchair.

Rita listened to his troubled breathing for a long time.

5

ALY SHOWED UP the next morning, but Rita was gone. She'd taken a suite at the Hotel Lancaster right inside the gates of Paris, near the edge of Neuilly. Rita could see the apartment-palaces of Aly's princely suburb from the windows of her hotel. Rita wasn't jealous of Aly's attention to Gene Tierney, wasn't jealous at all, though Gene was her only real rival as the most beautiful woman in the world. But Gene's life was already riven with despair. Her daughter Daria had been born with brain damage. Gene never fully recovered from that ordeal. She would fall in and out of deep depressions. And so Rita did not bear any grudge against her rival.

Still, she was startled when the concierge announced that Gene Tierney was at the front desk. Aly must have sent her as his envoy. And Rita didn't have the heart to send her away. They had never been friends, but both had danced with servicemen at the Hollywood Canteen, had prepared ham sandwiches in the canteen kitchen.

Gene was dressed all in white, with gloves and a floppy hat.

Her eyes didn't seem to focus, and Rita realized in an instant that Aly hadn't sent her as an envoy, hadn't sent her at all. Green Eyes, as Rita liked to call her, had come on her own from L'Horizon.

The two stars kissed.

Gene was born into high society and had studied French at a finishing school in Lausanne. Her father was a prominent investment broker and had never wanted Gene to become an actress, but an actress she was, estranged from fashion designer Oleg Cassini, the son of a Russian count and an Italian countess.

"Rita, dear, do you have any bourbon in the house?"

They both drank from the same bottle, which Rita kept in her luggage. Gene intended to marry the prince, once her own divorce was finalized. Rita relaxed, realizing she would soon be rid of Aly. I wish I could have been there in that room, voyeur as I am. How could anyone forget Gene's blazing beauty as Belle Starr, queen of the outlaws in the 1941 film that I often included at the Regina? I never tired of her cheekbones. Unlike Destry, Belle did wear a gun.

"I adore Aly," Gene said, the blaze gone out of her eyes, "adore him. But I wouldn't want to break up your marriage, dear. So I came to find out if—"

The phone rang. Aly was on the line. He barely said hello to Rita. "It's madness. Give me Gene. She does not have my authority to be there."

Rita handed her the phone. She could hear Aly shouting. "Yes, dearest," Gene said with tears in her eyes. She put down the receiver.

"Rita, I'm afraid I have to go. But it was a great pleasure, having our own whiskey breakfast."

The concierge arrived an hour later with a note from the Aga Khan and tickets on a liner leaving from Le Havre. The stationery wasn't embossed. It didn't even have the Aga's seal. It was written on the simplest sort of paper.

My Dearest Margarita,
You must not think ill of a tired old man.
You will always remain my daughter as long as I am alive.
Like you, I had my childhood taken from me.
I succeeded my father as the Aga Khan before I was nine.
You and my granddaughter have given me more pleasure than I ever
dreamed I could have.
Let the lawyers bicker. We will not.
Praise be to Allah.
The Aga Khan.

• EIGHT •

Pal Joey, 1954–1958

1

I T CAME UPON us like a thunderclap. All of a sudden Shorty and
I had entered the age of art houses, and the Regina was no longer a second-run flytrap. UCLA invited me to lecture in front of
their film classes, but I refused. The Regina was enough of a forum
for Regina X.

Still, we needed someone to build more seats. I found a carpenter listed on a bulletin board inside the Farmers Market. The
carpenter who arrived wore a ponytail and a denim jacket with the
sleeves cut off. His arms were long and sinewy. I didn't recognize
him at first. It was Nando. He'd given up his sea legs. He was no
longer Errol Flynn's first mate onboard the *Zaca*. He'd stopped
working for Errol a long time ago. He now lived in a bungalow
on a pissy canal in Venice Beach and had become a carpenter on
dry land.

"Nando," I said, with a stitch in my voice, "don't you recognize me?"

"I wasn't so sure you wanted to be recognized, Miss Rusty."

"Why the hell not?" I asked.

He looked at me with a measure of pain. "Well, Mr. Errol said I wouldn't amount to much on dry land."

"Well, he's a damn fool."

He put down his carpenter's box, and I can't tell you how it happened, but we kissed. He was wearing a trace of lipstick, just a touch. And that's what excited me. This ex-bosun lived in the uncertain territory between a guy and a gal.

Nando built the extra seats for us, beveled in an entire row of chairs; he flattened the tilt on the kitchen table in our bungalow, sanded our windowsills, repaired our toilet seat. As it turned out, he was also an unlicensed electrician; he fixed a few of our sockets and redid the wiring in our lamps. He also worked in the projection booth, and put in a new glass plate in our candy counter. He had a spray gun in his box, and got rid of an entire cluster of cockroaches in the women's toilet. He never left the Regina after that morning. He gave notice to his landlord and moved in with Shorty and me.

"I ought to give you a beating, Nando."

He had a puzzled look between his lashes. "Why?"

"For lettin' me live without you all this time."

He laughed and shook his lovely shoulder blades. "Rusty, I guess we'll have to tinker a bit with whatever time we have left."

2

I T WAS NANDO who discovered her wandering about. I hadn't
seen Red in several years, not since that time at Lake Tahoe.
She had moved into a tiny mansion on the street of stars, Roxbury Drive, in Beverly Hills. But she spent most of her time in
Europe, as her lawyers fought with Harry over her obligations to
Columbia, and her two girls vacationed with Aly on the Riviera
or visited with the Aga Khan, who couldn't breathe without his
oxygen mask.

So I was startled when Nando brought Rita to our bungalow
behind the Regina. It couldn't have been much after eight in the
morning. She'd been standing under the Regina's marquee when
Nando returned from the Farmers Market with cinnamon buns
for our breakfast. He didn't recognize Rita at all. She was disheveled, with her red hair all in knots, and Nando wondered if she
had escaped from a downtown shelter, or perhaps an insane asy-
lum. She'd been drinking, and hadn't bathed. One of her shoes
was missing.

"Rusty," she said, and Nando realized that this bizarre woman wasn't a stranger. He had to navigate her behind the theater, to our bungalow, with little twists of his free hand. "Rusty," he shouted as he opened the screen door. "She mentioned your name, and I . . ."

I couldn't believe what I saw—Rita in rags. Her coat was stained with whiskey. I was willing to bet she had been guzzling all night. Her hands were covered in filth. "Rusty," she cried. "I'm so ashamed. I can't remember my address."

I would have killed to keep her from getting hurt. I waltzed Big Red into the bathroom like a princess, removed her rags, sat her down in the tub, put on my terry-cloth mitt, and gave her a bath. I scrubbed as hard as I could. She had the beginnings of crow's nests around her eyes, and a deep pucker on one side of her mouth, though her legs were as long and beautiful as ever.

I lent her one of my robes, and we came out into the kitchen, where we had our coffee and cinnamon buns. She was much more coherent, but she still didn't remember her address.

"You live on Roxbury, with all the stars," I said.

She snapped at me with blazing suspicion in her brown eyes. "Who told you that?"

"Gosh," I said. "It's public knowledge. I read it in the *Reporter*."

She grew even wilder, and I could sense a mad fit coming on, like the fits I remembered from her years with Orson. "How come you never showed *Carmen* once at the Regina?"

I didn't coddle her. "We're an art house," I said. "And *Carmen* isn't art."

"Then what is it?"

"Paste," I said, "that poses as historical romance."

Some of her sense was coming back. "You used to be much kinder when I paid you a salary."

"Red, we've shown *Gilda* half a dozen times. And we had an entire festival around *The Lady from Shanghai*."

"On account of Orsie," she said.

"Not at all. Your performance was quite singular."

"Singular?" she asked. "What's that?"

"Unique," I said.

I gave her a sweater and blue jeans, socks, and my sandals. I washed her hair and untwisted all the knots.

She looked more like Gilda now, my Big Red. We took Shorty's car and drove to Beverly Hills, with its mansions and mock castles that represented a kind of self-styled royalty. I didn't need instructions from Red. I recognized her house from the photo shoot in the *Hollywood Reporter*.

She didn't have her keys, of course. Shorty had no trouble picking her lock and disabling the alarm. The neighborhood of the stars had its own private police, but Rita looked like Rita again, and we weren't bothered by any policemen, private or not.

I didn't know whom to call. Rita had a pad near her phone with a dozen numbers scribbled on them; none of the listings were local; they were all from overseas. I had the long-distance operator try them, one after another. No one answered except the Aga Khan, I mean his private secretary.

The Aga got on the line. I could hear him wheeze.

"Margarita," he said, "my dear Margarita," as he pushed out each word with its own swish of breath. He must have understood her condition. Red had me talk to the Aga.

"Let me introduce myself," he said.

"I know who you are. I placed the call."

"Then you will find her passport, please. You will pack a few items. A car will call for her in half an hour."

"Your Highness, we will need a little more time."

"Forty minutes, my dear. I should have been more diligent about the little one. She was supposed to confer with her lawyers about her obligations to Columbia. It's my fault. I shouldn't have left her alone. Forgive me—my breath is gone."

We dressed her and groomed her. Shorty found her passport under a silk cushion.

A black sedan was waiting for Rita outside on Roxbury Drive. The driver looked like a soldier in civilian clothes. Red insisted on sitting up front with him. She hugged the three of us and got into the car.

I was wistful as it drove away. I had betrayed her. I should have been less devoted to Orson and his art and a little more devoted to Red. Her children were in Europe with Aly, and Rita was all alone, battling with Columbia's lawyers. God knows what she did at night.

The next morning I received a telegram from the Aga himself.

MARGARITA HAS ARRIVED

And the day after there was a ten-thousand-dollar check sitting in our mailbox from a foundation I had never heard of, the Rainbow Trust. I was tempted to tear up the check. But Nando persuaded me not to.

"We can afford to repair the whole theater with that grant . . . and get a new screen."

"It's a bribe," I said.

"No, it's not," Shorty said. "We shouldn't begrudge that old man. He barely has the strength to breathe."

Rainbow Trust, my ass, but we used up every penny of that grant. I was still in a sour mood. And then a letter arrived from Red in that special blue airmail paper with an extra flap to seal it tight.

Pal Joey, 1954–1958

Rusty,

*The only thing I remember is you ironing my underwear.
I was much happier when you taught me about books and words.
You should not worry about me.*

Your friend,
Big Red

3

NOT ANOTHER WORD from her in two years. Then last year Rita was resurrected, or so it seemed. She must have made peace with Harry Cohn. She appeared in *Pal Joey*, Columbia's biggest hit of 1957. Rita got top billing over Frank Sinatra and Kim Novak, Columbia's new star, a blonde who was "stacked," as she says in the film. It's about a kindhearted heel, Pal Joey (Sinatra), who ends up as a two-bit entertainer at a nightclub on San Francisco's Barbary Coast, once a haven for pirates. I would learn from Louella that Harry had bought the rights to *Pal Joey* years ago, and meant it to be a kind of sequel to *Cover Girl*, starring Red and Gene Kelly. But MGM wouldn't allow the Janitor to borrow Gene now that he was a big star, and so the project languished until Kim Novak arrived at Columbia. Harry gave Kim Rita's role, and poor Rita was recast as the *other* woman, wealthy widow Vera Simpson, who invites Joey's troupe to perform at a charity auction on Nob Hill. And for a second she could almost be Gilda in a Jean Louis gown, with her red hair gathered up in a French twist. She moves with her old cat-like elegance. She's wearing a bit too much eye shadow, but that didn't really bother me.

'Frank, I mean Joey, is a bit of a louse. He exposes Vera, the society widow, as Vanessa the Undresser, and obliges her to do a sort of striptease to benefit the auction. He's quite clever, Frank is. It's Sinatra's film, not Rita's. Nor does it belong to Kim Novak, who plays Linda English, a Rubenesque blond chorus girl from Albuquerque. The deep tones of Sinatra's voice cast their spell over us, while Cohn was having his revenge on Rita—the mock-striptease that she does on Nob Hill is a self-punishing parody of her glove dance in *Gilda*.

I found it sad and insulting. No amount of retouching can hide the pucker of her mouth and the crow's nests around her eyes. All the bourbon and rye had bitten into Rita's thirty-eight years.

And yet she's perfect for the part. She scorns Joey—Sinatra— then pursues him, buys him his own nightclub, Chez Joey, calls him "Beauty," as she would a pet dog. He lives in one of her dead husband's abandoned properties, a houseboat, with a closetful of clothes.

And then the story strays. Joey romances the widow, but he's in love with the "mouse"—Kim Novak, naturally. The same camera that had fallen out of love with Rita Hayworth is now delirious over Kim; it kisses her with close-ups, sculpts her mouth and eyes in luscious contours and colors. Rita may sing "Bewitched, Bothered, and Bewildered" in her negligée, after a night with Sinatra, but I wasn't beguiled or bewitched. I was angry as hell. Red had been blindsided, to say the least; she had once beguiled half the planet as Gilda, a stripper who didn't have to strip. . . .

The wealthy widow threatens to shut down Chez Joey before it even opens if the mouse—Kim Novak—appears in the show. Joey tries to juggle Vera and the mouse, and finally he rebels. He leaves San Francisco, with its promise of Chez Joey, and heads for Sacramento, with the mouse at his heels.

I felt sorry for Rita. She should never have taken the part. She may have had top billing, but *Pal Joey* was a vehicle for Sinatra's voice and Kim Novak's languid beauty. It was Rita's last flick for Harry Cohn. She'd had tantrums in the studio. She was sullen on the set, I was told. She must have realized the dilemma she was in. She often forgot her lines. And it was punishment to have her play a society dame—that wasn't our Red.

I wanted to tear down Columbia's walls and preside over a firing squad—for the Janitor, Harry Cohn.

I ran into Viola Lawrence at the Regina. We'd just screened *The Lady from Shanghai* for perhaps the tenth time. Viola was as secretive as ever in her dark glasses. She was accompanied by three junior cutters, young women with faint blond mustaches, who didn't wear dark glasses, but had their mistress's unfathomable, pulsing eyes; like Vi, they were all dressed in dark leather jackets, green skirts, and high heels. Vi introduced them as Ramona, Marsha, and Millie—her minions, her disciples, her muses.

She was about to make one of her quick exits, but I wouldn't allow Vi and her three muses to vanish so easily. I knew Vi was the cutter on *Pal Joey*, and I wanted to learn whatever was going on with Rita. I almost had to kidnap Vi to get her to have a drink with me at Musso's with her cotillion of junior cutters.

Vi sat hunched over in one of the booths, half-hidden, but no one dared disturb her. Vi was in great demand. Cohn lent her out to other studios, and she could destroy many an actor or actress' career, cut into any scene she desired, with the help of her disciples.

"Rita." That's all I had to say.

Vi peered out from under her dark glasses. "Rusty, I did the best I could. She was incoherent half the time. I'm a cutter. That's all I can do—cut."

"Yes," said Millie, "we're all fond of that misfit. I rehearsed her, fed Miss Rita her lines, and she would forget them a moment later.

And we couldn't redo what was on the screen, you know. She aged overnight. Isn't that right, Ramona?"

"Oh, it wasn't the litheness of her body," Ramona said. "Miss Rita was supple enough. She could have danced rings around Frank and Kim. They were flat on their feet compared to Miss Rita. But her face was hard, hard, hard."

"And full of wrinkles," Marsha chimed in.

"That's enough, girls," Vi said. "It's Rita's presence on camera that has paid your bills all these years. She has been Columbia's most visible star ever since *Cover Girl.*"

"Bankable, too," said Marsha, parroting Vi.

Still, all their chatter told me nothing. They would echo whatever Vi said. I wasn't satisfied.

"Vi, you should have discouraged Rita from taking the part of an ex-stripper. Cohn set her up. He wanted Gilda's ghost, and he got it. And you were so careful with Kim Novak. Why couldn't you have saved a couple of caresses for Rita?"

I could see the sadness in Viola's scrunched eyes. "Rusty, I couldn't *save* Rita. Nobody could. It was a crash-dive. I'm a cutter, my dear. I don't produce."

Vi had more sway over Harry than she was willing to admit. "You could have prevented the massacre. Come on, you're Viola Lawrence."

She let out a bitter laugh. "Ha!" she said. "I'm queen of the scraps. Right, girls?"

"Yes, yes," the three of them trumpeted. I had a wild wish to relieve them of their smirks.

"I wielded my scalpel, I promise you," Vi said. "I tore away the stuttering moves, the missteps. But I wasn't on the set. I had to do it all in the cutting room. She might have stolen the film if she had been mean enough, if she had been a real bitch. But it's not in her nature. . . . Yes, Rusty. In the end, I was not pleased with *Pal Joey.*"

"Neither were we," said Ramona. "But we couldn't rescue Miss Rita. The camera tells its own tale, and it was a very sad tale to tell."

"Hush, now," Vi said. "Come, girls."

The three muses hadn't even had time to savor their gin and tonics. So they took their first and last sips. Vi was clearly uncomfortable. She hadn't ruined Rita on the cutting room floor. The film itself was Rita's ruin. But as Cohn's cutter of cutters, it seemed to bother Vi, as if the Janitor had used her as an instrument to get back at Rita.

Vi slid out from inside the booth with her three cutters and left me there. I watched the other faces at Musso's, the mingling of fear and awe at the sight of Viola's dark glasses and leather jacket. It was really Vi who owned Gower Street, not the Janitor and his hierarchy of directors and producers, not the bankers in Manhattan, not Harry's small stable of stars, but Vi and the satanic pull of her hand. Vi created the continuity and lyrical sweep of Columbia's chosen films. It was Vi who had created Gilda, and Gilda's feline prance, the movement of her glove like a velvet pendulum gone haywire. She dominated everyone but the Boy Wonder. She cut *The Lady from Shanghai* to shreds, turned it into "a little thriller," as she told Harry, but she couldn't find a way into the labyrinth of the mirror maze. It remained outside her provenance. She admired Orson and hated him, because he had composed a scene that was beyond a cutter's ability to cut. . . .

As for Orson himself, he, too, didn't fare well. Harry Lime had made him *recognizable* almost everywhere on the planet, with Lime's accompanying "tail" of zither music from *The Third Man*, but all that veneration couldn't give him back the tools of his trade. Not even Vi could have rescued him from the bumbling amateurs he had to hire for his film projects. He had better luck in England, with his Harry Lime radio dramas on the BBC, tailored just for him. But it felt like a bit of cannibalism, as if the master were feeding on his own tub of flesh.

He also tripped twice and broke both his legs while performing *King Lear* in Manhattan. The old king had to wheel himself about the stage, with the "cry" of his wheelchair competing with the deep tremors of his voice. Yet he was able to conquer and seduce at least a part of the audience. His moaning could be heard in the far terrain of the balcony, I'm told, as he cradled his dead daughter in his arms. I wish I could have been there with Nando. But I couldn't manage such a trip on our tight budget. Still, I was able to imagine him in his chair, grizzled as an old king would be, terrifying and pitiable in his pursuits.

But Hollywood did beckon him in a roundabout way, as if the fates hadn't utterly abandoned him. Universal decided to make its own "little thriller," starring Moses—I mean Chuck Heston—and according to the *Hollywood Reporter*, Moses had always dreamt of working with the director of *Citizen Kane*.

Universal promptly hired Orson to direct and act in *Touch of Evil* as a crooked border-town detective. In my schoolgirl's heart I had a secret wish that Orson would lure me back, even now, after so many years. But he never did. . . .

4

O N A WINTER morning, a month or so after I'd met Vi at
Musso's, Nando shook me out of bed. I stared at the lovely
leanness of his body, and I was still amazed. Both of us wore lipstick now, and had one pierced ear, like intertwining twins.

"Rusty, someone's waiting for you outside the Regina."

I squinted at the clock. "I'd call it high treason," I said. "It isn't
even seven."

I would have gotten up for Rita, but no one else.

"Who is it?" I growled in my ogre's early morning growl.

"Harry Cohn."

"Nando, send Harry away. Tell him I'll meet him for tea and
crumpets at a more reasonable hour."

"He says it's urgent. And he was very polite."

I couldn't stop squinting. "How the hell did you find out he
was here?"

"His chauffeur came to our bedroom window."

"That man has a lot of nerve," I said.

But I put on my robe and slippers. If Harry had summoned me

to Gower Street I wouldn't have come. I owed him nothing. Yet here he was at the Regina. I scraped across the rear alley in my slippers and went out to the marquee. Cohn was waiting in the back seat of a Chrysler sedan. He must have lost twenty pounds since I'd last seen him. His streetcar conductor's shoulders were gone. The collar of his sports shirt consumed most of his neck. His eyebrows had no discernible color. His cheeks were as dark and grim as gunpowder.

He was always blunt with me. "I'm dying," he said.

I was cruel to a very cruel man. "We're all dying, Mr. Cohn."

He popped a tablet into his mouth. It was nitroglycerin, I guessed. He must have had chronic chest pains.

"Rusty, my ticker has decided not to tick. My arteries are shot. I should have an operation. But I'd never survive it."

"I'm sorry," I said.

"I'm not here for sympathy. It's Rita I'm worried about."

I had to keep myself from laughing in his face. She'd made the Janitor a mint, and while she was on the lot she still had to punch in every morning like a canteen worker. I'd heard the gossip about her temper tantrums. During her last days at the studio, she had ripped into her dressing room, smashing the mirrors and writing on the walls with her lipstick and eyeliner—

COHN, COHN, COHN

—as if it were a magical omen that might undo the king of Columbia.

She was divorced from Aly, and the Aga Khan could no longer protect his beloved Margarita. He died in bed at his chateau in Switzerland. His weak heart couldn't withstand an outbreak of the flu. I can imagine how Rita felt, how she must have mourned him in silence. She never sent me a word about the Aga Khan.

"Harry, what would you like me to do?"

"Stay in touch with her. She could use a friend."

I was mystified about the Janitor's sudden concern for Rita. He'd tried to destroy her in *Pal Joey* and almost succeeded. Perhaps his own busted ticker had shaken him and softened his rage against Rita.

"Ah," Harry said, staring out the rear window of his Chrysler, "you've built yourself a little paradise, a temple to the Hollywood classics and all the other films I despise. Tell me what I can do for you. I always return a favor."

I wasn't shy. Orson's new film had been edited in utter silence. It disappeared a week after it was released. "I'd like a print of *Touch of Evil* from Universal, as soon as you can get it. Steal it from the bastards. I don't care."

"Done," he said and started to laugh. "Orson's latest catastrophe."

He shut his eyes—his eyelids were whiter than white. He was finished with me. I climbed out of the Chrysler. . . .

A week later Harry went on his annual vacation to the Biltmore in Phoenix, a resort on Camelback Road favored by that other king, Clark Gable—it was Hollywood's own Riviera in a sea of sand. It had a luxurious restaurant, the Gold Room, with gold leaves hammered into the walls, and an equally luxurious pool, where the Janitor loved to do the dead man's float while dreaming of the empire he had built on Gower Street, according to Louella. "I have my best ideas in the water, Lolly—brainstorms of atomic proportions."

Cohn stayed in a cottage near the pool with his second wife, Joan, a shiksa who had once been a starlet at his own studio. I still had a few friends in the basement of the Writers' Building, and they told me that Cohn hardly ever went to his office before he landed in Phoenix; he was no longer the janitor of his domain, turning off light bulbs after midnight. He had sniffed his own mortality and carried it with him to Camelback Road. Seems he'd been having chest pains for months, but wouldn't go near a hospital, because it might have caused mass hysteria in the movie market. He swallowed his nitroglycerin tablets, sat beside the pool in the desert sun, and suffered a heart attack in the middle of a meal at the Gold Room; Harry died en route to the hospital in a spanking-white ambulance, with the sirens screaming in his ears.

Joan had him baptized, because his last words had been, "Jesus, fuck, fuck," and she felt that her late husband had been communing with the Lord in his inimitable ferocious manner. The bar mitzvah boy from Manhattan ended up with the last rites *after* he became a corpse. His wife didn't waste any time. She had two soundstages at Columbia converted into a chapel; a priest conducted the services, while Harry lay on a bier, like a medieval prince, in a coffin smothered in orchids. There was a passel of Catholic "soldiers" at the funeral: Kim Novak, Loretta Young, Rosalind Russell, Maureen O'Hara, and John Ford, complete with his eye patch. I also recognized Dick Powell, Tony Curtis (né Bernie Schwartz), and Glenn Ford among the honorary pallbearers.

I wondered who had invited me. I'd never met the widow, who wore a stylish black cape and veil, designed by Jean Louis. Still, there was a great mob of people milling about—private secretaries, producers, technicians, screenwriters, directors, starlets, and Columbia's moneymen with grim, gray mouths; and I happened to notice the little tyrants and lords of the other studios, each with his entourage. They no longer had to compete with Harry, among the very last of the moguls, who had been both president and production chief of *his* studio—unlike Louis B. Mayer, who was ousted from his throne in 1951, and had never even been president at MGM. Mayer had died last year, a skeletal man stricken with leukemia, or I would have seen him at the services, with a handkerchief balled in his fist. Mayer was always crying, dead or alive.

I bumped into Louella, notebook in hand. "Child," she asked in a belligerent tone, her wattles larger than ever, "what on earth are you doing here? Harry was never fond of you."

"I'm the mystery guest," I told her and moved on, as people began to crowd the coffin and clutch the orchids, their one souvenir of Harry's reign. Studio guards had to pluck these scavengers from the bier as the widow grew hysterical beneath her veil.

I had hoped to run into Rita. But Rita wasn't there. She hid in Beverly Hills during the services.

Danny Kaye read the eulogy written by playwright Clifford Odets, himself a Boy Wonder of the 1930s with such proletarian masterpieces as *Waiting for Lefty* and *Awake and Sing!* . . . until he pitched his tent in Hollywood. He must have "flirted" with Cohn for a little while, but I never saw him once in the Writers' Building at Columbia. Perhaps the eulogy was just another work for hire. A handsome man in horn-rimmed glasses, Odets stood in a corner, while Danny Kaye compared Columbia Pictures to a cathedral. Forgive me, but I would call it a butcher's paradise.

Harry didn't have to travel very far. The Hollywood Memorial Park Cemetery was only six blocks south of the studio. It was the single cemetery Hollywood had, and Harry must have wanted to lie down as close to his domain as he could. I decided to walk the six blocks.

It had begun to rain. I could see the ribs of a lightning bolt. I shivered once and walked on, as a limousine stopped for me. "Get in," a voice echoed from deep within the cave of the limo. Viola Lawrence was inside, without her disciples. She wasn't wearing her dark glasses in that cave. Her eyes were all red. She had good reason to mourn that son of a bitch. They'd been a formidable team.

I could hear the pounding of the rain on the roof of the limo. A tempest had arrived to commemorate the passing of Harry Cohn. The wind whipped at the slanting rain and I could no longer see out the window. We might as well have been in Siberia rather than cruising along Sunset.

"Vi," I said, "*you* invited me to the services. Otherwise, I couldn't have gotten inside Harry's walls."

Vi didn't answer me at first. Her white skin shone like silver in the semidarkness. She put on her glasses.

"I didn't invite you, dear, but you're as welcome as anyone. I can assure you of that. You looked after Rita and you worked with Orson on *The Lady from Shanghai*."

"Vi, you butchered that film."

"Did not," she declared, indignant now. For a moment I thought she was going to shove me out of the limo—into Harry's rainstorm.

"Whatever I did, Rusty, had one purpose—to get that film released. Otherwise it would still be sitting in a can inside Columbia's vaults. . . . Where's Rita? She owed it to Harry. He made her a star."

I didn't feel the need to answer Vi. I hadn't worked for Harry or for Rita in years. And I'd never worked for Vi.

Finally we arrived at Hollywood Memorial. Hearst's longtime mistress Marion Davies had been buried there. Her supposed depiction in *Kane* as Susan Alexander, a reluctant opera singer, caused so much havoc for Orson. Hearst had his minions attack the film for Marion's sake. Orson should not have made Susan a devotee of mammoth jigsaw puzzles, one of Marion's pet passions. . . .

Page boys stood there with umbrellas for the stars and other important guests while I dove into the storm with an upturned collar.

The cemetery looked like a pharaoh's retreat on Santa Monica Boulevard. It had high impregnable walls and tall bending palm trees. Inside there were Egyptian temples and urns and green lawns that snaked across the cemetery like tiny mountains. Harry's grave site was near one of the urns. The grave diggers were dressed like eighteenth century savants in white wigs—and rubber raincoats.

Spencer Tracy shoveled earth over the coffin while the priest, who had scuffed heels, welcomed Harry's ghost to eternity. I watched the raindrops explode on Spencer's gray fedora.

Mourners kept arriving, stragglers with broken umbrellas that flew off into the wind like wounded crows. The cemetery was packed with people. I saw children and beggars who must have thought they were coming to a carnival. I'm sure none of them had ever met Harry.

It was Viola who spoke at the grave site—with neither an umbrella nor a raincoat.

"He was my boss," she said, as the rain twisted some of Vi's words into a crackling melody. "We hardly ever met outside his office. He did not like idle play. He loved to argue and question my cuts. He was adamant. 'Make it better, Vi.' He was a difficult man. I threatened to quit a dozen times. He laughed. 'Where would you go, Vi?' Columbia thrived because of Harry Cohn. I wasn't there during Harry's rise. But it must have been epic. He swallowed up entire lots. He had to be cruel or he couldn't have survived. . . ."

Vi lowered her head. It wasn't fatigue. She was stuck in some riddle that must have created havoc with all her memories of Harry Cohn. Mourning had turned her mute.

I stood there wondering about Rita, whether she mourned the Janitor in some secret part of her soul. She'd been crafted out of Cohn's clay. She was Cohn's creature no matter how hard she fought him. He hated her, loved her, and looked after her—lusted after her, too. He must have considered her his own special "child" at Columbia, or he never would have hired me to spy on her. Their relationship had been the grand duel of her life.

But even with all the time and money he had spent on Margarita Carmen Cansino's rebirth as Big Red, he couldn't have imagined that she would become Hollywood's "bombshell" of the forties. Harry had never had a *real* star in his terrain until Rita. Yet what mattered so much to him meant so little to her. She hated going to Gower Street, hated every moment. *Gilda* had been her revenge on Harry Cohn. Rita's brazenness in that film was her battle cry. It still made Harry a fortune. The harder she tried to break away from Harry, the more their lives remained entwined. Her absence from the funeral had somehow made her present *everywhere* in that crowd of mourners.

The patter of the rain might as well have been Rita's footprints. Even I was bewitched. . . .

· NINE ·
King Lear, 1958

1

THE DEAD MAN had kept his promise about *Touch of Evil*.
A print arrived from Universal the very week Harry was
buried. I decided not to screen the film in advance, without an
audience. I wanted to watch *Touch of Evil* for the first time with a
full house.

As usual with Welles, there was a line that wended its way
around the block, like the slow swish of a serpent's tail. We didn't
even advertise or display Universal's posters and signboards. We
just had Nando climb up on his ladder and spell out

TOUCH OF EVIL

in huge block letters.

I'd never been so jittery in my life. And it got worse when Orson
arrived with a mysterious dark-eyed lady fifteen minutes before the
screening. He must have weighed three hundred pounds. I had to
find two seats for him alone and one for his lady. The lights hadn't
gone down, and when the audience noticed him in the house there

was a moment of long, silent reverie. And then people applauded in a spontaneous explosion of joy. He had been mocked and reviled in America as a prodigal son who had wasted his talent, a firecracker that had fizzled. But the Regina had always championed his art. He'd come out of his exile in Europe to sit among cinephiles who didn't give a damn about cash receipts. We loved his daring, his bravura, his defiance, too.

I had to play Mussolini, and ask three fans in the first row to give up their seats, with a bribe of a monthly pass to the Regina. Then Nando had to pluck out the armrests between two seats, find a soft cushion, and create a throne for the *Maître*.

Orson grumbled a hello and said, "Rusty, have you met my wife? She's a countess, you know. Her blood is much, much bluer than mine."

The countess laughed. I kissed her on the cheek. And I could feel a wound right under my heart. I realized in a second that she was a better fit for Orson than Big Red. It was the curse of social class. She'd had a privileged upbringing, like Orson himself. He could discuss *Hamlet* and *Lear* with the countess. And Rita had grown up in a void. She could sing with her shoulders and her hips. That was her uniqueness and her limit. She'd become a princess by decree, but it didn't last. She would always remain Margarita.

Orson sat on his throne, which swayed under him as the lights went out. I didn't have much clarity as I looked at the screen. My head was in a swirl. But I wasn't blind to his new persona, Hank Quinlan, the crooked border town cop in *Touch of Evil*, who was as singular as Charles Foster Kane. Both were larger, more forceful, than anyone else around them. I knew that Maurice Seiderman, the makeup magician who had sculpted the Boy Wonder into a creaky old man in *Citizen Kane*, had also worked on him as Hank Quinlan. It took two hours each morning, I'm told. Maurice put plastic bags under Orson's eyes, redid his hairline, and gave him a squashed nose. Quinlan was the ultimate gargoyle that Orson had always longed to play. He wore pillows under his coat. Captain Quinlan had taken a bullet in one leg, and walked with a limp.

He had all the rot of a border town cop and a deep, scratchy voice that seemed to ruffle the space around him. His wife had been murdered. He planted evidence in every case. He had a turkey ranch, and he never took a bribe. He could only have been reinvented by a man addicted to Shakespeare. He was as sad and wild as Lear, without his daughters, without his kingdom, without his company of knights. He was a howling wound with a monstrous body and a monstrous face. I noticed nothing but Quinlan, and the tortured, ponderous ballet of his movements.

The lights went back on. Whatever Universal's own editors had done to the film, it still belonged to Orson. People roared, "Regina X, Regina X," and the ferocious pull of that sound propelled me onto the stage.

"Children, what can I tell you? I loved Hank Quinlan. He's the master's greatest creation, that monster who moves us beyond the possibility of our own repair. The entire film was like looking into the hall of mirrors in *The Lady from Shanghai* and never getting out of the maze. That's where Orson leaves us—stuck inside one of his many mirrors. None of us can escape his art, this relentless pull of cinematic gravity."

"More," people shouted, "more."

They didn't stop stamping their feet until Orson, leaning on a cane, just like Quinlan, stood up from his king's cushion. He couldn't have mounted the stage. We would have needed a catapult, and that might not have worked.

Orson held up one of his plump paws. "I put all my worth as an actor into Quinlan, all my worth. The folks at Universal said I'm lazy. I couldn't remember my lines. They don't understand that delivery is all—and I delivered."

"Mr. Welles," asked one of our acolytes, "how could you admire such a despicable man? He framed people, he murdered people."

"So have Shakespeare's kings, and Quinlan was a kingly man. I didn't use Quinlan as a mask. The pounds of makeup and the pillows soothed me. . . . Yes, Universal's cutters botched the film. They were merciless in their quest for a narrative line that didn't exist, and still doesn't. But they couldn't botch Quinlan no matter how they tried. When Quinlan strangles Uncle Joe Grandi, he's destroying Hollywood and its cult of uncluttered narratives."

Orson reveled in the strangulation of Grandi, a Mexican crime lord played by Akim Tamiroff. Each gory detail—the murderous gloved hands of Hank Quinlan as Uncle Joe's eyeballs begin to pop—literally stopped time and took us right out of the frame.

"But you couldn't have made the film without Hollywood's master technicians," said another one of our patrons.

"Yes," said Orson, with spittle flying. "But we aren't watching *Touch of Evil* at Grauman's Chinese. This is all the opening we'll ever have—at the Regina, and yes, with Rusty Redburn. We don't need the Rockettes or a Marilyn Monroe look-alike. We have nothing but a tiny kingdom in a tinier theater in the tiniest heart of Hollywood."

That night we had a late dinner at the Hollywood Derby. Orson was barely recognized. No one bothered him. Hollywood was the same old rigid society of producers. It wouldn't allow its films to be shown on television. So the little screen struck back, stole lesser stars from the studios, such as James Arness, who now played Marshal Matt Dillon in a weekly western, *Gunsmoke*, which kept even more viewers away from the big screen. I came to like *Gunsmoke*. I watched it with Nando at my side. It had the flavor of a fairy tale, with a child's toys—pistols and spurs and very tall hats.

And it had an added feature. Dennis Weaver, who plays Chester, Matt's sidekick and sometime deputy with a limp, also appeared in

Touch of Evil, as a loony loquacious motel clerk, who speaks entirely in Chester's voice. It's almost as if *Gunsmoke* had invaded the contours of Welles' film. . . .

We had our own touch of evil at the Hollywood Derby. Orson kept glaring at Shorty. "You abandoned me, you little shit. You should have followed me to Europe."

"I couldn't, boss," Shorty said. "I couldn't."

And that touch of evil turned into a smile. "The best valet I ever had. . . . Where's Rita? Didn't you invite her to the screening?"

"I can't find her," I confessed.

"That's ridiculous. I spoke to her last week—after Cohn was buried." He turned to his countess. "*Carina*, you must have her number *somewhere*." She peered into a little black book, while Orson summoned a waiter to bring him a telephone. He had her dial a number, plucked the receiver out of her hand, and said, "Rita, darling, is that you? We've been waiting for hours. We're having a little party at the Hollywood Derby." He stood up like a sea captain and searched the room with his Mongolian eyes. "No, I swear to you that Lolly Parsons isn't here. I'll pound her head on her table if she shows up. I promise."

And so we waited and waited—for well over ninety minutes—until Rita finally arrived. There were stark lines on her face in the dim light, as if she were being ravaged from within. But the restaurant recognized her right away.

"Princess Rita!"

Americans loved royalty and clung to her title. I didn't.

She was wearing a mink coat, which she thrust off and hurled at one of the waiters with all the élan of Gilda removing her glove. She'd come to us in her best pair of Juel Park's pajamas. Its silk was as fine as any of Christian Dior's evening suits. Shorty found a chair for her. She was now thirty-nine years old, and the bones of her face were as beautiful as ever. But one of her eyes kept blinking.

And the sadness had settled in so deep that I had to steel myself to remember the Rita I had first met on Woodrow Wilson Drive in the midst of World War II and the Mercury Wonder Show we had done on Cahuenga Boulevard. But that dancing step was still there. She danced with each breath.

It was Orson who toasted her with champagne. He had already devoured three steaks with a jar of Dijon retrieved from his pocket.

"Darling," he said to Rita, the champagne flute wavering in his hand, "I can't recall. Have you met my wife?"

"No, Orson," she said in that lifelong whisper of hers.

I could tell he was playing Lear and Falstaff tonight, not Hank Quinlan. "Then let me introduce the Countess di Girifalco, otherwise known as Paola Mori, my beloved."

"Stop it, Orson," Paola said. "Behave yourself, just once." And she reached across the table to clasp Rita's hand. "I have admired you for so long. I'm delighted that you could come. You have inspired a whole generation of young actresses. We worshipped your carnality in *Gilda*."

"Carnality?" Rita asked, bewildered by that word.

"Yes," Paola said. "Oh, men do what they want. They're pigs. But you were the first woman who ate up the screen, took an entire bite. We did not have a Gilda of our own."

"But it's simple," Rita said, with the first bit of blaze in her brown eyes. "I love to dance."

Paola stared right into that blaze. "Yes, but it is not so simple. And you were just as daring in *The Lady from Shanghai*."

Rita shook her head. "I'm afraid, Countess—"

"Call me Paola, please."

"Paola, I'm afraid the critics wouldn't agree. They laughed their heads off and said I was the champagne-blond murderess who got scalped. They said I didn't know how to act. Ask your husband."

I saw a curl of anger in Paola's forehead. "I don't have to ask.

You were the exact opposite of *Gilda.* The screen ate you alive.
I don't credit Orson. I credit you."

Orson had two more bottles of champagne delivered. "Am I
going mad? We have a mutual admiration society at my own table.
Rusty, do something. Bail me out."

"Paola's right," I said.

"Then perhaps we should thank the dead for Rita's performance in *Shanghai,* dig up Harry Cohn, and fete him at our table."

Rita crossed herself. "Don't blaspheme," she said. "And I do
owe a lot to Harry, even if he was a son of a bitch."

And now Orson rose up and roared. "But I directed you in
Shanghai, not Harry Cohn. . . . Jesus, Rusty, help me out."

"But there *was* a taste of Cohn in her performance," I said. "He
was his own hall of mirrors. He could vanish and rise right up
again. And we feel it in Rita's confusion and despair."

"She's a killer, a cold-blooded killer," Orson said.

"Like Harry Cohn," Shorty shouted.

And Orson moaned like the performer that he was. "Am I
betrayed by everyone?"

"Sit down, dear," Paola said. "And don't make a scandal. You
can't take credit for everything. Give the dead man his due."

We ate in silence after that. Rita's hand was shaking. I could
feel her descend into a slow, freighted world of silence. Once upon
a time, *every* move of hers was a dance step done with a delicious
grace. But she was losing the power of her language bit by bit.
She'd never find it again.

Oh, Orson would prosper with his countess. He'd wander across the planet. He'd appear on talk shows, but would that
whiplash—that clarity—of *Kane* ever come back? His performance
as Charles Forster Kane had been at the very beginning of Orson's
film career, and Quinlan, sadly, was at the very end. I knew he'd
never make another Hollywood film again. Orson had packed his

entire sense of the grotesque into Hank Quinlan's tub of flesh. Quinlan was *everything* he sought in a character—baroque and out of bounds. . . .

Rita left the table first. She had a driver, she said. She caressed Nando's hair, shook Shorty's hand, hugged Paola, Orson, and me, put on her mink coat, and danced her way to the door, signing autograph after autograph, the movie star who had a constant shriek inside her head.

"Will she be okay?" Paola asked me.

I lied. "Who can tell?"

Paola slapped her own head and cursed herself in Italian. "Orson, where's your sense of chivalry? You could have escorted Rita to her car. She was once your wife, you know."

"Yes," he said, "I could have taken her on a ride to the parking lot on my cane, *carina*."

Paola turned to me. "Rusty, can you believe this pig of a man?"

It was Shorty who paid the bill . . . as I ran after Rita.

I found Red just as she was getting into a pea-green Cadillac Coupe de Ville in front of the Derby. She seemed startled.

"Forgive me," I said. "I should have walked out with you."

"Like old times," she whispered, "when you followed me everywhere."

"Yes, Rita. Like old times."

Her left cheek began to twitch. "Rusty, I'm a bad girl. I just couldn't go to Harry's funeral. I couldn't bear to be around all those people. They would have pawed me—and pretended how much they loved Harry. And so I called Columbia and sent you as my . . ."

She couldn't catch hold of the word she wanted.

"Surrogate," I said. "Your surrogate."

The twitching stopped.

"That's a lovely word. You've always been my surrogate, even after you stopped spying on me and Orson. . . . And I have to tell you, Rusty, I do like Orsie's wife. She can get her way without having to throw a dish at him. Isn't she beautiful?"

"You're the beautiful one," I said under my breath.

She rubbed my hand with her lips, got into the Coupe de Ville, and Princess Rita rode away.

Sadness reigned. I missed my little wars with Orson, and the fun I had giving Big Red literature lessons. Her Cadillac suddenly lurched to a stop in the middle of Vine. "Rusty," she shouted from her window, "when will we do *War and Peace*?"

And then she disappeared into the haze of after-midnight traffic.

I had a bad case of the sniffles, I confess. I loved the Regina, but suddenly I could see Red in her Juel Park's negligée, preparing dinner for Orsie.

Call me a spy or whatever you want, but it was the only worthwhile family I ever had.

2

A S MUCH AS I mourned my past life with Big Red, I still had to deal with the Hollywood Merchants Association and its annual Christmas parade, since the Regina did make me sort of a merchant.

The parade had started in the 1920s, just around the time I was born, when Chaplin and Doug Fairbanks and Gloria Swanson were the wonders of the world, America's new royalty. Much more vital than Europe's eccentric, inbred kings and queens, they ruled Hollywood together with moguls and merchants who dreamt of becoming as rich as Kublai Khan. When Doug courted "America's Sweetheart," Mary Pickford, the whole world shivered. And while Doug and Mary were on their honeymoon in Paris and London, crowds pursued them everywhere. They—Mary and Doug—couldn't cross Piccadilly without the protection of an entire police brigade. The movies had *imagined* them. They were the most beloved newlyweds that had ever been. Their mock-Tudor mansion in Beverly Hills, Pickfair, a converted barn, had become as popular as the White House—Einstein visited Pickfair, so did

George Bernard Shaw. Mary, who loved to play young girls in her movies, was also the sharpest and richest producer in Hollywood. But neither of them really survived the conversion to sound. Doug, the acrobatic prince of the silent screen, played Don Juan in 1934, but with bloated features and a flabby neck. Movie fans didn't want to hear Doug woo the aristocratic ladies of Madrid in a voice that lacked the music of his lyrical leaps. He died in 1939, without ever leaping in another film. . . .

That still left me with the 1958 Christmas parade on Hollywood Boulevard. The trolley line was gone. Half the stores along the boulevard had closed. Many of the stars had moved to Europe to shield their assets. Others, like Dean Martin, had gone to Vegas, where they gambled and performed in that land of illuminated midnight. But here we were, with trolley tracks and no trolleys; Christmas decorations strung over lampposts, made with tinsel that broke off and flew into the streets. Still, we had our parade. This part of the boulevard, my part, was known as Santa Claus Lane. Santa sat in a simple float. He used to have two live reindeer, stabled at La Brea during the Christmas season. But that tradition stopped right before Pearl Harbor.

Orson happened to be doing a magic show in Vegas just then, and decided to participate at the last moment. He shared a Cadillac convertible with Rita. Shorty was their driver.

Orson and Rita were suddenly the ragged remains of whatever little royalty Hollywood had left. We had Susan Hayward and Gregory Peck in a second convertible; Jack Lemmon and Jennifer Jones in a third. No studio could have coerced them into joining the parade. These stars must have come out of loyalty to the *old* Hollywood, when the annual Christmas Parade highlighted a year of rocketing receipts, while reindeer pranced along the trolley tracks.

The fourth convertible carried the queen of the parade—Lolly

Parsons, wattles and all. She was now seventy-seven years old, and had lost most of her power with the studios that were still standing, still intact. Yet they must have feared Parsons a tiny bit, or they wouldn't have given her the queen's convertible. Here she was, bathed in rouge, and holding a silk handkerchief like a scepter, smiling at those who still greeted her.

Though she looked mummified, she stared right into my eyes. At first I played the bitch and pretended not to notice her. But damn it all, I felt sorry for Louella and the echo she had lost in movieland, despite the harm she had done. So I bowed and made Nando bow, too.

"Greetings, Your Highness."

And she brightened. "Why, is that you, Rusty?"

"Yes, ma'am."

She squinted. "Come closer, please."

I approached the queen's convertible. She flaunted her handkerchief over my head and waved her driver on.

There were floats that the depleted studios had prepared to celebrate their past victories, such as a monster image of Rhett Butler, his cheek as big as a barn. Kim Novak sat on top of a float that the publicists at Columbia had prepared; it featured a slide show from the studio's recent hits, with Kim in a red tuxedo and high heels. She was clutching a golden wand that pointed to images of Burt Lancaster in *From Here to Eternity* and Marlon Brando in *On the Waterfront*, a handsome palooka with razor cuts over his eyes.

There were majorettes from Hollywood High, the daughters of studio secretaries, file clerks, and technicians. There were writers and cutters dressed as clowns, acrobats who had once worked as stuntmen at the Columbia ranch. Leading the pack was the parade master himself, a clown who had appeared as a bit player in several films, but now performed at retirement colonies near the ocean. He had an electric step that reminded me of Rita in *Cover Girl*.

He pranced along Santa Claus Lane, wearing a pillbox hat and carrying a cane, with which he poked at majorettes and drummer boys who shattered the strict line of the parade. He had a smile smeared across his face that lent him a demonic look. His pronounced motion, that eager pantomime of his, seemed to signal the end of an era. I could imagine him disappearing into the dust with all the majorettes.

Nando had to jog alongside this tattered army of floats with his toolbox and repair wooden wheels that were spinning out of control. Some of the writers and cutters ran out of breath and had to leave the parade, despite the parade master's protests. I couldn't help but remember the late thirties, when I had come to Hollywood from Kalamazoo, and when every news outlet in America sent cameramen and reporters to follow the parade down Santa Claus Lane. There wasn't a single cameraman today.

I summoned Nando, and told him to stop chasing after stray wheels. We stood outside the Regina's marquee as the parade passed. The boulevard was half-empty except for Hollywood's homeless, who were having a grand time. The parade marshals had handed out little pies and sandwiches.

I was baffled. It never snowed in Los Angeles, yet I could *feel* a snowflake. I looked up and realized that the errant flakes were coming from a snow machine mounted on one of Universal's floats. A young man on the float was cranking Universal's "snow cannon." The flakes spat out of the cannon and created a blizzard right in front of the Regina.

We stood there, as if at attention, and then through the blizzard came Orson and Rita sitting on the rump of their convertible. They must have crossed Santa Claus Lane a second time, without the majorettes and the other Cadillacs and floats. Orson could have been that bad boy and provocateur I had met on Woodrow Wilson Drive, a rogue with a wicked smile, like Harry Lime, though

Orsie would never have bartered in penicillin and allowed children to die. . . .

I was like a cinephile who had been sitting in the dark too long. The movies had maddened me, more than just a little. It wasn't the Regina's fault. It was this parade. I expected the reindeer to arrive. And then I realized my dilemma. Somehow, I had summoned up Orson's mirror maze, hidden in a fun house, where time had its own acrobatics, as it kept replicating Rita's face. But the lady from Shanghai didn't have that feather bob in the convertible. Instead, Rita had her long cascade of red hair. The maze had emboldened me, perhaps. I swear I saw a glint of *love* in Orson's eyes. The mirrors I had summoned shone on Rita. Her shoulders had that magnificent sweep, while her hands had a melodic line that belonged to her alone, as if they were at the edge of some secret whisper.

That whisper called to me. And in my reverie, I realized that *Orson* had re-created movieland. His hall of mirrors was cinema itself, with its hypnotic power to enchant. . . .

Rita was beckoning me to ride with her in that convertible, as if she were Gilda again.

I wanted to jump up and join her, but I'd been Regina X long enough to tear myself away from this phantasmagoria in a Cadillac.

I realized that no movie house could be a magic mirror. Orsie was three hundred pounds, Quinlan without the putty and paint, our own King Lear on Hollywood Boulevard. Rita had deep marks under her mascara. But she wasn't lost. She wasn't alone. Princess Rita had Orsie on Santa Claus Lane.

"Red," I shouted, "Big Red. . . ."

But they had moved deeper into the blizzard and whatever glimpse I had was gone.

AUTHOR'S NOTE

Rescuing Rita

I never quite recovered from *Citizen Kane*. Its lyrical nightmare has haunted half my life. It's no accident. *Kane* begins with a warning on a wire: NO TRESPASSING. Yet we're trespassers, all. At least those of us who are willing to move beyond the wire into a film that never ceases to seduce, that is as modern now as when it was made. Small wonder, then, that I wished to tackle a novel about Orson, whom I revered despite his gargantuan faults, as if he were devoured by his own largeness.

There was so much mythology surrounding him, most of it supplied by Welles himself, that I just couldn't write a novel in his voice without surrendering to Welles' own bravura.

Like many geniuses, he never solved the enigma of his own genius. He saw himself as a circus master, who could hold the entire "circus" of a film together. He couldn't. He didn't know the first thing about screenwriting when he arrived in Hollywood. Yet he had a gift that went beyond all the technical wizards at RKO. Welles had the eye of a camera. There isn't a moment in *Citizen Kane* that doesn't explode with energy and hold us captive to whatever image is onscreen. And no one but Welles could have dreamt up the magic mirror maze in *The Lady from Shanghai*, where he weaponizes the cinematic machine, and leaves us all helpless victims in its wake, trapped forever in that maze as moviegoers. Like other directors, he had his failures and misfires. But he remains the most audacious director in the history of film. Hollywood moguls, led by Louis B. Mayer, tried to destroy every print of *Kane*, to render it invisible, as Welles had dared parody *their* Willie, William Randolph Hearst. It's *Kane* that has survived, not Louis B. Mayer, not the other moguls.

Yet the more I read about Rita Hayworth, Orson's second wife, the more I realized that *she* would become central to my novel. Still, I couldn't write in her voice—she had none. Her real voice was the glide of her body, her panther-like moves. And when I discovered that she had been violated by her own father, had become his sexual pawn as well as his dancing partner before she was thirteen, I sensed that Rita's voiceless voice would remain crucial to whatever I wrote.

And so I invented a narrator, Rusty Redburn, whose own sexual fluidity sets her apart from the other characters in the novel. She's an outlaw who can see beyond the provincialism and prejudices behind the male-dominated hierarchy of Hollywood's so-called "Golden Age." She's the perfect foil to Harry Cohn and his fellow moguls, since she possesses none of their structural power and they hardly care that she exists. But Rusty understands their "product"—their films—better than they do. She's a kind of Cassandra who realizes which films will last and which won't, and why the walled-in Hollywood citadel of Harry Cohn was destined to fail. She has her own movie house, the Regina, and becomes Hollywood's chronicler, Regina X. She's among the first to recognize Welles.

Hired by Harry to spy on Rita and Orson, she subverts his wishes, becomes Rita's protector and Orson's chief ally and part-

time collaborator. But she cannot save Orson from his own extravagances and wanderlust. Decreed the most beautiful woman in the
world, Rita was also one of the shyest. And that shyness would have
crippling consequences; it kept her from traveling to the White
House with Orson to meet FDR and Eleanor; she preferred the
company of hairstylists and makeup girls at Columbia who tattled
to her about Orson's peccadillos and helped ruin their marriage.
She would claim to love Orson all her life, after four other failed
marriages and years of drinking that would hasten her dementia.

I did not want to document her decline in *Big Red*, though
we do glimpse her in a bedraggled state. Instead, I tried to reveal
the music in her bones, as Rusty herself relates—Rita was always
dancing, even when she stood still. Her shyness was fully shown in
Jane Withers' poignant eulogy of Rita at her memorial service in
Beverly Hills on May 18, 1987. Jane, a child star of the 1930s, had to
tutor Rita on the set of *Paddy O'Day* (1936), or Rita couldn't have
recited her lines.

A gentle girl, Rita was pulled out of school at an early age and
felt inadequate for the rest of her life. Yet her language was in her
limbs. Much of the world could feel it when she danced with such
abandon in *Gilda*. But the aura around *Gilda* couldn't last, and as
Rita would lament: her suitors went to bed with Gilda and all of
Gilda's glamour and woke up to a girl who walked around in blue
jeans. Rita often confessed how happy she had once been with
Orson, who, adoring her as he did, still cheated on her with a
parade of other women, such as Judy Garland and Marilyn Monroe, to name a couple. Though he claimed he still loved her in
his very last interview (the day before he died), he did mock Rita
in a rather brutal manner. If being with him meant happiness, he
boasted to one of his biographers, then what could the rest of her
life have been like?

Perhaps that is the mystery of Big Red. She had a temper. She

drank. She succumbed to Alzheimer's. But there remained a grandeur to her beauty. She was, after all, Princess Rita, even if she preferred Margarita Carmen Cansino. And when she was dealing with
Harry Cohn and other powerful, predator-like males, her silence
was both her weapon and her song.

Pain is the word that defines her, perhaps *sadness*, too. It's curious that Jane Withers, a child herself in the 1930s, recognized the
child in Rita. That's why they got along so well. Both of them had
the stubbornness of children—Jane was most often a spoiled brat
onscreen. And when Jane first noticed Rita dancing in a Charlie
Chan movie, she might have been looking into a mirror of herself,
though Rita's movements were magical, and Jane's were not.

Rita of the red hair was a star long before the release of *Gilda*
in 1946, but the role of Gilda made her immortal to mid–twentieth
century America, and any distant land that had a movie screen.
Sexualized though she was, the child in her remained. She was
always the little girl locked in some unfamiliar dressing room with
a set of toy electric trains for company while her parents gambled
away whatever she earned. She kept these Lionel trains in her own
dressing room at Columbia, coveting them throughout her career.
Perhaps that sound of the trains as a locked-in child was the after-
echo of her entire life, and this was the music she heard, even while
she danced.

ACKNOWLEDGMENTS

I would like to thank Patricia Allyn Biggs, Ph.D., interpretive ranger at the Manzanar National Historic Site, for helping me gather information about the Manzanar War Relocation Center, where my invented characters Julie Tanaka and her father, the Baron, were interned.

I would also like to thank my editor, Robert Weil, for being a wonderful partner in the writing of this novel and for sharing a bit of his own family history, the letter his great-aunt Martha Landmann wrote to the commandant at Treblinka, asking for news about her daughter Sophie. This memory helped inspire me to write Rusty's letter to the director of Manzanar.

Without the keen eye and ear of Liveright's Haley Bracken, I might never have found Rita's inner song.

It was a special delight to work with satirist Edward Sorel again, since he designed the cover of my very first novel. Now his brilliant rendering of *Big Red* has evoked a powerful portrait of Orson Welles' perverse genius and also a wild, sad Rita that has never been revealed before.

I would like to thank Art Director Steve Attardo for his guiding hand, and we wouldn't have had the book's wonderful interior design without Julia Druskin. It was also a pleasure working once again with Dave Cole, whose heroic efforts made copyediting a real adventure.

I would like to thank my agent and ferocious ping-pong partner, Georges Borchardt, for encouraging me to write *Big Red*.

Finally, I would like to thank my own Big Red, Lenore Riegel, for seeing me through the various drafts of this novel. I would have been whistling in the dark without her devotion and good sense.